Love Finds You™

IN

LANCASTER
County
PENNSYLVANIA

Love Finds You™

IN

LANCASTER
County
PENNSYLVANIA

BY ANNALISA DAUGHETY

summerside
PRESS™

Summerside Press™
Minneapolis 55337
www.summersidepress.com

Love Finds You in Lancaster County, Pennsylvania
© 2011 by Annalisa Daughety

ISBN 978-1-60936-212-6

Unless otherwise indicated, Scripture references are from The Holy
Bible, King James Version (KJV). Scripture references marked NLT are
from the Holy Bible, New Living Translation (NLT), copyright © 1996,
2004. Used by permission of Tyndale House Publishers, Inc., Wheaton,
Illinois. All rights reserved.

The town depicted in this book is a real place, but all characters are
fictional. Any resemblances to actual people or events are purely
coincidental.

Cover Design by Koechel Peterson & Associates | www.kpadesign.com

Interior design by Müllerhaus Publishing Group | www.mullerhaus.net

Cover photo by Doyle Yoder, www.dypinc.com

The author is represented by MacGregor Literary, Inc.,
Hillsboro, Oregon.

Summerside Press™ is an inspirational publisher offering fresh,
irresistible books to uplift the heart and engage the mind.

Printed in USA.

Dedication

....

This book is dedicated in memory of my
grandpa, H. B. "Pudge" Pearle.
Not a day goes by that I don't miss his smile,
his laugh, and his words of wisdom.
He was the consummate storyteller, and each
novel I write carries some of him inside it.
His legacy lives on through the many lives he touched.
Although I miss him terribly, I'm comforted by
the knowledge that he is in a better place.

Acknowledgments
....

The people in my life continue to amaze me with their support as I chase my dream. My mom, Vicky Daughety, is always my first reader. Thanks, Mom, for sacrificing sleep so you could read about Caroline and Lydia Ann and the scrapes I put them in. Sandy Gaskin and Jan Reynolds offered not only their honest and helpful critiques but also encouragement and prayers. Thanks to both of you for your help! Thanks to my editor, Rachel Meisel, and my agent, Sandra Bishop, for their input, encouragement, and prayers.

The Lord is my rock, my fortress, and my savior;
my God is my rock, in whom I find protection.
He is my shield, the power that saves me, and my place of safety.

PSALM 18:2 NLT

Lancaster County, Pennsylvania

LANCASTER COUNTY, PENNSYLVANIA, IS LOCATED IN THE HEART OF Pennsylvania Dutch Country. Settled in the early 1700s by immigrants in search of religious freedom, the area was named after the English city of Lancaster. Today, tourists flock to the area to visit Amish farms, enjoy local culinary delights, and take in the beautiful scenery. Because Lancaster County encompasses both urban (the city of Lancaster) and rural (Strasburg, Bird-in-Hand, Paradise, Intercourse) settings, there truly is something there for everyone. Local businesses cater to tourists, offering a variety of Amish-made goods. Beautiful quilts, handmade furniture, and baked goods are just some of the things that can be found in the quaint shops. Roadside stands are scattered around the countryside and usually run by Amish women and children selling delicious baked goods and homemade root beer. Visitors of all ages can enjoy spending the night on a working dairy farm, riding the Strasburg Railroad, touring the Sturgis Pretzel House, and visiting the Bird-in-Hand

Farmer's Market. No visit to Lancaster County is complete without stopping to see one of the county's twenty-nine historic covered
bridges and indulging in a slice of the local specialty, shoofly pie.
A visit to Lancaster County is one that won't soon be forgotten—
and one that visitors will likely want to repeat.

Annalisa Daughety

Chapter One

....

The swirling clouds were growing darker by the minute. Lydia Ann Raber looked up at the sky then quickened her step, hoping she could reach the safety of her quilt shop before the storm arrived. The air was warm and thick, and she could smell the rain in the distance.

"Lydia Ann!" Mrs. Troyer called out from the bakery across the street. "They're saying the storm will be a bad one. Come with me to the General Store basement." The older woman locked the door of her shop and cast a worried glance at the clouds. Most of the buildings in downtown Charm, Ohio, were only one story, but the Charm General Store had a good-sized basement.

Lydia Ann gave the sky another look. She'd always hated storms. When she was a little girl, she'd tried to convince her *dat* to let her bring the horses inside the house so they'd be safe. He'd laughed. "They're fine in the barn where they belong," he'd said. "And the *gut* Lord will keep us safe."

She didn't know why those words, spoken so many years ago, came back to her now. "Oh, I'll be fine in the shop. The girls will be there soon; school is almost over." Her twin daughters, Mary and Katie, had just turned six. They always came to the quilt shop after school. Lydia Ann could see Mrs. Troyer's furrowed brow from across the street. "Go on without me." She smiled. "It's probably just going to be a little rain. Nothing to worry about."

Mrs. Troyer didn't look convinced. "But the man on the radio said things could get ugly fast." She wrapped her arms around her body and shuddered. "It just doesn't feel right out here."

Lydia Ann bit her lip. It did seem too muggy outside to be only late April. "I'll come over as soon as the girls get here." She tucked a wayward strand of blond hair into her *kapp.*

Her answer seemed to satisfy the Englisher. "See you in a bit, then." Mrs. Troyer rushed off in the direction of the General Store.

Five minutes later, Mary and Katie burst through the door of the quilt shop. "It's going to be a gulley-washer," Mary exclaimed, parroting one of her *dawdi*'s favorite expressions. She plopped her lunch cooler on top of the counter. "Teacher told us to come straight here."

"She's a wise woman." Lydia Ann smiled at her girls.

Katie gave her a gap-toothed grin. "I like it when it rains. It makes the frogs and worms come out."

"Eww." Mary turned up her nose. "I don't like those slimy things."

Identical all the way down to a dimple in their right cheeks, Katie and Mary had always shared everything. It was only recently that they'd begun to develop individual likes and dislikes.

"All of God's creatures are beautiful," Katie said matter-of-factly. "Right, *Mamm*?"

"Indeed." Lydia Ann grabbed a notebook from the top drawer. She might as well go over the recent quilt orders while they waited for the storm to pass. "Come on, girls. We're going to the General Store for a bit."

They hurried through the door and set out for the store. Thunder boomed in the distance.

"We'll wait out the storm there," Lydia Ann explained, catching sight of Katie's worried expression. "I'm sure we won't be the only ones."

As she held open the door to the General Store, a jagged streak of lightning flashed. The little girls squealed and ran inside.

"That one went all the way to the ground," Mrs. Troyer said from her perch by the window. "The storm is getting closer."

"Go on downstairs, girls." Lydia Ann motioned toward the stairs that led to the basement.

"I'm glad you decided to come over," Anna Glick said. The teenage girl stood at her usual spot at the cash register. She'd helped out at Lydia Ann's quilt shop until she'd gotten a full-time job at the General Store. Lydia Ann had always appreciated her sweet disposition and knew the girl was a great asset. Worry flashed across her pretty face. "The weather radio is on downstairs. Sounds like it isn't safe to be outside." Bad storms had swept through the area a couple of years ago and made a lasting impression. Lydia Ann had gone with her mother-in-law to take baskets of food to the men cleaning up the debris after the storm. It had been a real mess, with so many homes and businesses damaged.

"Everyone needs to come to the basement now," the store owner said from the top of the stairs, his voice strained. "We're under a tornado warning."

Lydia Ann cast one last glance out the window. It was almost as dark as night. She said a silent prayer for their safety and followed Anna and Mrs. Troyer down the stairs.

* * * * *

Caroline DeMarco sat numbly on the arm of the leather couch in the expansive living room of her Atlanta mansion. Lance hated it when she sat there. "This isn't your mawmaw's house in Hiram," he'd say mockingly when she reverted to behavior he considered uncouth. Like sitting on the arm of a couch.

She stood and walked the length of the room, her arms wrapped tightly around her thin frame. She couldn't remember the last time she'd eaten, but for some reason she didn't feel hungry at all. Cold, though. She was cold. Which for some people might be weird considering the fact that it was nearly May. But Caroline was always cold…except for maybe in July when Atlanta was practically boiling.

She had to figure out what to do. What would her mama's advice be? She quickly pushed that thought away. Thinking of Mama only made her sad, and for this moment, she already had all the sadness in her that she could handle. She knew there were reporters outside the house right now—waiting out there in the dark of night, like predators surrounding their prey. And she was the prey.

Lance. Stupid Lance. He'd had to go and mess up everything… and now there wasn't even a way for him to fix things.

Because earlier that afternoon, under the glare of TV cameras and flashing bulbs, her husband—the star pitcher for the Atlanta Braves—had made his last public appearance.

At his funeral.

And as the nation mourned the young baseball phenomenon, Caroline was left to pick up the pieces of her shattered life.

Alone.

Chapter Two

. . . .

Simon Zook climbed down from his buggy and tried to ignore the numbness in his left foot. He stomped the ground a few times to get the blood flowing. *Must've laced my boot too tight this morning.*

"Welcome, Simon." Inside, Jeremiah Bellar looked up from the shelf he was filling with jars of his wife's homemade pepper jelly. "What can I help you with today?" The Bellars' store sold everything from pastries to postcards.

Simon smiled. "I'm actually here on behalf of my mamm. She's not feeling well. I came to get some of that herbal tea she likes to drink when she has a cold."

Jeremiah nodded. "Leah always makes me drink some when I so much as sniffle. She says the combination of the herbs will fix me right up." He grinned sheepishly. "And I suppose she's right. I haven't missed a day of work in two years." He grabbed a bag of tea from the shelf and handed it to Simon. "Is that all you need today?"

"I think I'll look around." Simon knew he should get back to the farm, but his foot was still asleep. Maybe walking around a bit would help.

"Good morning," Jeremiah greeted an English couple. "Is this your first time in Lancaster County?"

"Yes, sir," the young woman said. "We're headed to Philly to see some friends, but we wanted to stop here first."

"She's looking for quilts," the man with her said. "We've been to every market and roadside stand in the county, I think."

Jeremiah chuckled. "Then I suspect you've made a lot of stops."

"It's a beautiful place," the woman gushed. "We adore Amish Country. Wasn't it a shame what happened a few days ago?"

Simon stepped around the corner, curious to hear what the woman was going to say. He hadn't heard of any bad news lately.

"A shame, you say?" Jeremiah asked.

"The tornado that went through that little town in Ohio. We saw it last night on the news. Right in the middle of Amish Country there." The woman pulled on her husband's sleeve. "What was the name of the place, honey? It was something so cute."

"Charm. Charm, Ohio."

Jeremiah backed up, knocking over a display of postcards.

Simon hurried forward to help his friend. "Are you okay?" He reached out to steady Jeremiah. All the color had gone out of the older man's face.

"You know I have family in Charm." He looked pleadingly at Simon. "Can you look out for things here? I need to go find a phone."

* * * * *

Michael Landis tapped on the steering wheel of his SUV. He'd forgotten how annoying it was to be stuck behind a horse and buggy. He considered turning around and heading back to DC—except that he didn't have a job there anymore. Or an apartment. No girlfriend, either. And when he thought of the dismal situation going on with his checking account right now, just filling up his vehicle with gas would be a challenge. No way he was dipping into his savings just because he happened to be down on his luck.

Thankfully, his parents had been elated at the thought of having him back in Lancaster County. If he knew them, they'd already planned a big Landis family get-together complete with distant cousins and his elementary-school friends.

But his older brother had been quiet so far about the decision to move back. Not a huge surprise, though, considering the fact that they hadn't spoken but twice in the past year. And both of those times, it was only because Phillip happened to answer the telephone at their parents' house.

A break in oncoming traffic gave Michael the chance to go around the buggy. Finally. He nodded at the Amish gentleman as he passed.

His growling stomach reminded him that breakfast had been long ago, and a Pop-Tart at that. For a second he considered stopping at the Bird-in-Hand Farmer's Market for a quick snack. But by doing that, he was only postponing the inevitable homecoming that awaited him. *Might as well get it over with.*

Michael waited at the light and turned onto Old Philadelphia Pike. It was even more congested than he remembered. His mom had mentioned that there were new businesses cropping up, and she hadn't been exaggerating. He cast a wistful look at the Farmer's Market but kept driving. The crowded parking lot and multiple tour buses made it easier to pass up.

Ten minutes and two left turns later, he found himself on the long gravel driveway that led to his childhood home. Even though it had been years since he'd been back, things looked exactly the same.

A Border collie ran from behind the house, circling the SUV and barking a greeting.

"Hey, boy." Michael stepped down from the vehicle and stretched. "I don't think we've met."

"That's Toby," his brother said from the door of the large storage shed.

Michael bent down and scratched the dog behind the ears. "He's a good-lookin' dog."

"He's from the same line as Scrappy." Phillip forced a smile.

Scrappy had been Michael's constant companion until the day he'd gone off to college. He still remembered the day Mom had called to tell him that Scrappy had gone to that great hunting ground in the sky. The news had caused him so much heartbreak, he'd refused to ever own another pet.

Michael's mouth broke into a wide grin as he spotted his parents hurrying down the porch steps. He fought the urge to run and meet them halfway. That seemed a little childish. He wanted everyone to be clear that although he was the youngest member of the family, he was still a grown man.

"How long you planning on staying?" Phillip peered into the crowded SUV and cast a wary glance at his younger brother.

Michael sighed. So much for niceties. "I'm not sure. Not long. I'll probably try to find a place to rent or something."

"Now why would you want to do that?" Ellen Landis shot Phillip a scowl before pulling Michael into a hug. "You can stay here as long as you like." She reached up and patted his face. "You've missed Christmas the past two years. At least let me enjoy having you around for a little while before you move out again." Her face had a few more wrinkles than he was used to seeing, but her eyes were the same shade of blue.

"Son, I'm so glad you're home." Dad caught him in a tight bear hug and pounded on his back. "We were beginning to think we were going to have to send out a search party to get you here."

"I guess you'll be wanting me to go slaughter the fatted calf," Phillip muttered.

Mom chuckled. "Now, Phillip, don't be like that. We're just happy to have him home."

Phillip raised an eyebrow in his brother's direction. "Welcome back," he said curtly. "Now if you'll excuse me, I have work to do." With that, he turned on his heel and headed toward the barn, leaving Michael alone with their parents.

"I know you'll be losing money every night I'm here. I don't want to be a burden." Despite being a working dairy farm, his parents had turned their home into a bed-and-breakfast after Michael and his siblings had left home. The old farmhouse was a tourist favorite, and it wasn't unusual to have repeat guests.

"Don't be silly. You'll even be staying in your old room." Mom smiled.

His dad clapped him on the back again. "And I suspect you'll earn your keep. Unless you've forgotten how to milk a cow." He chuckled.

"I'm sure it's just like riding a bike." Michael grinned. He'd missed them.

"Now, come on inside. Let's get you fed." Mom looped her arm through his and led him toward the large farmhouse.

He wasn't going to argue with that. But the fact that at least one member of the family didn't share in the happiness of having him home made him a little uneasy.

One day at a time. Worst-case scenario, he'd go sleep in the barn.

Chapter Three

. . . .

Lydia Ann liked to think of herself as a survivor. When her mamm had been killed in an accident eight years ago, she'd leaned on Dat and her husband, Levi.

And five years ago, when Levi had succumbed to cancer, she'd gotten through it by focusing on the twins.

Standing in the rubble of what used to be her quilt shop, Lydia Ann wondered if she'd finally reached her breaking point. She'd always been careful not to question the Lord, but it was hard not to, especially after she'd been dealt yet another blow. Was her faith being tested?

"Mamm, are you sad?" Katie asked, tugging on her apron. "Your smile is turned upside down."

She looked down at her daughter. "I'm a little bit sad. You know, your dat and I worked together to build this shop. So it makes me sad that it's gone." She and Levi had been so young then. He'd wanted her to have a place to display and sell her quilts. That small idea had turned into a successful business, especially in the past couple of years.

She knelt down and put an arm around each of her daughters. "But things can be replaced. People can't." She squeezed them tightly. "I'm just thankful no one was hurt during such an awful storm." The Lord had been watching over them, that was for sure. Multiple funnel clouds had been spotted and several businesses and homes had sustained damage—yet there weren't even any minor injuries. Some people might call it lucky, but Lydia Ann knew better. She called it blessed.

"As soon as the debris is cleared, we can start rebuilding." Levi's mamm came to stand next to them. "I'm just sorry to see all your merchandise ruined." She patted Lydia Ann on the arm. "It's a good thing you're a fast quilter. And of course I'll help however I can."

Lydia Ann stood quietly. She'd been dreading this moment since she'd gotten off the phone with her cousin Emma earlier in the day. Levi's parents had been so wonderful to her and the girls over the years. "That's so sweet of you, Susanna. But I'd like to hold off on rebuilding, at least for a little while." She cleared her throat. "I spoke to Emma this morning. They've invited me to bring the girls to Shipshewana for a visit." Lydia Ann's cousins Emma and Abby lived in Shipshewana, Indiana. Despite the distance, they were her closest friends. Not a week went by that they didn't exchange letters. And it would be wonderful for Mary and Katie to get to know her family.

Susanna nodded. "I think that is a wonderful-gut idea. I know how you miss them." She smiled down at Katie and Mary. "And I know two little girls who will love to go on an adventure."

Lydia Ann breathed a sigh of relief. She'd been so afraid of hurting Susanna's feelings. She should've known better. Susanna was now the closest thing she had to a mother. Of course she'd understand how a tragedy would make Lydia Ann long to be surrounded by her family.

"When are you leaving?" Susanna asked.

Lydia Ann knelt to pick up a quilt square. "Day after tomorrow. The van will pick us up at the house."

Susanna smiled. "I'll look after things while you're gone."

"*Danki*," Lydia Ann said. Despite everything that had happened, she was looking forward to being with Emma and Abby. She knew they would lift her spirits. "Come on, girls." She motioned for Mary and Katie to follow her. "There's nothing more that can be salvaged here." With one final glance at the rubble, she ushered the girls into the waiting buggy.

* * * * *

Caroline buried her head underneath her lavender-scented pillow and pretended not to hear the knocking. The persistent knocking. Between the phone ringing, the doorbell chiming, and now this, it was no wonder she couldn't get any sleep.

"Caroline?" Robyn Wilson stuck her head into the dark bedroom. "I know you don't want to be bothered." She walked in and closed the door behind her. "But I want to make sure you're okay."

A groan escaped Caroline's mouth, and she pressed the pillow to her face. "I'm as okay as I can be." She tossed the pillow aside and sat up, drawing her legs to her chest. "Sorry to leave you to deal with everything. I can only imagine how crazy it is out there." Robyn had been Lance's personal assistant for the past two years, and since the news of his death broke, she'd been working overtime. Caroline wondered briefly if Robyn had even left the house over the past few days. Not that she cared. There were so many rooms, Robyn could probably invite her whole family to stay and Caroline would never know.

"That's okay." Robyn perched on the end of the king-sized bed. "But I need your input on a few things." Ever efficient, she whipped out her notepad. "Several members of the team have stopped by, and some of their wives as well. Greg, especially, wants to talk to you in person." Greg Jenkins had been Lance's closest friend. They'd come up through the minors together. "Also, I have a number of calls that you'll need to return yourself. The lawyer. The lady from the funeral home. Lance's agent." She ticked them off with her fingers. "I've handled everything I can handle. But I'll be glad to stay here a few more days and continue to take care of things." Robyn met Caroline's gaze.

"Are they still camped outside?"

Robyn nodded. "Just outside the gate. If it makes you feel any better, there aren't as many today as there were yesterday."

"Vultures."

"People are concerned about you. Although this is probably not the time to tell you, your picture is on the cover of pretty much every tabloid in the country."

Caroline rolled her eyes. "Please tell me it won't be like this forever."

Robyn hesitated for a moment too long. "Not forever. But for a while." She sighed. "Lance was probably the most recognizable athlete over the past decade. And after what happened…" She trailed off. "People are curious about the private details."

"Did you know?" Caroline leveled her gaze on Robyn. She'd wanted to ask the question for more than a week now.

"What?" Robyn asked, avoiding her eyes.

Caroline shook her head. "Did you know what was going on? About all the women?" She sighed. "I won't be mad if you did. But I want to know the truth."

Robyn bit her lip. "I didn't know for sure. I mean, I suspected he might have a girlfriend, but I certainly didn't know there were so many."

"One in every major city." When the story broke last week, Lance had tried to convince her that some of the women coming out of the woodwork were lying. Even if that were true, it didn't change the fact that her husband had been a serial cheater—and she'd never had a clue.

"But I didn't know about Valerie," Robyn continued. "It never occurred to me that she was anything more to him than a business associate."

Caroline snorted. "I guess that's one way of putting it." She leaned her head back against the headboard and shut her eyes. "How did I not see it? Valerie was the best friend I had in this town." She sat up. "Or at least I thought she was."

"Have you talked to her since…?" Robyn hesitated, uncertainty written all over her face. "No, I guess you wouldn't have." The cell phone in Robyn's hand began to buzz. She held it up. "It's Lance's agent. He's called a million times."

The last thing Caroline wanted was to discuss the business side of Lance's image. But she knew how persistent Mitch could be. Robyn shouldn't have to keep putting him off. She held out her hand. "Let me get this over with."

Mitch didn't even bother with condolences. "I have a couple of options for you to consider," he began. "I know you're still reeling, but babe, you're a hot commodity right now."

Caroline furrowed her brow. "*I'm* a hot commodity?" She raised her eyebrows in question at Robyn.

The younger woman shrugged and went back to her list.

"All the major talk shows want you. And that housewives reality show has also put out feelers. They think viewers would love to see how you're coping."

Had the world gone mental? Her life had fallen apart and people were looking for ways to cash in on it. "No. I'm not interested in any of it."

"The housewives thing I get. But how do you feel about dancing on live TV? You took ballet, right?"

"*Dancing with the Stars*? Seriously?"

The pen Robyn was using flew out of her hand and hit the hardwood floor with a bang. "Sorry," she whispered, scrambling to pick it up.

"I'm as serious as a heart attack. At this moment in time, you are the most fascinating woman in the world."

"Look, Mitch. I appreciate everything you've done for Lance." It was true. Lance had been one of the most marketable athletes of all time and Mitch had done a lot to see that the endorsement deals had been as sweet as possible. But this was too much. "I'm really not interested in pursuing anything that puts me in the public eye."

"I know you've been dealt a blow here, but—"

"No buts. I'm really not interested."

She tossed the phone onto the bed. "I'm not news. I don't get it."

Robyn scratched her head. "Your wedding pictures were in *People*. That kind of makes you news. No matter what the reason, people have always identified with your story."

Caroline clicked on the TV.

"*The Weather Channel*?"

"It's the only channel I can be sure won't talk about me or Lance. The day Jim Cantore starts rambling about my life instead of a natural disaster is the day I cancel my cable. Besides, there's something soothing about it. It helps me fall asleep."

"Beats sleeping pills," Robyn admitted.

"See, *this* is news." Caroline pointed to the screen. The pictures that flashed across the screen showed the aftermath of a tornado.

"The tiny Amish town of Charm, Ohio, saw tornadic activity earlier in the week," the reporter said as the camera panned the area. "Despite the forceful winds, only a handful of homes and businesses reported any damage. Residents are thankful there were no injuries."

"Didn't you visit there last year?" Robyn asked.

Caroline nodded. "That was the last trip I took with Mama. She'd always wanted to visit Ohio's Amish Country. We had such a wonderful time. The food was delicious...the shops were neat... And the people—so kind. Mama and I had the best time." She smiled at the memory. "We'd planned to take a trip this summer to Lancaster County, Pennsylvania." Caroline shrugged. She'd give anything to go back in time and take her mama to all the places she'd hoped to see someday. It was too late now, though.

"Members of the tightly knit community have spent the days since the storm lending a hand to those in need," the reporter said as the camera panned images of neighbors helping neighbors.

"Looks like they've really got things figured out," Robyn said, her eyes glued to the screen.

Caroline climbed out of bed and flung open the doors to her massive closet. She emerged with a suitcase. "And you know what? I think I've got things figured out too." She smiled broadly. "There's somewhere I need to go." For the first time in a week—no, for the first time in years—Caroline finally had some direction.

Chapter Four

....

Lydia Ann sat on a porch swing, sandwiched between her cousins. Emma Weaver and Abby Yoder might be sisters, but they were total opposites all the way down to the color of their hair. Emma's dark auburn hair and olive complexion contrasted Abby's blond hair and fair skin.

"I can't believe the two of you work together now."

Abby giggled. "Mamm was a little skeptical at first too. But it works very well."

"We're good at different things, so we're able to split up the duties," Emma explained. "We sell a little bit of everything—quilts, baked goods, even books." She smiled. "And Noah's paintings, of course."

Lydia Ann returned her cousin's smile. She remembered the day two years ago when she'd introduced Emma to Noah Weaver. Noah and Lydia Ann's late husband, Levi, had been cousins. She'd seen the spark between Emma and Noah immediately, although it had taken them a little longer to realize it. "I'm so glad he's still painting." Noah's paintings depicting the town of Charm had been very popular in Lydia Ann's own shop back home. At the thought of her store, now in rubble, she grew somber.

Abby reached over and patted Lydia Ann's hand. "I see that look on your face. Tell us how you're holding up." One of Abby's special gifts was empathy. Even when they were small children, it had always been Abby who'd tried to make everyone feel better.

Lydia Ann forced a smile. "I know not to store up treasures on earth. And I know this is probably going to sound silly." She looked from Abby to Emma. "But I feel like losing the shop means I lost my last connection to Levi." She shook her head. "Besides the girls, I mean." She thanked God daily for Mary and Katie. Besides reminding her of Levi, they brought such joy to her life.

"I think it's only natural for you to feel that way," Emma said.

Abby nodded. "*Jah*, she's right." She smiled. "And didn't you say Levi's parents would help you rebuild the shop quickly?"

Lydia Ann nodded. "Rebuilding isn't the problem. My friends and neighbors will have the building up in no time." She sighed. "It's just that I'm not sure I even want to rebuild."

Emma cast a worried look at her cousin. "But you love the store. I've seen how much you enjoy helping your customers. And your quilts are so beautiful."

She spoke the truth. Lydia Ann loved talking to the customers who came into her shop. Especially when they asked her advice on quilting. She'd had many customers come back to her shop weeks or months later to show her their progress. "I guess you're right...," she trailed off. The truth of the matter was that she'd been feeling at loose ends lately. Something wasn't right, but she couldn't put her finger on it. That was part of the reason she'd been so quick to travel to Shipshewana. She hoped that spending time with Emma, Abby, and their families would help her to get back to normal. Whatever that meant. "Enough about me." She patted Emma on the knee. "I want to hear how things are going here."

Abby chimed in. "Oh, things are wonderful. Clara is growing like a weed." She grinned. "But you already know that."

Clara had been Lydia Ann's mamm's name, and Lydia Ann was pleased that Abby and Jacob had chosen the name for their daughter.

"They do grow up fast." She glanced at Emma. Her normally outspoken cousin was being awfully quiet. "And how about you, Emma? Anything new?"

Emma shook her head. "Nothing much. My garden is doing well. Noah has found work that he enjoys." She smiled. "We're planning a trip to Chicago soon. Neither of us have ever been there."

Lydia Ann smiled. Her cousin had always loved to visit new places. She could see the excitement in Emma's eyes. "That sounds wonderful. I'm so glad to hear that you're happy." Although, if she were being honest, she had to wonder if Emma and Noah were ever going to have a baby. They'd been married for two years now...but she hated to bring it up.

The sound of a buggy coming up the road broke the silence.

"It's Dat," Abby said. "I wonder what brings him here."

Mose Miller was Lydia Ann's mamm's eldest brother. She knew her mamm had always thought highly of him.

"Lydia Ann," he said, climbing out of the buggy, "I had a phone call for you at the store."

She wrinkled her brow. "Is everything okay at home?" She'd given Susanna and Ben the number of the furniture store where Mose worked just in case they needed to get in touch with her.

He shook his head. "It wasn't a call from Charm." He came to stand on the bottom step of the porch. "It was from Jeremiah."

She sank onto the porch swing. Her dat had tracked her down. He must've heard about the tornado. "I didn't think about trying to get in touch with him."

"Oh, Lydia Ann," Abby murmured. "He must be so worried."

Emma shot her sister a look. "Lydia Ann has had a lot on her mind. I'm sure she just forgot."

Two years after Mamm's accident, Dat had remarried and moved to Lancaster County, Pennsylvania. He'd come back to Charm for Levi's funeral, but other than that, they'd had little contact. At first, he'd written her every few weeks, but the correspondence had waned. She knew that probably had something to do with how unenthusiastic she'd been about him finding love again. It just didn't seem right to her.

"I should've sent him a letter. I will write one now." She stood to go into the house.

"That won't be necessary," Mose said. "He's anxious to speak to you himself. I told him I'd come and fetch you. He'll be calling again in an hour."

"He will?" She gripped the banister with white knuckles.

Abby gently patted her on the back. "Do you want me to go with you?"

"Jah. That would be nice." She could use the support. It wasn't that she didn't want to speak to him, but she wasn't sure what to say. And she wasn't fond of using the telephone either, even though sometimes it was a necessity.

"I'll stay here with baby Clara and the twins," Emma volunteered. "Take your time."

Lydia Ann let Abby lead her to the waiting buggy.

There was a time when she'd been so close to her father…but she couldn't help feeling betrayed by his decision to get married and move away. She said a silent prayer that she'd be able to find the right words.

* * * * *

Michael hated to admit it, but he'd really enjoyed the past couple of days in his childhood home. Not that he was going to turn into one of those thirtysomething guys who lived with his parents and whose main social interaction was playing online video games. Nope. This was just a temporary stop until he figured out the next chapter in his life. Besides, he still had two years before he actually turned thirty, and there was no way he'd still be at the farm then.

There had only been a couple of tense moments, both involving Phillip. It seemed that instead of things glossing over between them during the years Michael had been away, the division had only grown. Other than that, being back in Lancaster County was pretty sweet.

Michael walked down the creaky stairs that led from the guest rooms to the dining room. One thing he could get used to about being back home was his mother's cooking.

"Morning, Michael." Dad nodded at him. "We only have three guests eating with us this morning, so you have your pick of seats."

A home-cooked breakfast was included with the price of the guest rooms. It was served family-style and gave guests the chance to visit with each other and the Landis family. The long table in the dining room could accommodate as many as twenty people, and Michael knew that there were certain times of the year when every seat was filled. It was a far cry from the smaller table that had been there when he was growing up. But his parents seemed to love having guests, and he knew the extra income was nice.

An older couple came through the door. "Good morning," the woman said, smiling.

"Did you sleep well?" Dad asked.

The man nodded. "Very well, thank you." He took a seat opposite Michael. "I don't know if it is the fresh air or the delicious food, but I slept like a baby."

"How about you?" Dad asked, nodding at the woman.

"Oh, yes. I'm just sorry we missed helping milk the cows this morning."

Overnight guests were welcome to get up early and help out with the farm chores. Michael didn't understand the novelty, but he knew it was one of the aspects many people found most appealing about staying on a working dairy farm.

"There's always tomorrow." Dad grinned.

"Looks like almost everyone is here." Mom poked her head in from the kitchen. "We're just waiting on one more guest. She arrived late last night but told me she'd be joining us for breakfast."

Michael picked up a biscuit from the basket in front of him and smeared a pat of butter on it. The butter began to melt on contact. Much better than the typical breakfast bar he'd eaten on the Metro on the way to his office. Just a few days in Lancaster County and his life in DC seemed like it had happened to someone else. He couldn't help but wonder about his coworkers, though. When the magazine he had worked for decided to go to an online-only version, the lay-offs had been widespread.

The door opened, bringing his musings to a halt.

"Sorry I'm late," a beautiful blond woman said. She slid into the chair next to Michael without making eye contact with anyone in the room.

"Caroline," Mom said, stepping into the room with a platter of bacon in her hands, "I'm so glad you could make it. I'm sure you're tired from your trip." She set the platter in the center of the table.

Michael glanced at the woman next to him. Suddenly his stay in Lancaster was looking up.

Chapter Five

....

Having people stare at her was nothing new. Caroline and Lance had been in the spotlight so many times, she'd become accustomed to photographers pointing their cameras at her. Even just a trip to the mall meant being stopped multiple times by people who wanted to talk about Lance's last game or ask her about an outfit she'd worn that had ended up on the pages of *People*.

But now the scrutiny made her feel self-conscious.

She'd stopped at a hotel in Nashville and the girl at the front desk had recognized her immediately. "I'm so sorry for your loss," she'd said. After a quick trip to a nearby Walgreens, Caroline's normally honey-brown hair was transformed into blond. She'd had blond hair as a child and figured she could pull it off. Maybe changing her hair would give her enough of a disguise. Today, though, she felt as if her blond hair was a neon sign screaming, "Look at me!" And that was not at all what she'd hoped for. Still, though, no one had recognized her.

Yet.

"Everything looks delicious." She smiled at Mrs. Landis, who hovered over her with a worried expression on her face. "I'm starving."

"Good, good." Mrs. Landis set a casserole on the table. "This should do it." She glanced at her husband. "Will you offer thanks before we eat?"

Caroline bowed her head as Mr. Landis gave thanks for the food. It reminded her of when she'd been a little girl at her grandparents' house. Her grandpa always thanked God for the food before anyone ate a bite.

"I'm Michael," the guy next to her said with a grin once the amens had been said. "Michael Landis."

Caroline wrinkled her forehead. "As in kin to the owners?" she asked.

"As in their youngest son." His green eyes twinkled. "I've been living out-of-state for the past few years but am back home for a little while."

"I see." She pulled apart a steaming biscuit and reached for the butter knife. "I'm Caroline Jennings." When she'd arrived at the guesthouse last night, she'd decided to use her maiden name. Maybe no one would put two and two together.

"Do I detect a Southern accent?" Michael asked.

She gave him a small smile. "I'm from Hiram, Georgia."

He looked at her for a long minute. "You look very familiar."

Caroline's heart quickened. This was it. Her cover was blown. She'd been stupid to think she could hide her identity. "Maybe I have one of those faces?"

"Has anyone ever told you that you look like Carrie Underwood?"

She let out a breath she hadn't realized she was holding. "I've heard that one a time or two."

"With your blond hair and brown eyes, you could be her sister." He smiled. "Her prettier sister."

Caroline felt the blood rush to her cheeks. "Thanks," she murmured.

"So what brings you to the area?" Michael asked. "Sightseeing? Visiting family?"

Caroline shifted uncomfortably, wishing there were a polite way to get him to leave her alone. Sure, he seemed nice. But the more questions she had to answer, the more likely the truth would come out. "Just seeing a new part of the country. I visited part of Ohio's Amish Country last year, so I thought visiting Lancaster County could be fun." She turned her attention to the breakfast casserole on her plate. Maybe if her mouth was full of food, he'd get the hint.

"That's what brought us here too," the older woman across from Caroline said. "I've been reading about the Amish, so when we were planning our vacation, we decided this would be the perfect place to visit." She patted her husband on the arm. "And Gordon told me he'd go wherever I wanted, as long as it made me happy." Her eyes danced.

The man next to her chuckled. "I've spent forty years trying to make her happy. It's one of my greatest pleasures in life."

Caroline wanted to gag. Seriously? Seeing a couple so obviously in love only reminded her of what she'd lost. Or what she'd never really had to begin with, depending on how she looked at it.

* * * * *

"I can't believe I let you talk me into this," Lydia Ann said.

Emma laughed. "Abby deserves as much of the blame as I do. If she hadn't insisted that Noah and I accompany you and the twins on the trip, you never would've agreed to go."

Lydia Ann glanced over at Noah, who was quietly reading the twins a story. The five of them had left Shipshewana early that morning, traveling by van to Lancaster County, Pennsylvania. "I'm thankful the two of you are coming with us, even though you're only staying a few days." She managed a smile. "It gives us a little more time to visit. But I'm not too excited about spending the summer in Lancaster County." Lydia Ann's nervousness seemed to grow with each passing mile.

"Look at it this way," Emma said. "It will be a wonderful blessing for your girls to get to know their dawdi. They deserve to know him. And he deserves to know them."

"You sound just like your sister," Lydia Ann grumbled. But she couldn't help but smile. As soon as her dat had asked her to bring the girls and spend some time in Lancaster County, Emma and Abby had been completely for it. "Besides, am I to believe that you weren't a little bit excited at the prospect of accompanying us there? I know you and Noah plan to visit Hershey on the way home after you leave us." She grinned.

Emma at least had the decency to look sheepish. "Well, I am a bit happy to visit a state I've never been to. And the Fishers had such wonderful things to say about their visit to Hershey, I just thought we may as well stop there on our way back home." She chuckled. "But mostly I think it is the right decision for you and your girls."

"But…" Lydia Ann trailed off, sure that her thoughts would make her sound like an awful person.

"Are you afraid you'll feel uncomfortable being in their home?" Emma asked.

Lydia Ann nodded. "I haven't been around Leah too many times. When he first met her, I'd just married Levi. Soon after that, they moved to Lancaster County." She sighed. "Dat told me at Levi's funeral that he never would've left if he'd had any inkling what was about to happen."

"And I'm sure that was the truth. Lydia Ann, I know you've had a hard time, but your dat was so lost without your mamm. You know that."

Mamm's death had been out of the blue. Since it was an accident, there had been no time to prepare for the loss. At least with Levi, Lydia Ann had somewhat prepared herself for the worst.

The women fell silent as laughter came from the middle row. Noah and the twins chuckled over the story he was reading.

"He's very good with them," Lydia Ann observed.

Emma nodded. "He has a way with children. You should see him with Clara. Sometimes when she's fussy, Noah can get her to stop crying better than anyone. He's a wonderful uncle." She smiled at the thought.

Lydia Ann met her cousin's gaze. "Do you hope to have children of your own?"

"Oh, we'd love nothing more. I try and tell myself that it will happen someday. But I get so discouraged." Emma's normally sunny face grew sad.

Abby had confessed to Lydia Ann last night that she was expecting another child. It had to be hard on Emma. "I'm sure it will happen. And you'll be wonderful parents."

Emma leaned closer to Lydia Ann. "We know a couple from our church who recently adopted a baby. Noah and I have been talking about it lately. The thought of providing a good home for a baby in need makes me very happy. Noah too."

Lydia Ann nodded. "That sounds like an idea worth looking

into." It was true. Emma and Noah were two of the most kind-hearted people Lydia Ann knew. She grinned. "I hope you'll write me these next few weeks and let me know what's going on."

"Of course. Abby will too. And you'll have to do the same." She reached over and patted Lydia Ann's hand. "It will be fine. I suspect the time will fly by and you'll be back in Charm in no time."

"Jah. I know you're right." Lydia Ann stifled a yawn. "Sorry. I guess I didn't get much sleep last night."

Emma chuckled. "I'll bet Abby kept you up late last night, talking." She reached into her bag and pulled out a book. "Now you try to get a nap. We should be there soon."

Lydia Ann leaned over and rested her head against the cool window. She wasn't sure whether to feel nervous or excited, so she settled on both. It had been such a long time since she'd seen Dat. It would be nice to catch up with him in person. She just wished she felt the same way about getting to know his wife.

Chapter Six
....

Simon Zook walked into the Landis barn, eager to get started with the day's work. He'd already been up for hours, tending to chores at his own home. A lone figure seated on an overturned bucket startled him. A closer look told him it was his old friend, Michael Landis. "Mornin', Michael."

"Simon!" Michael exclaimed, standing up and brushing the dirt from his jeans. "I came looking for you yesterday, but you were gone to town." He grinned. "So I figured I'd catch you this morning before the day got too busy."

"I heard you were back in town." Simon grinned. Michael's upcoming visit had been all Mr. Landis could talk about for the past couple of weeks. "You've been away for such a long time." The Landis farm was the nearest property to the Zooks' place. Simon and Michael had known one another since they were small boys. In fact, Michael had been the first friend Simon ever had who wasn't Amish.

"I know. I never could get away from work." Michael looked sheepish. "But I'm back for a while this time."

"For good?" Simon asked.

Michael wrinkled his nose. "I don't know about that. But I am looking for a job around here."

Simon drew his brows together. "Surely your father can find work for you to do on the farm."

"I think I'll leave that to Phillip. I'm trying to find something at one of the local newspapers. There's a magazine directed at tourists that has an opening. I'd like to keep building my resume while I'm here." He grinned. "And not with milking cows and feeding chickens, either."

Simon chuckled. He should've known Michael would want to avoid working with Phillip at all costs. Those two had never been close. "I hope you find something soon." He reached over and patted a calf on the head. "Did your dad tell you that I'm working here full-time now?"

Michael nodded. "Yes. Sounds like you've been a real help."

"It's good work. And it works out well for all of us that they're operating a guesthouse. Mamm comes with me a few days a week to help out with the cooking and take care of the guest rooms. She really enjoys working here."

"It looks like the guesthouse is getting busier and busier." Michael pointed out the window at a trio of vehicles in the driveway. "I don't understand the draw, but the guests seem to love it."

Simon laughed. "I know what you mean. Imagine, paying good money to do farm chores. But they seem to enjoy it."

"Well, I guess once you're used to the hustle and bustle of the city, it might seem relaxing to be out here with the animals and open land."

"I suppose. I meet the guests here every mornin' before breakfast is served. I'm always surprised at how many of them want to get up so early to help."

Michael looked at him suspiciously. "Has a Southern woman been out here to feed the animals? Her name is Caroline."

Simon shook his head. "I don't remember her."

"You'd remember this woman. She's a beautiful blond with the sweetest voice."

"Sounds like someone might be a little smitten." Simon chuckled.

"Not smitten." Michael shot his old friend a look. "Just concerned. She left the breakfast table pretty quickly. Not that I'm all that great at reading women, but she seemed kind of upset."

Simon shrugged. "Maybe she doesn't like the way it smells like cows out here." He waved his hands around the barn.

Michael chuckled. "Maybe." He leveled his gaze at Simon. "Speaking of pretty women, I can't believe you and Sarah aren't married yet. I expected to come home to find you with a full beard."

Amish men grew their beards out once they were married. No need for wedding rings. That beard signified to the world the man's status. "I thought your parents would've told you." Simon absently rubbed his smooth chin. "She left. It's been almost two years."

"Left? As in for good?"

Simon nodded. "Seems that way. I heard she married some Englisher. I think they live in Philadelphia."

Michael let out a low whistle. "I don't know what to say. That must've been tough for you."

Tough didn't even cover it. Sarah had been the only girl he'd ever courted. He saw the way everyone in his community looked at him now. The pity in their eyes. "It has been difficult. I guess we never know what the morrow will bring."

"Guess not." Michael shook his head. "I should probably get out of here and let you get to work."

Simon followed Michael to the barn door. "It was good to see you again, Michael. I hope you'll be happy during your visit." He knew the Landises were glad to have their youngest son at home.

"You too. Let's get together again soon." Michael grinned. "I'm pretty sure I'll be bored out of my mind after another few days here."

"There's always work to be done." Simon balled his hand into a fist to get the circulation going. The numbness in his hand had seemed to come out of nowhere. "And I'd be glad for the help."

Michael chuckled. "Maybe I'll be out here tomorrow morning to help milk the cows."

"Especially if a certain blond woman happens to join the work crew?" Simon teased, ducking as his friend tossed a stray clump of hay in his direction.

* * * * *

Caroline had been driving around aimlessly for the past hour, enjoying the views of the farmhouses and pastures. Mama would've loved this place, that was for sure. The simplicity reminded Caroline a little of growing up in rural Georgia.

But those days were long gone. Besides, no matter how simple things seemed, her life was one giant ball of complicated. Even if the paparazzi were no longer camped outside, it didn't mean the story had died down. A conversation with Robyn earlier that morning had told her that the exact opposite seemed to be happening.

"It's like they're rabid. All the tabloids are speculating about where you are. And the fact that you were spotted in Nashville has brought about all kinds of rumors."

"Like what?" she'd asked.

Robyn had groaned. "You don't even want to know. But let's just say you've been romantically linked to a country singer."

Caroline sat in the parking lot of the Bird-in-Hand Farmer's Market, wondering if she'd ever get her life back.

Except that she knew what it would take for that to happen.

A time machine.

Lance had been so charming. He'd done and said all the right things. And she'd bought every line. Sighing, she pushed it out of her mind. She was safe here. With her newly colored hair in a pony-tail, clad in simple jeans and a T-shirt, no one would mistake her for the girl she used to be.

She grabbed her wallet and went inside, inhaling the sweet smells of freshly baked goods. Ten minutes later she emerged, armed with bags full of whoopie pies, several jars of jam, and an assortment of handmade pot holders. The jams and pot holders were gifts for Robyn and Mrs. Landis. The pies were to eat later. She hadn't been able to choose, so she'd gotten one in every flavor.

Caroline put her bags on the empty passenger seat and tapped her fingers against the steering wheel. It was awfully early to go back to the farm, but she had nowhere else to go. Except that she was afraid of running into Michael Landis. Something about him set her on edge. She'd overheard him tell the happy couple at breakfast that he'd been in Washington, DC, for the past few years. What if he recognized her? He'd certainly scrutinized her face.

She turned her car down the long driveway leading to the farmhouse. Michael was nowhere in sight. Thank goodness. She made her way to the guest entrance, trying to maneuver around the menagerie of cats that seemed determined to wind around her ankles.

"Did you enjoy your shopping?" A male voice behind her almost made her drop her packages.

She twirled around, expecting to see Michael.

Instead, a shorter, stockier man in work clothes stood before her. He chuckled. "Where are my manners? I can see I scared you."

He wiped his hand on his worn jeans and held it out. "I'm Phillip Landis." He grinned. "My parents own this place."

Caroline introduced herself. "I've been out to the Farmer's Market," she explained.

"One of my favorite spots. I'd be glad to give you directions to a couple of the bakeries, if you'd like. They sell a lot of the same stuff."

She nodded. "I've been to one of them already." She held up her bags and nodded in the direction of the house. "Do you live here?"

He shook his head. "Not anymore. I grew up here, though." He motioned down the driveway. "My house is the first one out by the main road." He gave her another smile. "I don't want to keep you. I usually come up for breakfast, but these past few mornings I haven't made it in time. Otherwise I would've introduced myself already." With a wave, he headed toward the barn.

Caroline watched him go, thankful he wasn't as inquisitive as his brother.

Chapter Seven

....

Lydia Ann silently nibbled a slice of homemade bread. It looked like Leah had gone all out for dinner, with heaping servings of chicken, fresh vegetables, bread, and a variety of baked goods that had made Mary's and Katie's eyes grow big.

"Lydia Ann?" Dat watched her, a concerned expression covering his weathered face.

Emma nudged her. "I think they'll be staying for at least two months, right, Lydia Ann?" she asked sweetly.

"Oh, yes." She'd been so lost in thought, she hadn't even heard the conversation around her. "We can stay for the summer. We just need to be home in time for the girls to start back to school."

Dat's face lit up with a smile. "I can't tell you how glad I am that you're here."

Leah nodded. "Jah. It's all he's been able to talk about for days." Her mouth turned upward. "And I'm thankful for the chance to get to spend some time with you and the girls."

"Thanks for having us," Lydia Ann murmured.

"That goes for us too," Emma said. "Even though we'll only be staying for a few days, I know having so many extra people in the house is a burden."

Dat shook his head. "It's nice to have a full house." He beamed at Mary and Katie. "And it's been so many years since there've been little ones around. They bring such joy to a home. I'm thankful to have my whole family under one roof." He nodded in Emma's direction. "Please give your parents my regards."

"Of course," Emma said with a smile.

Leah rose from the table. "Does anyone need anything else? A second helping of pie?"

Everyone chuckled.

"I think we're all full," Noah said. "Everything was delicious."

Leah beamed and began to gather dishes.

Emma stood and took the plates from Leah's hand. "Let Lydia Ann and me do that," she said. "You've done so much already."

Lydia Ann jumped up from her seat and began to help her cousin clear the table.

Once they were in the kitchen and out of earshot, Emma pulled Lydia Ann aside. "What is wrong with you? Couldn't you at least try to look happy to be here?" she whispered.

"I know. I'm sorry. I didn't realize that being around Dat again would make me miss Mamm so much." Lydia Ann frowned.

"I think it's only natural," Emma said.

Lydia Ann sighed. "I keep remembering times the three of us had together as I grew up. Remember when you and Abby used to come and stay with us during the summer?"

Emma laughed. "Those were fun days." She reached over and patted Lydia Ann's arm. "And good memories."

Lydia Ann nodded. "You're right."

"But I think you should try hard to make the most of your time while you're here." Emma looked intently at her cousin. "Give Leah a chance. I know it won't be easy, but she means a lot to your dat. And

I know him well enough to know she must be pretty special if he was willing to move away from his home for her."

Lydia Ann thought about her cousin's words. Emma was exactly right. If the past few years had taught Lydia Ann anything, it was that there were no guarantees in this life. And Dat wasn't getting any younger. Maybe she should try to give him the benefit of the doubt, even if it meant getting to know his wife.

* * * * *

"I hear you had an interview," Phillip said.

Michael tried to read his brother's face. He wasn't in the mood to be drawn into an argument, but maybe Phillip was just making small talk. This was the first morning he'd actually come to breakfast since Michael had been back home. "I sure did. I'm hoping to hear something soon."

Phillip took a sip of orange juice. "So does that mean you're back home for good?"

Michael wrinkled his brow. "No. It means that I'm trying to find gainful employment for a few months."

"Until something better comes along?" Phillip asked gruffly.

"Just something that's more along the lines of what I want to do."

His brother bristled. "You know, Michael, that's exactly what your problem is."

Michael shook his head. "I don't recall having a problem." He glanced at the dining room door, hoping the guests would come in soon and put an end to the conversation.

"Of course you don't. That's typical." Phillip took an angry bite from his biscuit. "When are you going to learn that we don't always get to do exactly what we want to do? Sometimes life just doesn't turn out that way."

"Why are you so angry? I haven't done anything but follow my dreams." Michael had had enough of his brother's lousy attitude. Why did he have to be so difficult?

"That's just the problem." Phillip stood. "*Your* dreams." He tossed his wadded-up napkin onto the table. "When are you going to learn that it isn't always about *you*?"

With those words Phillip strode off, leaving Michael seething.

His brother was impossible. He held such a grudge against Michael.

And Michael had no idea what it was all about.

Chapter Eight
....

Caroline looked over the tourist map she'd grabbed from the local visitors' center. She was proud of the way she'd learned her way around. Yesterday she'd only gotten lost a couple of times. It seemed like over the past few days she'd been to every roadside stand and store in the county. Well, maybe not *every* stand, but it sure seemed like it.

She'd even visited the big outlet mall in Lancaster proper. There were tons of people there and no one had recognized her. Not one single person. She tossed the map onto the desk in her guest room. Maybe she'd just wing it today and leave the map behind. One last glance in the mirror before she headed downstairs to what she knew would be a delicious breakfast. And despite the fact that her jeans already seemed a bit tighter than they had been when she'd arrived, she planned to indulge.

"Morning." Michael said, grinning as she walked into the dining room.

She nodded her head in greeting. "Hi."

He'd been missing from the table yesterday. Not that she was keeping tabs. But after two mornings of his chatter, she couldn't help but notice the quietness.

"Mind if I sit here?" She motioned at the empty seat next to him.

"Of course not." He grinned.

She filled a mug with coffee from the carafe that sat in the middle of the table. "Can you pass me the cream, please?"

Michael handed her a tiny container. "It's fresh cream," he said with a smile.

She poured a heaping amount of creamer into her coffee, enjoying the way it swirled into the darker liquid. Back at her old job, her coworkers had teased that she used as much creamer as she did coffee. She'd broken the habit because Lance had given her a hard time too. But now…she was free to use as much creamer as she pleased.

"So how long are you planning to stay here?" Michael's green eyes searched her face.

She shrugged. "I'm not sure." Her mouth turned upward in a tiny smile. "Why? Are you trying to get rid of me?"

He chuckled. "No, no. Nothing like that." He rubbed his chin. "Actually, I was going to see if maybe you'd like for me to show you around." Suddenly he looked unsure. "You know, like a tour."

Caroline bit her lip. "I don't know." She had to admit, it was getting a little old going everywhere alone. And surely if Michael was going to recognize her, he would've already done so by now.

"Have you seen any of the covered bridges?"

She shook her head. "Not yet." However, they were on her list of things to see.

"Well, if you decide you'd like to go on a little driving tour to see some of them, just say the word." He grinned.

Caroline took a sip of coffee. There was nothing to be afraid of. Even though his questions over the past few days had annoyed her, his persistence was endearing. "You know, I think that sounds nice." She smiled.

"I think everyone is here," Mr. Landis said from the kitchen doorway. He greeted a couple with two small children who'd just entered the dining room. Once they were seated, he turned to Michael. "Will you offer thanks, son?"

Caroline bowed her head. The morning prayers here seemed so normal. Not forced. Not for show. She was once again left with a longing for her childhood, when mealtime and bedtime prayers were important parts of her day. These past years, her talks with God seemed to only come when she was facing tough times. When had she stopped giving thanks?

"You okay?" Michael whispered, leaning so close that she could smell his soapy scent.

She jerked her head up and met curious stares around the table. Prayer was over. For how long, she wasn't sure. Heat flamed her face. "Sorry."

He grinned, and she noticed a tiny dimple in his cheek. "Don't be. I was afraid maybe I'd put you to sleep."

She couldn't help but chuckle. "Nothing like that."

"So, can you be ready to leave here around ten? I have a couple of things I need to do before then."

"Ten is perfect." She found herself looking forward to their outing. The past weeks were a blur of loneliness for her. Not that she expected Michael to turn out to be a real friend or anything—just that having some company would be nice for a change. She watched him from the corners of her eyes.

And some cute company at that.

* * * * *

"I'm thrilled for the opportunity," Michael said into his phone. "Since I grew up here, I'm familiar with all the popular places. And hopefully I'll know of some hidden gems that don't get as much attention."

"We're happy to have you onboard," Mr. Sinclair said. "With your background and experience, you'll be a great fit. See you Monday."

Michael clicked off the phone and tossed it onto his bed. Man, gainful employment felt good. He glanced at the clock on his nightstand. Just enough time to tell his parents the good news before he met up with Caroline. He took the stairs two at a time and burst into the kitchen.

Mom looked up from the cookbook she was perusing. "Is there a fire somewhere?"

"You're not going to believe this," he said, grinning. "But Mr. Sinclair offered me the job. I start Monday."

Mom pulled him into a quick hug. "Congratulations. I know you'll be glad to get back to work."

"I will." He grinned and motioned toward the barn. "See you later." He gave her a kiss on the cheek and headed outside to tell his dad the good news.

"Have you seen Dad?" he called to Phillip in the driveway.

His surly brother nodded. "He's out in the field."

"Okay." Michael pondered telling Phillip but thought better of it. He wouldn't care one way or the other. Their earlier conversation was testament to that.

"I've got work to do," Phillip said gruffly. "See you later."

"Where are you off to today?" Simon asked, walking up to hear the tail end of Phillip's words.

Michael couldn't hide his grin. "I'm, uh, taking Caroline to do a little sightseeing." He jerked his head toward the main road. "We're going to go see some of the covered bridges."

"The kissing bridges, you mean?" Simon chuckled.

"Just sightseeing today, man."

"Looks like your friend is ready." Simon nodded toward Michael's SUV.

Caroline stood next to the vehicle with uncertainty written all over her face.

"Hey there," Michael called. "You ready to go?"

She glanced up and smiled. "Sure am."

"See you later." Michael nodded at Simon.

"Have fun," Simon called, still chuckling.

Michael walked around to the passenger side and opened the door. "Your carriage awaits."

"I didn't expect to find a Southern gentleman all the way up here in Yankee territory." Caroline flashed him a smile as she climbed into the SUV.

"Guess you never know what's waiting around the corner." He jumped into the driver's seat and started the vehicle. "That's what makes life exciting, right?" he asked, driving the SUV slowly down the gravel driveway. At the end, he flipped on the blinker and waited to turn onto the paved road.

"I guess so," Caroline said. "But I kind of like knowing. That way I can be prepared for whatever situation arises." She pulled a pair of sunglasses out of her bag and put them on.

"Those things are so big, they're like a disguise or something," he said, giving her a sideways glance.

Her jaw hardened. "Don't be silly. Oversized sunglasses are practically all there is on the market today."

Great. He'd somehow managed to tick her off and they weren't even off of his parents' property yet. "They look fine. Just kidding." He pulled the SUV onto the main road.

"So tell me what we're going to see today."

"Well, I'm sure you've heard about the famed bridges of Lancaster County." He slowed down as they came up behind a horse and buggy. "There are twenty-nine covered bridges here. Most of them are historic landmarks. Some you can still drive through, but some you can't." He flipped on his signal and went around the buggy.

"Honestly, I didn't know anything about Lancaster County before I came here. Just that it was in the middle of Amish Country."

Michael rolled his eyes. "Yes. That's all most people know of the area."

"You say that like it's a bad thing."

He shrugged. "I grew up among the Amish. I guess it irritates me sometimes to see people treat them like they're some kind of tourist attraction. They're just good, hardworking people."

"I can see how you'd feel that way, but it's really sort of flattering. Think about it. People from all over the country come here to try to capture a little bit of what they have."

"What do you mean?"

"Peace. Contentment. From the outside looking in, it seems like an ideal way to live." She chuckled. "I mean, don't get me wrong. There's no way I could give up certain things like TV or air conditioning. But their sense of community is amazing, and the way they take care of one another is inspiring. Where I live, my neighbors barely know me. At least not the real me." She let out a tiny sigh.

"So who does know the real you?" He cast a quick glance in her direction.

A long moment of silence filled the car.

"No one, really."

"Don't give me that. Surely someone does. Your family? Your childhood best friend? College roommate? Boyfriend?" He knew he was out on a limb, but he couldn't seem to stop himself.

"Can you pull in here at this bakery?" she asked. "I'd like to get a couple of things."

"Why do I get the feeling that your sudden urge for baked goods is just a way to avoid my questions?" Even so, he slowed down and turned into the small gravel parking lot. The last girl he dated used to accuse him of deflecting personal questions. Maybe this was some kind of cosmic payback, because Caroline certainly seemed to have a thick wall around herself.

She grinned. "I just have a hankerin' for some whoopie pies."

"Well, if you have a hankerin', then by all means, let's take care of it." He chuckled and followed her into the bakery.

Chapter Nine

Caroline walked down an aisle filled with a variety of candy. Her personal trainer back in Atlanta would have a conniption fit if she saw this place. Caroline thought it was actually kind of liberating.

"See anything you like?" Michael asked from behind her.

Despite his questions, she had to admit that she was beginning to enjoy his company.

"Are you kidding? I'd like to buy one of everything."

He smiled. "I know what you mean. When I lived in DC, I was one of those super-healthy eaters. Lots of vegetables, no red meat… you know the drill." He shook his head. "But here I can't seem to help myself."

She laughed. "I keep telling myself it's the fresh air."

"Right. The fresh air—tinged with just a hint of cow smell."

Caroline couldn't help but grin. "Actually, it doesn't bother me. I'm a country girl at heart. My granddaddy had a couple of cows."

"No kidding? You don't strike me as a farm girl."

"There's a lot you don't know about me." *That might be the understatement of the year.*

Michael let out a soft chuckle. "Tell me about it." He grinned. "There's plenty of time for you to fill me in, though." He grabbed a bottled water from the refrigerated case. "Do you want something to drink? Water, soda?"

"Water is fine, thanks." She flashed him a smile and turned her attention to the freshly baked goods. "I love these little whoopie pies. They're just the right size." Despite the name, whoopie pie wasn't really pie at all, but two round pieces of cake with a creamy frosting sandwiched between them. "I think the red velvet cake with cream-cheese frosting in the middle is my favorite," she said.

"They are pretty good," Michael agreed, "although I prefer the chocolate kind with vanilla frosting."

They finally made their selections—whoopie pie for her and shoofly pie for him—and climbed back into the vehicle.

"So I'm thinking we'll stop at one of the bridges in the south-eastern part of the county. We can eat our pies picnic-style."

"Sounds divine." She glanced over at him. Long eyelashes, the kind women would kill for, framed his green eyes. He wore his blond hair in a spiky style. She could only imagine what the women from her neighborhood would say about him.

Ten minutes later, Michael parked the car on a side road. "I think I have an old stadium blanket in the back," he said. "I'll grab it. You get the snacks."

She followed him to a wide-open plot of grass where they had a great view of the bridge.

"It's so peaceful out here," Caroline said. The red covered bridge looked like something straight off a movie set. "Seriously. Even the flowers are all perfectly bloomed."

Michael met her gaze. "It is a thing of beauty."

She felt her face grow hot. "You're talking about the bridge, right?"

He shrugged. "The bridge is pretty. You have it beat, though."

"Thanks," she said softly. She couldn't help but feel flattered at his admiration. Lance had refused to compliment her looks once they got married. He always said it was to keep her from getting a big head. And although she told herself she didn't need a man to tell her she was pretty, there was no denying that it made her feel good to know Michael found her attractive.

He reached his hand out. "Toss me that bag. I think I need some shoofly pie."

She obliged. "So, tell me about you. What exactly brought you back home?"

Michael groaned. "It makes me sound like a failure."

"Believe me when I say I'm the least judgmental person you'll ever meet." It was true. She had no room to judge anyone else's life choices. Especially since she seemed to be the queen of choosing incorrectly.

"Fine." He gave her a tentative grin. "Let me start by saying that I love my parents. Really. My leaving home had nothing to do with them."

"Fair enough."

"But I never felt like I fit in here," he explained. "My brother was all about the farm, even when we were kids. But I'd rather be inside, reading or on the computer."

"So you're not into the outdoors?"

He shook his head. "It isn't that. I love to hike and fish." He grinned. "Even camp. I'm not some kind of prissy guy who hates to get dirty, if that's what you're getting at. I just grew up knowing that I didn't want to spend the rest of my life working on a dairy farm, that's all."

Caroline nodded. "Believe me, I understand. I think when you grow up in a rural area, there is a real need to leave and see the world. I know a lot of my friends growing up did that. They left home as soon as we got out of high school and headed for the city." She met his gaze. "But a lot of them returned to their roots, especially when they were ready to have children. So I think your choice to leave and find your own career sounds reasonable."

"Maybe to you. But to everyone in my family, it was like I was somehow disloyal. Especially according to Phillip." Disgust washed over Michael's handsome face. "I got good grades in school and was offered a nice scholarship to a school in Virginia. Their journalism department had a great reputation, so I jumped at the chance."

She wrapped the remainder of her whoopie pie in cellophane wrapping. It would be a nice treat later. "How'd that go?"

"I loved it. And then right after college I was offered a job in DC, writing for a weekly political magazine. Nonpartisan, but it leaned a little right."

"So that's what you've been doing for the past few years?"

He nodded. "Yep. I even won a couple of awards. But earlier this year, our format changed. We went to an online-only version and our pay scale changed." He shook his head. "Under the new system, we got paid based on the number of times people clicked on our articles."

She drew her brows together. "Ugh. That doesn't sound very stable."

"That's an understatement. Let's just say that there was no way of guessing what my salary was going to be. And with the cost of living in DC, there was no way I could keep on that way."

"So you came home."

"I tried cutting back at first. And I had enough contacts that I picked up some freelance work. Even so, my salary wasn't steady enough to justify staying." He shrugged. "I've been sending my resume out, but times are tough."

She sighed. "I'm sorry. But I'll bet you'll find something soon."

He grinned. "Actually, I found a job here. I officially start on Monday." He raked his fingers through his hair. "It isn't hard-hitting journalism or anything, though. I'll be writing for a magazine geared toward tourists."

"That sounds like fun."

"Yeah. It will be different than what I'm used to. I'll also be starting a blog, highlighting some of the fun things to do in Lancaster County and the surrounding areas. Plus, they want me to really beef up the social-media aspect of things."

"So you'll be like the Twitter king of Lancaster County?"

He chuckled. "Something like that."

"Well, it sounds like you've landed on your feet." Would she ever be able to say that about herself? At this point, it felt like she'd been knocked down so many times that she might not be able to recover.

"Let's hope so." He took a sip from his bottled water. "But enough about me." He waggled his eyebrows. "I want to hear about you."

"Nothing to tell."

"I'm going to have to call your bluff on that one."

She wrinkled her nose. "What do you mean?"

He ticked them off on his hand. "Beautiful. Single. Staying on a dairy farm thousands of miles from home. Avoids questions like a fighter avoids punches. Need I say more?"

"Please don't." She gave him a tiny smile. "Good genes. Haven't found the right man. Likes to travel. Takes awhile to warm up." She mimicked him, ticking off each statement with her fingers.

"You aren't going to make this easy, are you?" He grinned. "Okay. Let's start with the basics. What do you do for a living?"

Caroline bit her lip. If he only knew how complicated such a simple question could be. "I used to be a kindergarten teacher." She'd loved teaching. Her students had brought her such joy. And then one day, the Atlanta Braves all-star pitcher came to visit for a fund-raiser. Her principal had introduced the two of them. And the rest was history. Well-documented history.

"Used to be? So you aren't a teacher any longer?" He drew his brows together.

"Not exactly. I mean, I still have my license, but I'm not currently employed as a teacher."

Michael reached over and patted her hand. "And I now officially proclaim you the queen of evasiveness."

She recoiled at his touch, but not before she felt the electricity between them. "I'm just between jobs."

He gave her a long stare. "Okay. Fine. I'll accept that. But tell me—what brought you here alone? Most people who come and stay at the farm are with their families."

Didn't she know it. All week, she'd felt like a pariah in the midst of all the happy couples and families with small children. So far she'd been the only single guest at the farm. But she was used to being alone. Most of the past two years had been spent that way. "I didn't see any signs that said singles weren't welcome." She grinned. "I guess I just wanted to visit the area and figured I'd do it. If I had to wait to find someone to travel with me everywhere I went, I'd probably never go anywhere."

"But why here?"

"Peace. Quiet. A change of scenery." She shrugged. "My mama and I went to Ohio Amish Country last year and had a wonderful time. I guess I was just trying to recapture some of that."

"So why didn't you bring her with you?"

Caroline hated to say the answer aloud. "Mama passed away a few months ago. But she always wanted to come here." She felt hot tears fill her eyes. "So I guess I'm here for her."

Michael scooted closer and put his arm around her. "I'm so sorry for your loss. That must've been terribly difficult."

For a long moment, Caroline leaned into him. It had been so long since she'd been held by anyone. She'd forgotten how comforting a simple hug could feel. She let a tiny sob escape.

"Shh." He pulled her closer and smoothed her hair. "You'll be okay."

She shrugged out of his embrace. "I'm not so sure about that." Some days she questioned whether she'd ever get her life back on track. She felt his eyes on her and hated the pity she knew was reflected in them. "Sorry for unloading on you." She'd learned to be self-reliant and deal with her feelings on her own. Her outburst, though small, embarrassed her.

"Nothing to apologize for. I'm glad to see some of those walls come down."

She smiled through her tears. "Don't get used to it. It doesn't happen very often." She wiped her face. "But I do miss her. A lot. And now you know why I'm here." At least he knew part of the reason.

He stood and offered her his hand. "How about we go take some pictures?"

She let him help her up. "Sounds like a plan." The ease of conversation between them surprised her. But she couldn't help but feel deceitful. If he knew who she really was and what had happened with Lance, she knew he'd see her in a different way. At least she didn't plan to stick around Lancaster County too much longer. There'd never be a reason to tell him the whole truth.

* * * * *

Lydia Ann sat alone in the kitchen. She'd always been an early riser, relishing the time before anyone else awoke. Years ago she'd gotten into the habit of reading her Bible in the quiet of the morning. She flipped it open, wondering what message the Lord would have for her today, and soon found herself lost in the Psalms. It seemed as if she learned something new every time she studied.

In the eighteenth psalm, second verse, she found words to dwell on: "*The LORD is my rock, and my fortress, and my deliverer.*" Lydia Ann tried to live her life by putting her complete trust in the Lord, but sometimes that was hard. Sometimes she tried to put trust in man instead. She stared at the words. She'd faced adversity in the past. Mamm's accident. Levi's cancer. And now the tornado. She must remember that no matter what happened in her life, the Lord was in control. And she would trust in Him.

"Lydia Ann?" Dat whispered. "Is that you?"

She turned to see her father standing in the doorway. "Good morning," Lydia Ann said. "I was just spending some time with the Word."

Dat smiled broadly. "You remind me so much of your mamm. She used to do the same thing. Said the Lord spoke to her the loudest when the house was quiet."

How had Lydia Ann forgotten that? She'd heard Mamm say that so many times. It scared her a bit. Would the day come when she'd completely forget the loved ones who'd gone on before?

"Comparing me to Mamm is the greatest compliment you can give me."

Dat poured himself a cup of coffee and sat down across from her. "I'm thankful you decided to visit. I'm just sorry it took a tornado to make it happen."

Lydia Ann nodded. "I'm glad to be here. The girls are so excited to see a new place...and get to know you." She tried to push away her feelings of anger. He could've visited her. She'd been the one who'd lost a mother and a husband just a few years apart. She'd been the one left alone to raise two children. And he'd chosen to fall in love and make a new life with Leah.

He reached across the table and clasped Lydia Ann's hand. "Why don't you come to the store with me today?"

She pulled her hand back. "Oh, I shouldn't. I need to stay here and look after the girls."

"I'll bet Emma and Noah would be glad to spend the day with them."

"Spend the day with who?" Emma asked, appearing at the kitchen door.

"Dat asked me to go to his store today. But I need to stay here and look after the girls." She shot a pleading look at her cousin.

Emma narrowed her eyes. "Noah and I would be glad to keep them. In fact, maybe later on we'll bring them up to the store to see you."

"It's settled, then." Dat smiled and stood. "Come along, Lydia Ann. You can help me open up."

Lydia Ann glared at Emma. "You knew I didn't want to go," she whispered once Dat was out of earshot.

"I know. But I also know that you need to spend some time with him." She patted Lydia Ann on the back. "Give him a chance to explain himself. You of all people know that everyone handles grief in a different way."

Lydia Ann heaved a great sigh. "I suppose you're right. But that doesn't mean I'm happy about it." She left the kitchen and went to fetch her bag.

She climbed into the buggy and stared out at the changing scenery as they drove to Dat's store. Things in Lancaster County were different than what she was used to in Charm. Some of the differences were just because there were more people and more businesses here. But there were other things that had taken her by surprise and would probably take some getting used to. Buggies here were solid gray, but in Charm, they were black. Even the style of dress wasn't exactly the same. And Lydia Ann knew that some of the church rules were a little different too. Even so, there were enough things that felt familiar that it shouldn't be too hard to adjust to life in Lancaster County for a few weeks.

"We've worked hard on the store," Dat explained once they arrived at the little shop. "It's a busy little place. We get lots of tourists, but just as many locals come here for different things."

"Lots of herbs and spices," Lydia Ann said, looking at the variety of goods.

Dat came over to stand next to her. "Leah is known for her herbal teas. She says they're almost as good as the medicine you get from a doctor." He chuckled.

Lydia Ann bit her lip to keep a sigh from escaping. According to Dat, there was nothing Leah couldn't do. How could he have forgotten Mamm so quickly?

The bells that hung above the door rang as a customer came inside. "Simon." Dat rushed toward the entrance. "There's someone I want you to meet."

Lydia Ann cringed. Of course he'd want to introduce her to all of his friends and acquaintances. She wondered if the people who lived around here even knew he had a daughter and granddaughters. She peered around the aisle.

The man wasn't quite as tall as Dat, and dark brown hair peeked out from underneath his traditional Amish hat. His square jaw reminded her of pictures she'd seen of statues.

Dat spotted her watching them. "Lydia Ann, come over here and meet my friend, Simon Zook."

She walked toward where they stood. Simon's face lit up in a huge smile. His blue eyes were a nice contrast to his dark hair.

"Nice to meet you, Lydia Ann. I've heard so much about you."

He had? Maybe Dat hadn't forgotten about her after all. "It's nice to meet you too. I'm glad to be here." Despite her reservations about things, she had to admit that it was nice to be with Dat again.

"Simon works on a dairy farm not far from our house. But he also does some woodworking." Dat grinned. "We sell some of his goods in our store. Very popular with the tourists."

Simon lowered his eyes. "I enjoy doing it. It's a nice way to unwind after a long day at the farm."

Lydia couldn't help but smile. Simon seemed to bring a ray of sunshine into the shop.

The bell rang as another customer opened the door.

"Excuse me," Dat said, rushing forward to greet the couple who came inside.

"So…" Simon trailed off as if unsure what to say next.

Lydia Ann smiled encouragingly.

"Jeremiah says this is your first time in Lancaster."

Lydia Ann nodded. "Jah. This is the farthest I've ever been from home."

"I hope you had a nice trip." He smiled kindly. "And I was sorry to hear about your shop."

Lydia Ann couldn't hide her surprise. Dat had told people about the tornado? "I'm just thankful that no one was injured in the storm. But losing the shop was difficult."

"I was here the day he found out about the storm. He was so worried, I feared he was going to have an accident of his own as he set out to find a phone."

"I should've tried to get in touch with him immediately."

Simon locked eyes with her. "I'm sure you had a lot to deal with. No harm done."

Lydia Ann smiled. "Thanks for not making me feel worse about it."

"Are your daughters excited to be here?"

Lydia Ann's eyes grew wide. "Dat told you about them too?"

Simon grinned. "We're friends." He chuckled. "I know all about you."

She nodded. "Of course. I'm sorry. I just didn't know if everyone in the community knew about his life back in Ohio."

"It's been hard for him, being separated from you. Not being there as his grandchildren grew up." He leveled his gaze at her. "Losing his wife."

"Well, he sure seemed to move on pretty fast." Lydia Ann couldn't believe the words had actually escaped. She clapped her hands over her mouth, wishing she could take them back.

Simon took it all in stride. "Leah makes him very happy. But of course he hasn't forgotten you. Or your mamm."

Lydia Ann fell silent. Maybe she'd been too harsh on her father. "That's nice to know."

"I should get what I came for and head back to work." He smiled. "I'm just here to pick up a couple of things for the Landises. They own the dairy farm where I work, but they also run a guesthouse."

He motioned at a row of groceries for sale. "Mrs. Landis needs a few things for her evening meal."

"I'll leave you to your shopping." Lydia Ann gave him a final glance and went to join Dat at the counter.

"I'll ring you up," Dat said when Simon set his items on the counter.

"Danki," Simon said. Glancing at Lydia Ann, he smiled. "You know, you should bring your daughters out to the farm sometime. I'll bet they'd love to help bottle-feed the calves."

She laughed at the thought. "Katie would. Mary, not so much." She grinned. "But that's a wonderful idea. We'll have to stop by soon."

With one final smile, Simon picked up his bag and left the store.

"Such a nice young man," Dat observed. "Hardworking. And so helpful." He wiped a smudge from the glass counter with his handkerchief. "The two of you are about the same age, I think."

Lydia Ann had never been good at guessing ages. Even though she would turn twenty-six in a few months, she knew people usually thought she was younger. She had noticed Simon's clean-shaven face, though. Most people in their midtwenties were already married, so that surprised her a bit. But for all she knew, he could be about to marry in the fall.

"Let me show you the quilts we have for sale," Dat said. She followed him to the back of the store, observing the variety of merchandise the store held along the way.

Chapter Ten

. . . .

"Well, well." Phillip smirked. "If it isn't the resident journalist."

Michael narrowed his eyes at his brother. "What's it to you?" Ever since their parents had thrown a celebratory dinner in honor of Michael's new job, Phillip had been needling him.

Phillip guffawed. "Yep. Those fluffy pieces you'll be doing about the best bakeries in Lancaster County are certain to put you on the map. Heck, you'll probably win a Pulitzer." He clapped Michael on the back. "I can see it now." He waved his arm in an arc. " 'From Shoofly to Whoopie and Every Pie in Between.' " He chuckled again.

"I'm actually excited about my new position. So, really, nothing you can say will bring me down." Except that Phillip's words were echoes of the thoughts in Michael's head. It was almost as if his brother had a special talent for picking up on his biggest insecurities and using them as ammunition.

"No?" Phillip cocked his head. "I bet I know one thing that will." He pointed toward the driveway. "Your Southern belle is all packed up. Guess she's had her fill of this place." He raised an eyebrow. "And of you."

Michael felt as if someone had punched him in the stomach. Caroline was leaving today? He knew she couldn't stay forever, but he hadn't realized she'd be going so soon.

Michael tried to keep his face neutral, but with one glance at Phillip, he knew he'd failed.

"Guess she didn't plan on saying bye, huh?" Phillip jeered.

Michael looked down at his watch. If he didn't leave within the next few minutes, he'd be late. Not a good impression for his first day on the job. "Later, Phillip." He walked off without another glance. Maybe she was in the kitchen talking to his mother. She hadn't made it down for breakfast this morning, and now he knew why—she'd been packing. He hurried up the three steps to the door that led right into the kitchen.

Disappointment hit him immediately. Mom and Mrs. Zook were the only ones there.

"Hon, you're going to be late if you don't leave." Mom smiled. "Did you forget something?"

Just his heart.

"No. Just saying bye." He grinned and gave his mom a side hug. "See you this afternoon. Wish me luck." Michael went to his vehicle and fished around for a scrap of paper. He quickly scribbled a note for Caroline on an old gas receipt and left it underneath her windshield wipers. Not exactly the most romantic gesture, but it was all he had time for this morning. He hopped in his car and headed towards downtown Lancaster.

Surely she wouldn't leave without saying good-bye.

Would she?

* * * * *

Caroline sat on the middle of the bed and ran her fingers along the quilt pattern. She'd been such a chicken this morning, not even able to go downstairs for breakfast. Over the past week, she'd gotten used to the family-style breakfasts. Last night, the Landises had even invited her to eat dinner with their family as they celebrated Michael's new job. There'd been so much joy around the table. So much happiness. It only reminded her of the loneliness that waited for her back home.

But she couldn't stay here forever.

She knew Michael already wondered the reasons behind her extended stay. No, it was definitely time for her to leave. She planned to do a bit more sightseeing and then hit the road. She wouldn't go straight home, though. Maybe she'd find an interesting place to stop along the way.

She grabbed her shoulder bag and went downstairs. Mrs. Landis and Mrs. Zook were talking and laughing in the kitchen. She poked her head inside the doorway. "I guess it's time to say good-bye," she said softly.

Mrs. Landis tossed the pot holder on the counter. "We're certainly going to miss you around here." She grinned and held up a sheet of paper. "But we'll always remember you, thanks to your grandmother's biscuit recipe."

Caroline had written down the recipe last night. "She'd be honored." Caroline stood stiffly. Good-byes weren't her forte. "Please tell the rest of the family how much I enjoyed my stay."

Mrs. Landis raised an eyebrow. "I wish you'd have given us more notice of your departure. We could've had a big going-away meal tonight." She narrowed her eyes. "Are you sure you don't want to stay just one more day?" She slung an arm around Caroline's shoulder. "You've already set the record for the most nights stayed here. We'd be glad to give you a free night's stay tonight if that's the problem." She smiled kindly.

Caroline was touched. "Oh, that's awfully generous of you, but I couldn't. I really need to get on the road."

"Are you certain?" Mrs. Landis asked. "I know Michael will be so disappointed that he didn't get to say good-bye."

Caroline considered her words. She and Michael had gotten to be pretty good friends, especially after their outing to the covered bridges a couple of days ago. And last night after dinner, they'd sat in the family room, playing Scrabble with his parents. It had been the most fun she'd had in ages. One more night wouldn't hurt, right? She grinned. "You've talked me into it. But I insist on paying."

Mrs. Landis laughed. "We'll discuss that later."

"In the meantime, I'm going to visit the shops at Kitchen Kettle Village." The popular tourist area was filled with quaint shops and eateries.

"Sounds perfect."

Caroline went out to her car. The slip of paper underneath her wiper blades drew her attention. Trash? She fished the paper from the car, and scrawled writing caught her eye.

"Leaving without saying good-bye? And I had to hear about it from my brother? You sure know how to wound a man." He'd followed his message with his phone number.

She couldn't keep from smiling. Staying one more day had been the right decision.

But tomorrow...

Tomorrow she had to leave.

Chapter Eleven

....

"Here's your computer." Jenny Stafford pointed into a cubicle. "Everything is pretty basic—phone, computer, supplies. But if you prefer a laptop, just let me know and I'll see what I can do." She smiled prettily. "And can I just say, I can't believe you're here."

Neither could he. Or at least he couldn't believe he was here with her. Jenny and Michael had been high school and college sweethearts. Everyone had expected them to get married. But he'd opted to head to DC after graduation, and she'd been determined to come back home. After a few months of long distance, the relationship had ended. "It's nice to see you again." Except that he'd been around her for only a few minutes and he already felt tense. Working with an ex wasn't exactly at the top of his list of fun things to do.

She smiled. "I'm very much looking forward to catching up." The glint in her eye spoke volumes. "I'd better get back to work. Mr. Sinclair will be in soon and he'll probably want to talk to you. In the meantime, why don't you look over some of our past issues?" She pointed to a stack on his desk.

As soon as she was gone, he whipped his phone out of his pocket. No calls. No texts. Caroline had surely had time to read his note. He sank down into the seat. How had she managed to get under his skin in such a short amount of time? Even though he still got the feeling she was hiding something, he felt like she was finally starting to open up to him. The phone buzzed in his hand. He glanced down and rolled his eyes. His brother. What could Phillip possibly have to say? Probably just wanted to get in one final zinger. A sinking feeling washed over him. Phillip's phone call could only mean one thing: Caroline had left. Without calling him. Glumly, he ignored the phone and picked up a back issue of *Lancaster County Visitor*.

* * * * *

Caroline admired the older two-story home. The sign out front proclaimed it to be a bookstore and coffee shop, but it clearly had been a residential home at one time. She'd always been a sucker for a house with a wraparound porch. She stepped inside.

"Good afternoon," an elderly woman said from behind the counter.

Caroline smiled. "Hi." The shop looked like something she herself might have decorated. Three large square paintings depicting various parts of a red gerbera daisy hung over a red love seat.

"Could I help you with something?" the woman asked.

"I'm just looking." Caroline glanced around. "It's a lovely place."

"Thanks." The woman's kindly, round face lit up in a smile. "Please feel free to look around." She pointed toward the back of the store. "There's a coffee bar back there. It's self-serve."

"I'll have to check it out." Caroline wandered through the shelves lined with used books. "Some of these look like collectibles."

The woman nodded. "Sure are. I've always been somewhat of a collector. My favorite thing is to get signed first editions." She pointed to the front of the store. "Most of the books are used, but I also have some new releases displayed up front."

Caroline walked to the back of the store where the coffee bar was housed. The tables were hand-painted with whimsical designs. "These are great," she remarked. "I love the way the chairs don't all match."

The woman chuckled. "I guess you could say I have a flea-market problem. I bought those tables and had a local girl paint them but then realized I didn't have any chairs. So I started going to flea markets and tag sales to find chairs."

Caroline ran her hand over a wooden chair that had been painted pink. "And then you painted them different colors."

"Exactly. I thought it was a nice touch with the painted tables."

"Well, I love it." Caroline walked over to the coffee bar and stopped in her tracks. "I have this same coffee mug at home." She lifted an oversized mug from the shelf. "Except that mine has a dog wearing a Santa hat instead of a cat on the front." Mama had gotten it for her last Christmas. When Lance had seen her drinking out of it, he'd made fun of the design—called it "too kitchy" for his tastes.

The woman laughed. "My daughter got that one." She motioned toward the coffeepot. "Do you want me to make a fresh pot?"

"Oh, no, that's okay. I don't want you to go to any trouble." Caroline sat down at the table and ran her hand over the glossy surface. "This is such a cute little place."

"Thanks. It's been my home for quite a while."

"Your home?" Caroline asked.

The woman nodded. "I live upstairs." She sat down across from Caroline. "I'm Lottie, by the way."

"Caroline."

"Well, Miss Caroline, I can tell by your accent that you aren't from these parts."

"No, ma'am. I'm from Georgia."

Lottie grinned. "Georgia. That borders my new home state." She chuckled at Caroline's surprise expression. "I'm moving to Florida… to one of those retirement places." She shook her head. "My old bones can't take another Pennsylvania winter. Plus my daughter and son-in-law live in Jacksonville."

"Wow. When are you moving?"

Lottie's face grew sad. "Just as soon as I can get rid of my inventory." She gestured at one of the tables. "So if there's anything here you'd like, even the fixtures, I'd be glad to make you a great deal."

"Are you selling the house?"

Lottie shook her head. "No. I don't have the heart to sell it. This is the home my husband and I bought when we were first married." She sighed. "David went home three years ago to be with the Lord. But I'm still not ready to let go of the place we built together." Tears filled the old lady's brown eyes. "That must seem so silly."

Caroline reached over and clasped Lottie's weathered hands. "I don't blame you at all."

"Thanks." Lottie managed a smile. "I'm going to try to rent the place out once the merchandise is sold."

An idea formed in the back of Caroline's head. Had she lost her mind?

Chapter Twelve

....

Simon picked up a bale of hay and threw it over the gate. He couldn't remember another day like this when he'd made so many dumb mistakes. He'd forgotten two of the things Mrs. Landis had asked him to get at the store. Then he'd left the gate open and some of the cows had gotten out. And to top it off, he'd dropped and spilled an entire bottle of milk meant for one of the calves. The cats had been thrilled. Phillip, on the other hand, hadn't been amused.

"Where is your mind today, Simon?" he'd asked.

Meeting Jeremiah's daughter had shaken him. He'd heard all about her but hadn't expected her to be young and pretty. For some reason, when he'd heard she was a widow, he'd expected her to be closer to his mamm's age. But upon meeting her, he wasn't even sure she was as old as he was. Imagine, being widowed and raising two children at such a young age. And then losing her shop to the tornado. Not to mention her mamm's death. That was more than anyone should have to handle. So Simon knew where his mind was. It was reeling, trying to figure out when he might be able to spend some more time getting to know Lydia Ann. If there was anyone who must need a friend right now, it had to be her.

He grabbed the lawn hose and began the task of cleaning out one of the barn stalls. At the sound of a car door closing outside, he glanced through the open barn door. Michael was home. Simon dropped the hose and went out to see his friend. "How do you like the new job?" he asked once he reached Michael.

Michael wrinkled his nose. "Man, you are not going to believe it."

Simon raised his eyebrows. "Not a good day?" He could certainly sympathize.

"The job itself is great. I'm actually excited about showcasing some of the lesser-known attractions around here. It's just that one of my coworkers happens to be an old friend of mine."

Simon shrugged. "That doesn't sound so bad. What's wrong with working with an old friend?"

"It's an old girlfriend." Michael raked his fingers through his hair and leaned against his vehicle. "The only serious relationship I've ever been in. Do you remember Jenny?"

Simon nodded. "Of course. She was a permanent fixture here during your high school years."

"Yeah, well, I'm not so sure about working with her. I get the idea that she might want to rekindle things."

"And you're not interested?" Simon asked.

"Let's just say it ended badly the first time. Once we left Lancaster County, we realized we were pretty incompatible." He sighed. "I don't want things to be awkward at work."

"Just keep your mind on your job." After the day Simon had experienced, dispensing that advice was comical. He noticed Michael's glum expression. "It will all work out."

Michael sighed. "Jenny isn't the only bad part of my day." He crossed his arms and leaned against the SUV. "I guess you know that Caroline left. I thought she might call me before she headed out, but she didn't."

Simon shook his head. "She was going to leave, but she didn't."

"What do you mean, she didn't leave?" Michael's eyes lit up. "Her car's not here."

"I'm sure she hasn't left. In fact, I had to go over to Jeremiah's store to get some things for your mom. It sounds like your family is hosting a going-away dinner for her tonight."

"So she's staying another day?"

Simon almost teased his friend about the gleeful tone that had taken over his voice, but he thought better of it. "She's staying at least another day."

* * * * *

The bells jingled on the door and Lydia Ann looked up from her perch behind the counter. She grinned broadly at Emma's excited expression. "Good afternoon, cousin. Did you get some good news?"

Emma laughed. "We passed a bookstore on our way here. It's just a few stores down. I thought we might stop in before we go back to your dat's house."

"I see." Lydia Ann chuckled. "You and your books."

Noah piped up. "This is a wonderful store."

Dat looked up from where he was stocking the front shelf. "Let me give you the tour." He grinned. "We'll start in the back. Follow me."

Noah and Dat sauntered off, Dat pointing out merchandise as they went.

"How has today been?" Emma asked, once the men were out of earshot.

Lydia Ann shrugged. "Better than I expected. Dat and I haven't had a whole lot to say to each other, but we've also stayed pretty busy today." She thought of Simon. "And I met one of his friends. The man knew all about me already."

"See? I told you your dat hadn't forgotten about you." Emma smiled. "Give him some time. I'll bet your relationship with him will be back to normal before you know it."

Lydia Ann nodded. "I hope you're right. He's always been a man of few words. And it seems like after time passed without us seeing each other, he doesn't know what to say to me anymore."

Emma patted Lydia Ann on the back. "You know that old saying about time healing wounds? I think it might be true. It's almost as if you're starting over from scratch, getting to know him again. But what a blessing it is for you and your girls."

"I guess you're right," Lydia Ann admitted. She couldn't expect things to be just like they used to be. And she and Dat had warmed up to one another as the day had passed, even laughing together about memories of Lydia Ann's childhood.

Noah and Dat returned from their tour.

"Are you ready to go?" Noah asked. He grinned in Emma's direction. "We don't want the bookstore to close."

Ten minutes later, Noah stopped the buggy outside an old house that had a sign in front declaring it a bookstore.

"What a pretty place," Emma observed.

They walked past the lone vehicle in the parking lot.

Emma stopped in her tracks. "Look," she said softly, pointing to the driver's side window.

Lydia Ann peered into the window. A young woman sat hunched over the steering wheel. Loud sobs racked her body.

"Do you think we should check on her?" Lydia Ann asked.

Emma nodded. "I do." She turned to Noah. "You go on inside. She might not feel comfortable if we're all staring at her."

He smiled. "Of course. I'll be inside if you need me."

Emma rapped softly on the window.

The woman looked up, a surprised expression on her face. She opened the door. "Y–yes?" she stammered.

"Are you okay?" Lydia Ann asked.

The woman stared at her blankly for a long moment.

"Are you okay?" Lydia Ann repeated. She cast a worried glance at Emma.

The Englisher's blond hair fell over her face, and she pushed it away. Her tearstained cheeks were pale. "I don't know if I'll ever be okay again," she whispered.

"Are you hurt?" Emma asked. "Do we need to call someone?"

At Emma's words, the woman began to cry again softly. "That's just it. There's no one to call." She caught Lydia Ann's gaze, her brown eyes shiny with tears. "I'm all alone."

"Surely there's someone," Emma said. "Your parents? A friend?"

The woman closed her eyes. "My parents are dead. And I don't have any friends. At least not any that live near here."

Lydia Ann leaned into the vehicle. "Please tell us how we can help you."

The woman gave them a small smile. "You're so kind." She wiped her eyes. "And I seem to have forgotten my manners. I'm Caroline Jennings."

Chapter Thirteen
....

Caroline tried to pull herself together. Of all the embarrassing situations... The two Amish women peered at her as if she had horns.

"I'm Emma," said the one with dark hair. She motioned toward the blond. "And this is my cousin, Lydia Ann." She smiled broadly. "Now I'm going to go see if I can find you some water inside."

Caroline watched her walk away then looked back at Lydia Ann. "You don't have to stay out here with me," she murmured. "I'll be fine."

Lydia Ann gave her a comforting smile. "I don't mind staying with you. Maybe I can help."

"I just made a big decision today and realized that I didn't have anyone to consult about it."

Lydia Ann furrowed her smooth brow. Her blue eyes were kind. "Do you want to tell me about it?" She motioned at the wraparound porch. Two white wicker chairs sat in front of a large window. "How about we go have a seat?"

Caroline nodded. She climbed out of her vehicle and followed the Amish woman to the porch. "I guess you figured out that I'm not from around here," Caroline said once they were seated.

Lydia Ann smiled. "If it makes you feel any better, neither am I."

Caroline listened as Lydia Ann explained about the tornado and her spur-of-the-moment trip to visit her father.

"Wow. I saw that on TV," Caroline explained. "My mama and I visited Charm last year." She managed a tiny smile. "That's one reason I came to Lancaster County—because Mama had always wanted to visit." She shrugged. "I guess I figured I could see the place for her."

Lydia Ann placed her hand on Caroline's arm. "I'm so sorry. Losing a parent is truly awful."

Caroline could see the empathy in the woman's eyes. For the first time in a long time, she felt like someone understood her. The irony that it was an Amish woman wasn't lost on her. She'd never thought of the Amish as having anything in common with her. "Thanks. It has been a tough year for me. I lost my mama and my husband within a few months of each other." She shook her head. "I'm not sure how to recover."

Lydia Ann nodded. "My husband lost his battle with cancer when our twin daughters were only a year old." She gave Caroline a tiny smile. "They're six now, but I still miss him."

"I'm so sorry to hear it." Caroline couldn't help but think of the difference in their situations. Lydia Ann and her husband had obviously been in love. But the more Caroline learned about her own husband, the more she realized that the love she'd thought existed had been little more than an elaborate PR stunt.

"Well, the Lord knows what He's doing," Lydia Ann said matter-of-factly. "He will see us through the trying times."

Caroline admired her faith. "I guess you're right."

Lydia Ann nodded. "Truly." She sat quietly for a moment. "What kind of decision did you make today?"

"I decided to stay in Lancaster County." She laughed. "Can you believe that? The only people I know here is the family whose guesthouse I've been staying in. And I've been paying them to let me stay there."

"Staying here doesn't sound like such a bad decision," Lydia Ann said gently.

"That's not exactly the crazy part," Caroline said.

The bookshop door burst open. "Here's a bottle of water for you," Emma said, handing Caroline the cold drink. "Lottie is so nice, she got it out of her own refrigerator."

"Thanks." Caroline smiled. She turned back to Lydia Ann. "I just agreed to rent this place." She motioned at the house. "I'm going to live in the upstairs part and run the bookstore."

"Well, that sounds like a wonderful plan," Lydia Ann said sweetly.

Caroline wrinkled her forehead. "It would be if I knew anything about running a store." She let out a chuckle. "I don't even know how to work a cash register."

"Lydia Ann does," Emma said. "She's been running a quilt store for years."

Lydia Ann nodded. "It's not too bad once you get the hang of it."

Caroline blinked. "How long did you say you'd be in the area?" Lydia Ann could be the answer to her problems. Well, at least one problem.

"About another month or so."

"I don't guess you'd want a job, would you?" Caroline asked hopefully.

Lydia Ann and Emma exchanged glances.

"I hadn't planned on it, but you know, that might not be a bad idea." Lydia Ann bit her lip. "Emma and Noah leave in a couple of days."

Emma nodded. "And you're so close to your dat's store, you could walk there from here."

"True." Lydia Ann furrowed her brow. "But I'm not sure what the girls would do."

"You're welcome to bring them with you. There's a big yard in the back and also a children's area in the store." Caroline smiled. "I was a kindergarten teacher, so the thought of having children around makes me happy."

Lydia Ann nodded her head. "Well then, I guess you've found some help."

"I can't thank you enough," Caroline said. She couldn't believe her luck. All of a sudden she didn't feel quite so alone. She glanced over at the Amish women. "Emma, it was so nice to meet you. Lydia Ann, can you be here on Thursday?"

Lydia Ann nodded. "See you then."

* * * * *

Caroline drove past Kitchen Kettle Village. Normally the quaint shops and restaurants caught her eye, but today she barely noticed them. Meeting Lydia Ann had calmed her down some, but she still wished she could discuss her decision with someone. For a second she considered calling Michael. She had the receipt with his number in her pocket. But he was at his first day on a new job and she didn't want to bother him. There was no one else to consult with. Except for her lawyer. Or her accountant. But they would only want to talk about the financial ramifications of her decision.

She finally decided to go back to the farmhouse. Maybe she could help Mrs. Landis in the kitchen. There had been a time when baking brought her great joy. But once she married Lance, he preferred dining out or hiring a cook. He'd said the country-style dishes she made were too unhealthy for an athlete.

Fifteen minutes later, she pulled into a spot at the guesthouse.

"Hello there," Phillip called as she got out of her car.

She waved a greeting.

"I hear you're staying another night." He sauntered over to where she stood.

She nodded. "Your mom talked me into it. She can be very persuasive when she wants to be."

He chuckled. "Have you told Michael the news yet? I think he was looking for you this morning."

"No. I haven't seen him." She motioned toward his SUV. "But it looks like he's home from his first day on the job."

"Looks that way." Phillip adjusted the baseball hat on his head. "I'd better finish up. Sounds like we're having some kind of feast tonight." He grinned and walked back to the barn.

Caroline grabbed her bag and went to the guest entrance. She couldn't figure out the vibe between Michael and Phillip. There seemed to be underlying tension. Most of the time when she'd been around them at the same time, they'd just ignored one another. Their behavior didn't fit into the otherwise closely knit family. Even their grandmother and uncles came over for breakfast sometimes.

She poked her head into the kitchen. Mrs. Landis was bustling around and didn't even look up when the door opened. "Is there anything I can do to help?" Caroline asked.

Mrs. Landis's mouth broke into a big smile. "Oh, I can't let the guest of honor help cook her own dinner."

Caroline wrinkled her forehead. "Of course you can. I love to cook and never get the chance." She held up her bag. "Just let me put this upstairs and I'll be right back down." She went upstairs to the room she'd started thinking of as "hers" and tossed her things onto the bed. A quick glance in the mirror showed her that her long blond hair desperately needed a ponytail. She peered closer and saw tiny dark roots. Ugh. She needed a touch-up too. Being blond might not be all it was cracked up to be.

"Here's an apron." Mrs. Landis tossed a gingham-printed fabric in her direction when Caroline returned to the kitchen. "It was my mother-in-law's."

Caroline grinned. She adored things with a history. She quickly tied the apron strings behind her back. "Okay. What's my job?"

Mrs. Landis held out the recipe written in Caroline's handwriting. "How about you whip up your grandma's biscuits? We're having fried chicken and mashed potatoes." She smiled. "And Mrs. Zook made homemade apple cobbler for dessert."

"Yum." Caroline took the recipe and then washed her hands in the deep sink. "It's a good thing this is my last night here or I might have had to take up running again."

Mrs. Landis chuckled.

"Mom, have you seen my blue—" The door burst open, and a shirtless Michael trailed off and turned a deep shade of red at the sight of Caroline.

She averted her eyes, but not before she caught sight of six-pack abs. Clearly he didn't need to take up running, despite his mother's cooking.

"Your blue shirt?" Mrs. Landis laughed. "Check the dryer."

He quickly exited from where he came.

"I'm not sure I've ever seen him look that embarrassed," Mrs.

Landis said, still chuckling. "I think it's safe to say that you've got him a little rattled."

Caroline blushed. So his mother had picked up on their blossoming friendship. She'd hoped that had gone unnoticed. "He seems like a great guy."

"I like to think so." Mrs. Landis dropped a chicken leg into the sizzling grease. "Of course, I'm not blind to his faults, either." She grinned. "That's the beauty of motherhood. You learn to love the good and the bad about your kids."

"I'm sure."

"So…" Mrs. Landis glanced at her. "You don't have children of your own?"

If it had been anyone else, Caroline would've felt like the question was prying. But coming from Mrs. Landis, it seemed to be sincere. "No kids. Not even a pet."

"I'm sure your time will come." She smiled kindly. "If that's the kind of life you want."

Caroline wondered if she'd ever considered the kind of life she wanted. She'd sort of fallen into the life she had without really planning for it. "Oh, I do. I'd like nothing more than to be a mother. Someday." Lance had been the holdout where kids were concerned. It was never the right time. Either he was busy with the season, busy with the off-season, or working on endorsement deals. He always had an excuse as to why they should wait. And she hadn't argued, just gone along with his plans. Maybe it was for the best. With the current state of her life, she couldn't imagine trying to raise a child.

The door opened again and Michael walked in, a sheepish grin on his face. "Sorry about before." He thumbed his blue polo shirt. "I didn't realize anyone else would be in the kitchen."

Caroline laughed. "I insisted that your mom let me help her. I hate the thought of anyone going to trouble on my account."

He shook his head. "That's just crazy. We have to eat whether you're here or not." His green eyes twinkled. "But I'm glad you decided to stay one more night. I understand that you tried to run off this morning without even saying good-bye to me."

"I would've called."

He raised an eyebrow. "That's easy to say now."

"Seriously. I would've. Besides, I have your number now. And on that fancy notepaper, even."

Michael chuckled. "Yeah, a gas station receipt was my only option. Either that or a McDonald's napkin." He winked. "I figured real paper was classier even if it was a little crumpled."

"Well, you're nothing if not classy," Mrs. Landis chimed in. "And if you're going to stand here and distract my star biscuit-maker, why don't you make yourself useful?" She took out an apron and tossed it at him. "Tie this on first, though. We don't want you to have to go around shirtless anymore."

He pulled on a tattered "Kiss the Cook" apron and shot his mother a look.

Mrs. Landis chuckled. "Sorry, son. That's your dad's apron and the only one that will fit you."

"Whatever," he mumbled. "What's my job?"

She handed him a box of tea bags. "How about you make another pitcher of tea?"

Caroline enjoyed the easy back-and-forth between Michael and his mom. And she had to admit, he looked kind of cute in his apron.

Chapter Fourteen

....

Lydia Ann sat on the porch and watched Mary and Katie dance around the yard.

"They sure have a lot of energy," Leah said. "It's hard for me to remember when my kids were that young."

Lydia Ann nodded. "They certainly keep me busy."

"How many children do you have?" Emma asked. "I don't think Lydia Ann ever told me."

That was true. Lydia Ann didn't talk about Leah much. So of course she hadn't thought to tell Emma many details about her.

"I have two boys." Leah smoothed her skirt. "They live near Strasburg with their families." She smiled in Lydia Ann's direction. "You'll meet them on Sunday. Since it's an off week from church, they're bringing their families here for a visit. I think you'll get along very well with my daughters-in-law, especially Becky," Leah said. "She is about your age and works in a quilt shop in Strasburg. She's married to my youngest son, Joseph, and they have a little boy who is just a year younger than Mary and Katie." Her eyes twinkled as she spoke of her family.

"It sounds like we will have a wonderful-gut time," Lydia Ann said. "I know Mary and Katie will be happy to meet a new friend." She felt Emma's eyes on her. "And so will I."

Leah rose from her wicker chair. "I'd better go inside and do a little tidying up before we eat."

Lydia Ann jumped up. "I'll help."

Leah shook her head. "No, stay here and visit with your cousin. I know you'll miss her after she's gone." With a smile, she went inside and closed the door behind her.

"I wish you could stay here with me," Lydia Ann said glumly.

Emma laughed. "Someone needs to get a better attitude." She waved her hand toward the twins. "They are having a wonderful time. Your dat is so happy to have you here. I don't think he's stopped smiling since we arrived. And Leah is trying very hard to get to know you."

Lydia Ann knew that Emma spoke the truth. "I can't help but feel so alone here, though. Once you're gone, who will I talk to?"

Emma rolled her eyes. "You could get to know Leah better. Or maybe you'll become friends with Caroline as you work together. And it sounds like you have a lot in common with Leah's daughter-in-law." She met Lydia Ann's gaze. "But it isn't like you're being forced to stay here forever. You'll be headed back to Charm before you know it." She grinned. "And I hope you'll plan another visit to Shipshewana later in the fall. By then, Abby will be great with child and I know you'll get a kick out of seeing her that way."

"Okay. You're right. From this moment forward, I will work to have a better attitude." Lydia Ann smiled. "And since tomorrow is your last day here, you can plan the day."

Emma grinned. "Let's visit that farm you mentioned so Mary and Katie can feed the baby cows." Lydia Ann's heart quickened. A visit to the farm meant running into Simon. For some reason, he'd popped into her mind a few times since their introduction.

"If that's what you want."

"It is," Emma said. "And after that, I think Noah wants to go see some of the covered bridges."

Lydia Ann smiled again. "That sounds like a gut way to spend the day to me." She rose. "I'm going to go insist that Leah let me help her." She headed toward the kitchen feeling lighter somehow. And as much as she didn't want to admit it, the prospect of seeing Simon tomorrow had a lot to do with it.

* * * * *

"Michael, will you ask the blessing?" Mr. Landis asked.

Caroline bowed her head. She blushed when Michael mentioned her by name in the prayer—but it was flattering that he'd think to pray specifically for her.

"Thanks," she mouthed once the amens had been said.

He grinned in return.

"Well, Caroline, I guess I don't have to tell you that we don't normally have going-away dinners for our boardinghouse guests," Mr. Landis said. "But we've all come to enjoy having you here."

"And these biscuits are delicious," Phillip said. "Most guests don't share their cooking skills either."

She laughed. "Thanks on both counts. You've all made me feel like part of your family, and I really appreciate it." It had been a long time since she'd felt like part of a family.

"Some of us more than others," Phillip muttered in Michael's direction.

Caroline bristled. Conflict made her uneasy.

Thankfully Michael took it all in stride. "I, for one, am glad you decided to stay an extra night." He grinned. "It would've been a shame if you'd had to leave before you tasted Mom's fried chicken." He held up a perfectly fried chicken leg and took a bite.

"So, you're headed back to Georgia tomorrow?" Mrs. Landis asked, heaping mashed potatoes on her plate.

Caroline swallowed. She'd be able to tell from their reactions whether she'd made a terrible mistake. She cleared her throat. "Actually, no." She took a sip of tea. "I decided I wasn't quite ready to go back home." She noted their puzzled expressions and plunged ahead. "You know the bookstore that Mrs. Lottie Harris runs?"

Mrs. Landis nodded. "I love Lottie's place. That poor woman. She's really had a time of it since her husband died."

"Well, she's moving to Florida to be near her daughter. She doesn't want to sell the house, though. Just wants to rent it out. " She bit her lip. "So I decided to rent it from her." She looked around the speechless table. "I didn't have to sign a lease or anything. She's going to leave the place furnished and I'm just going to buy the merchandise from her."

Michael's eyes grew wide. "So you're…moving here?"

She halfway smiled. "Not permanently. But yes. For a little while." She laughed. "I know nothing about running a bookstore, though, so I might end up out of business."

"Caroline, that's wonderful news!" Mrs. Landis exclaimed. "But won't your family back home miss you?"

Four pairs of eyes landed on her face. She shifted in her seat. "I don't really have any family," she said quietly. "So there's really nothing tying me to Georgia." Except for a mansion and a foundation that bore her last name. But that was it. And those things could do without her for a little while longer.

Mrs. Landis reached over and patted her on the arm. "I'm sorry, dear. I didn't know. But we're glad to have you nearby. I hope you'll stop in to visit even though you won't be staying here any longer."

She grinned. "Of course. I'd like that." She glanced at Michael. "Y'all have been so wonderful to me during my stay. I hope you'll come visit me at the store as well."

Once the last bit of apple cobbler had been eaten, Mr. Landis pushed back from the table. "That was delicious." He leaned over and gave his wife a quick kiss on the cheek. "How about I help you with the dishes? We'll let the young people get out of here."

Caroline thanked them for dinner and turned to go toward the guest rooms.

"Not so fast." Michael walked up behind her. "It's early yet, and barely dark. Do you have somewhere to rush off to or something?"

She shook her head. "Guess not." She smiled. "Why?"

"I thought you might like to go for a ride."

"A ride?"

He chuckled. "On one of our four-wheelers. I thought you might like to see some of the farm. It's a full moon tonight, so we should be able to see pretty well." He grinned. "Plus, one of our dogs just had a litter of puppies."

She returned his smile. "Lead the way."

He led her to a building behind the barn. "Wait here," he said. A few minutes later, he drove out of the building on a red four-wheeler. "You're not scared, are you?" He grinned.

She climbed onto the back. "Are you a good driver?"

He reached back, grabbed her hands, and wrapped them around his waist. "I am, but you'll still need to hold on tightly."

"Is that so?" She couldn't help but laugh. The warm night air washed over her, and the way she felt with her arms wrapped around Michael almost made her forget about the past few years.

Almost.

They drove around the perimeter of the farm, Michael pointing out various landmarks. He finally came to a stop near a building. "You feel like exploring a little?"

She grinned. "Sure."

"Don't worry—I brought a flashlight." He held up a small Maglite.

Caroline waved her hand toward the full moon. "I'm not worried. It seems that God is providing the light tonight."

"True." He opened the rickety door on the building. "The puppies are in here. They should have their eyes open by now." He grinned. "I thought we could check on them."

She followed him into the dark building.

Michael reached out and grabbed her hand. "Just for safety purposes," he whispered. "I wouldn't want you to fall down or anything."

In that moment, with her hand in his, she wondered what kind of fire she was playing with. Once he found out everything about her—who she was, what the last couple of years had been like—there was no way he'd want anything to do with her.

He shined the light behind a bale of hay. "There they are." He let go of her hand and wrapped an arm around her waist, pulling her close. "Do you see them?"

"They're so cute," she murmured. "Five perfect puppies."

He turned her toward him so they were face-to-face. She could barely make out his outline in the dark.

"Caroline," he whispered.

Her heart pounded in her chest. She knew what was about to happen. She wanted it to happen. But it terrified her so much, she could barely breathe. "No, Michael." She pulled out of his embrace and turned quickly on her heel. She ran through the blinding darkness, feeling for the door. She pushed against it with her shoulder, losing her balance and landing with a thud on the hard ground outside.

"Caroline," Michael said, coming up behind her. "Are you okay?"

She tried to collect herself by doing some deep breathing. "No." She shook her head. "I'm not."

He knelt down next to her. "I'm sorry. I didn't mean to come on too strong. I was just so happy to find out that you hadn't left… and then to learn that you are staying for a while knocked me for a loop. In a good way."

"Don't apologize." She pushed against the ground into a sitting position and leaned against the building. "It's just…" She took a breath. "There are things you don't know."

"I'm a great listener." He stood and held out his hand to help her up. "Do you want to head back to the house? We can talk there."

She shook her head. "No. Let's just stay right here." She patted the ground next to her. "Sit back down."

He obliged.

"There's something you need to know." Her voice trembled.

He reached out to her. "You can tell me anything."

"I was married. Until recently." She wasn't ready to tell him the whole story. But he at least deserved part of it.

Michael's face registered shock. "Married?"

She nodded. "My husband passed away a few weeks ago." She left out the part where her husband was gunned down in their driveway by his scorned mistress. Because, frankly, it was a little much to take.

"I'm sorry to hear that." His voice was strained.

She pondered her words. "The truth is, we'd been living apart for the past couple of years." She shook her head. "Our marriage has been in name only for quite some time. But still, his death has been difficult to deal with."

Michael's expression was one of compassion. "You've had a lot to deal with. It's no wonder you sought refuge here."

He didn't know the half of it. "I feel so safe here." She waved a hand around the expansive farmland. "It's part of the reason I decided to stay." She shrugged. "What I told your mother at dinner is true. There's really nothing waiting for me at home."

"Not even your kindergarten class?" He looked puzzled.

"I'm still licensed, but I'm not sure I'll go back to teaching." She didn't even dare imagine that her life could go back to that kind of normal.

He smiled. "Well then, I hope you'll end up with a very successful bookstore."

"And, don't forget, coffee shop." She returned his smile.

"What do you say we get out of here?" He stood up and offered her his hand. "I'll bet Mom and Dad will let us into their Scrabble game if we ask."

She laughed and let him help her to her feet. "That sounds wonderful." He pulled her to him in a hug, and she let herself relax against him for a long moment. Now that he at least knew part of her story, she felt better. But she knew that, eventually, the whole truth would have to come out. And if the fact that she was once married shocked him, she could only imagine how he'd feel when he found out who she'd been married to.

Chapter Fifteen

....

Simon looked up from his task of feeding the chickens. The unmistakable sound of a horse and buggy coming up the drive told him guests were coming. He stepped out of the barn and was pleased to see Lydia Ann. "Mornin'," he called.

Two little girls scurried out of the buggy, along with a woman about Lydia Ann's age.

Lydia Ann smiled as they walked over to where he stood. "This is Mary." She put a hand on the shoulder of one blond-headed twin. "And this is Katie." She put her hand on the shoulder of the other one. "They've been so excited about visiting the farm, they barely slept last night."

"Mamm says we might get to feed a baby calf!" Mary exclaimed.

"That's right. They're very hungry this morning." Simon smiled. "If the two of you want to go into the barn, you can look at them while I prepare their food."

The girls hurried off, laughing and giggling.

"This is my cousin Emma," Lydia Ann said. "She and her husband rode with us from Shipshewana." She grinned. "I think she just wanted to see a new part of the country, but she says she came along to help us get settled."

Emma laughed. "Both are true."

Simon smiled at the two women. They shared a bond; that was obvious. "Well, either way, I'm glad you decided to visit the farm."

"We'd better get to the barn," Lydia Ann said. "There's no telling what the girls have gotten into."

Simon chuckled. "Oh, they'll be fine. Believe me. We have a number of children through here, especially in the summertime. The barn is pretty kid-friendly."

"So, Simon," Emma said as they walked, "are you originally from Lancaster?"

Simon grinned. "I was born less than a mile from this very spot." He ushered the women into the barn.

"Aren't they cute?" Katie exclaimed, running over to her mother and taking her hand.

Mary followed. "I think the babies are very hungry today." She grinned, displaying a missing front tooth.

"Let me fix their bottles and we'll get them taken care of." Simon had to hide his smile. The little girls' excitement was contagious.

Katie and Mary bounced around as Simon stirred the bucket to mix the formula for the calves. He felt an odd twinge in his hand. "Would one of you like to stir?"

"Jah!" Katie exclaimed. She took over, taking great pains to stir the milky liquid.

"It's just like mixing cake batter, isn't it, sister?" Mary asked.

Simon grinned at Emma and Lydia Ann. "I wish I had such good helpers every mornin'."

"We can come back again, can't we, Mamm?"

Lydia Ann smiled down at Mary. "If Mr. Simon allows it, I think that's a wonderful-gut idea."

Simon gazed at Lydia Ann. She had the prettiest face of any

woman he'd ever seen…and it was made even prettier by the love she clearly had for her daughters. He felt Emma's eyes on him and quickly looked away as his face flushed.

"Is it ready yet?" Katie asked, looking up at Simon.

He leaned over to check. "Let me get the bottles filled and then we can feed them." He worked quickly to fill four bottles. He handed one to each little girl, and then he turned to Emma and Lydia Ann. "Would either of you like to try?"

Emma laughed. "I think Lydia Ann should do the honors."

He nodded. "Here you go." He held a bottle out for Lydia Ann.

She took it, grinning. "Danki."

Simon led them over to where four black-and-white calves waited impatiently. The largest of the four threw back her head in anticipation. "Hold the bottle up so the milk flows." He showed them how. "And make sure you keep a tight grip on the bottle. They will pull on it, and if you aren't careful, they'll pull it right out of your hands."

"Ooh," Mary squealed. "They're slobbering."

Katie laughed. "Don't be such a baby. Slobber won't hurt you." She held her bottle with one hand and stroked the calf on the head with the other.

"Do they only eat once a day?" Mary asked.

Simon held onto the bottle and watched as the calf drank hungrily. "Once in the morning and again in the afternoon."

"Mine's empty," Mary announced, pulling the bottle from the calf's mouth. "It must've been the hungriest."

Simon grinned. "Go put the bottle back in the bucket. I'll rinse them out later."

When the rest of the bottles were empty, Simon pointed in the direction of a big sink. "You can go wash up over there. I'll bet everyone has cow slobber on their hands."

The little girls laughed, debating over whose hands were covered in the most slobber. Once everyone had washed their hands, Simon walked them out of the barn.

"Too bad you missed the milking," he said. He pointed at a wide swinging door. "That's the milking room."

Katie tugged on Lydia Ann's apron. "Can we come back sometime to see the milking?"

Lydia Ann laughed. "If we get invited back."

"You're welcome any time." Simon grinned. "And we've just had a litter of puppies born. If you come back in a couple of weeks, they'll be big enough to play with."

"Puppies!" Mary exclaimed. "We love puppies."

"You might've just made two friends for the summer," Lydia Ann said, chuckling. "We'll definitely be back now."

Simon joined in her laughter. "I'm looking forward to it."

They herded the twins back toward the waiting buggy.

"It was nice to meet you, Emma," Simon said. "And nice to see you again, Lydia Ann."

With a final wave, Lydia Ann climbed into the buggy. He waved back, but not before he caught the knowing look on Emma's face. Simon wondered if Emma would tell her cousin that he'd had a hard time keeping his eyes off of her. And if she did, what Lydia Ann would think.

* * * * *

Lydia Ann bustled about the kitchen. She and Emma had insisted that Leah take a night off and let them cook.

"That smells so good," Emma said, grinning.

Lydia Ann laughed. "I hope it tastes good too." She set the chicken-and-noodle dish on the table.

"Your apple dumplings smell good too."

"I've gotten better at cooking since I married Noah." Emma laughed.

She'd always labeled herself a bad cook, but Lydia Ann knew better. "I believe Noah would be happy even if you burned the dinner every night."

Emma's face colored prettily. "I guess you're right." She raised an eyebrow in Lydia Ann's direction. "This morning was fun."

Lydia Ann nodded. "Mary and Katie had a great time."

"I think Simon had a good time too."

"I hope we weren't too much of an imposition on him." Lydia Ann knew he'd meant it when he'd invited them, but she hadn't wanted to disrupt his workday.

"Oh, I'm pretty sure he was glad you were there."

Something in Emma's voice made Lydia Ann stop what she was doing. She slowly turned from the counter to face her cousin. "What do you mean?"

Emma cocked her head innocently. "Just what I said. I think he was glad you were there. He seems like a nice man."

"I think you're right. He's very helpful. I thought he was great with the twins." She shrugged. "He told me that he was used to having children tour the farm, so I'm sure he must enjoy them."

"I wonder why he isn't married." Emma played with the strings on her kapp.

Lydia Ann furrowed her brow. "For all you know, he could be ready to be published in the fall."

"I have my doubts about that."

"Why? Neither of us know him well enough to think that." She narrowed her eyes at her cousin.

Emma shrugged. "I think that if he were courting someone, he wouldn't have been so affected by you."

"By me?" Lydia Ann drew back as if she'd been slapped. "What are you talking about?"

"Don't play dumb. You had to have seen the way he looked at you—like a lovesick puppy."

"No." The word came out sharper than Lydia Ann intended. "You must be imagining things."

Emma walked over to Lydia Ann. "No, cousin, I was not."

"You know that I have no interest in another man." Lydia Ann met Emma's gaze. "Ever."

Emma bit her lip. "Lydia Ann, there was a time when I didn't listen to the advice of others. You included." Before Emma had married Noah, she'd spent time sneaking around with an Englisher. The man had ended up treating her poorly, and the relationship had almost ruined things between her and Noah. But once everything was out in the open, Emma had admitted that she didn't want to leave the Amish community. Once she'd made that decision, she'd joined the church and married Noah soon afterward. Lydia Ann knew that Emma was happier now than she ever thought she'd be. "I'm not going to harp on this, but I think you might want to at least open yourself up to a friendship with Simon."

Lydia let out a breath. "Friendship, yes." She nodded. "I can handle friendship. But nothing more."

Emma reached over and hugged her cousin. "I only want you to be happy, Lydia Ann. And happiness means surrounding yourself with people who love you."

Lydia Ann lifted her chin. Her cousin meant well, but she knew nothing of loss. Lydia Ann had been surrounded by people who loved her, a long time ago. And now they were gone. Why would she want to risk her heart again?

Chapter Sixteen

....

Caroline lifted the tiny puppy and nuzzled it against her face. "Hey, sweetie," she cooed.

Michael laughed. "He's already got you wrapped around his little finger." He grinned. "Or paw, as the case may be."

"Would you believe that I've never had a pet? At least not one that was truly mine." Her grandparents had let her claim both a cat and a dog as "hers" on their farm, and she'd spent hours on end playing with them. But once she and Lance married and she'd wanted to get a pet, he'd nixed the idea. He was allergic to cats and said dogs were too much trouble. She'd told herself it was for the best. They were away from home so much of the time that it wouldn't have been fair to the dog. But now she had all the time in the world.

"That's a shame," Michael said. "Because the two of you together make a very cute pair." He lifted his camera and snapped a picture.

"Stop that," Caroline said. His constant picture-taking was disconcerting. But the only way to explain her aversion would be to tell him the whole truth.

He snapped another one. "Come on," he said, laughing. "You're a natural. Every picture I take of you looks like it could go on the cover of a magazine."

She snorted. If he only knew. "Don't be silly." She gave the puppy another nuzzle. "I can't wait to take him home with me."

"And I feel certain he'll be happy to go with you."

She gently placed the tiny puppy with the rest of the litter. "He'll be great company for me, don't you think?"

Michael grinned. "Yes. But you know, if you want the kind of company that can actually carry on a conversation, you can always call me."

She couldn't help but laugh. "What if I want the kind of company that can help me move furniture?" Caroline had ended up staying at the Landis guesthouse for a few more days to give Lottie the chance to pack up. Lottie was leaving all her furniture except for the mattress set. Caroline knew she'd need some help getting a set moved upstairs into her new space.

"Hmm. I might know someone who happens to be a multitalented furniture-mover." He raised an eyebrow. "But I'm pretty sure you'd have to have dinner with him as payment."

Caroline's mouth turned upward into a smile. "That might be arranged." She slapped his arm as he raised the camera again. "If you'd stop taking those pictures."

Michael laughed. "You drive a hard bargain." He motioned toward the farmhouse. "You know, I think my parents are really going to miss you when you move into the new place."

Caroline had grown very fond of his parents too. Mrs. Landis had been so nice to her, even offering to do her laundry. "They're very sweet."

"So about our upcoming dinner…" Michael trailed off. "Is there anywhere you want to try?"

Caroline shrugged. "Several places, actually." She grinned. "But you know, I've been wanting to visit Lititz. It seems like such a quaint little town." Lititz was a historic town in the northwestern part of the county.

Michael's eyes lit up. "Perfect. I've been meaning to go up there for work."

She narrowed her eyes. She hadn't realized his dinner invitation included work. "Oh?"

He seemed to catch her mood. "It won't take any time away from our outing. I just meant that I'd like to write a blog post about some of the stores and restaurants." He grinned. "No big deal."

She realized how unreasonable she was being. But she couldn't help but be reminded of Lance and how every date they'd had, especially over the last two years, had somehow been related to his work. Michael was different, though. She knew that. "Sounds like a plan." She forced a smile. "Speaking of work, how is the new job going?"

He bit his lip. "The job itself is great. I'm really getting a handle on the social-media aspect. Our contacts are growing, and it's getting to the point where part of my day is actually spent answering questions that people are posting in different online forums." He shrugged. "So things seem to be going pretty well."

"Why do I sense that there's more to the story?"

A shadow passed over his handsome face. "My ex-girlfriend works there." He sighed. "She's starting to be awfully friendly."

Caroline bristled. The idea of him working with an old girl-friend felt like a sucker punch…except that she didn't have a claim on him. She was in no place to even go on a real date, much less be romantically involved. But despite that, the thought of him and a friendly ex didn't sit well. "Well, have you thought about rekindling things?" she asked, trying to keep her voice casual.

He scrunched his face up. "Are you serious?"

When she didn't respond, he continued. "Of course not. Our relationship ended for a reason. She was super jealous. When I moved to DC, she actually used to quiz me about how many females I knew there." He sighed. "And I'd never given her any reason not to trust me. It was like her insecurities grew as the years went on."

"Wow. That doesn't sound like much fun."

Michael nodded. "It wasn't. Besides, I don't plan on being in Lancaster County long-term. And I have no use for a long-distance relationship." He grinned. "Now, speaking of work, I'd better get going. I'm already late."

She nodded but couldn't help but try to read into what his words meant. He knew she was only in Lancaster County for a short while. Was this his way of telling her that she was just a way to pass the time? Probably. And really, that was fine. She'd just have to view him in the same way—as a pleasant distraction. But she couldn't shake the deflated feeling that stayed with her the rest of the day.

* * * * *

Michael tried to concentrate on the work in front of him. So far he'd set up Twitter and Facebook pages, and now he was trying to come up with a good name for the blog. He sighed. He was used to dealing with political facts, but this job was clearly going to test his creative skills.

"How's it goin'?" Jenny asked, walking into his cubicle. She leaned against the desk and crossed her arms. "Have you settled in yet?"

He tensed. "Yes. It's a little different from DC, though." He tried to keep his tone conversational. "I'm just working on the blog now."

Maybe she'd get the hint that he was in the middle of something.

"Cool." She grabbed the lone seat from the corner of the cubicle and slid it next to Michael's desk chair before plopping down next to him. "You think all the social-media stuff is going to be useful?"

He shrugged. "Seems to be the wave of the future. I think it will at least help get the word out about some of the interesting sights to see around here."

She leaned closer to him. "There are a lot of interesting sights to see."

Michael swallowed. "I'm thinking of doing a photo essay."

"You always were a talented photographer. I think that's a great idea."

He hated that she knew enough about him to know that. There had been a time when Jenny was one of his favorite subjects to photograph. When they were in college, he'd even entered some pictures of her in a contest. He'd received an honorable mention and a brand-new camera. He met her gaze. "I hope so."

"Well, I just thought I'd see if you might want to have lunch sometime," she said. "I've noticed that you usually eat at your desk." She laughed. "And that's no fun."

He kept his face neutral. "I like to power through lunch so I can get home at a decent hour."

"Whatever." Her tinkling laugh filled the cubicle, and suddenly he was back in high school, hiding out in his parents' barn with Jenny. They'd had some good times together. Especially in high school. It wasn't until college that things had started to change between them. And by the time they'd graduated from college, her unfounded jealousy had begun to drive him crazy.

She leaned closer to him. "Come on, Michael. Don't you think it might be karma or fate or something that not only are you back, but you're working with me?"

He looked into her crystal-blue eyes and shook his head. "Jen, we had some good times. But that is all way in the past."

She trailed her finger along his arm. "It doesn't have to be," she said quietly.

Before he could respond, Jenny stood and put the chair back in the corner. "One lunch. That's all I'm asking."

Michael sighed. On the one hand, if he agreed to lunch, she might think he would actually consider rekindling things. But on the other hand, if he didn't agree, she would probably keep bugging him. Jenny was nothing if not persistent. Always had been.

He looked up at her and nodded. "Fine. One lunch. For old time's sake."

Jenny's mouth broke into a huge smile. "Awesome. Maybe next week? I'll make a reservation at the Pressroom Restaurant. You know that's one of my favorites."

She would pick a place that had a reputation for being intimate. And it had been their special place when they were together. "Just name the day."

Jenny gave him one last over-the-shoulder grin and left his cubicle.

Michael sighed. Funny how the past raised its head when you least expected it.

Chapter Seventeen

....

Caroline straightened the stacks of books on the shelf in front of her. "Do you think we should rearrange the store?" she asked.

Lydia Ann stood in the middle of the room, looking around. "Maybe." She pointed toward a large armoire that held knickknacks for sale. "But some of these furnishings look heavy."

Caroline walked over to where the Amish woman stood. "A friend of mine is supposed to stop in to help me move a couple of things upstairs." She smiled. "He's borrowing his dad's truck and picking up my mattress."

Lydia Ann raised her eyebrows and then cast a puzzled glance at Caroline. "I thought you didn't know anyone here."

"His parents own the guesthouse I stayed at." She shrugged. "I guess I can call him my friend."

"If he volunteered to go pick up your mattress and move it inside for you, I'd say you can." Lydia Ann chuckled.

"Do you think the girls are okay?" Caroline asked. Mary and Katie were two of the sweetest children Caroline had ever been around. They'd played inside for a few minutes then decided to explore the backyard.

"The minute they found out you had a new puppy, they were so excited to come to work with me." Lydia Ann smiled. "We had a puppy for a short time, but he dug up the yard. Our neighbors ended up taking him. Thankfully." She shook her head. "Mary and Katie were only four, and I was working at the quilt shop. The last thing I had time to do was fill in the holes."

Caroline laughed. "I haven't had a pet since I was a little girl. But as soon as I saw him, I knew I had to take him." She smiled.

"He'll be great company for you," Lydia Ann affirmed.

And company was something Caroline needed. She didn't regret her decision to stay in Lancaster, but she still lived in fear that someone would eventually recognize her. Robyn kept her informed of everything going on back home, and the offers to share her story were still coming in. In fact, she'd had a frantic voice mail from Lance's agent yesterday, who wanted to discuss her feelings about a tell-all book about Lance's rise and fall. The two bright spots in her life were Lydia Ann and Michael. Both had been genuinely nice to her. It was refreshing to be treated that way and know that it had nothing to do with who she'd been married to.

"Have your cousin and her husband already gone back home?" she asked Lydia Ann.

The Amish woman nodded. "They left yesterday. They were going to stop in Hershey and spend a day there, but they should get back to Shipshewana tonight." She frowned. "I'm going to miss them a lot."

"I'm sure. And you'll be here for a few more weeks?" Caroline was unclear about Lydia Ann's reasons for being in Lancaster but didn't want to pry.

"Yes. My dat lives here. And his wife, Leah." A cloud crossed Lydia Ann's normally sunny face. "He's been wanting me to bring the girls for a visit for the past few years, but I haven't been able to.

Then the tornado hit and he was so worried…." She trailed off. "So I decided it was time to visit."

Caroline picked up some uncertainty in Lydia Ann's voice. "And are you enjoying yourself?"

Lydia Ann sighed. "I don't want to complain." One corner of her mouth turned up. "But it's difficult for me. I guess I don't understand how Dat moved on so quickly." Her face grew sad. "Mamm was killed in an accident two years before the girls were born."

"I'm so sorry. I know from experience how that is a difficult time."

"You've lost your husband. Would you marry someone else after losing the love of your life?" Lydia Ann asked.

Caroline bit her lip. She didn't want to shock the woman. But if they were going to work together, she may as well let out the truth. "My situation was a little complicated. In fact, my husband and I lived apart for the two years before his death." She sighed. "As it turned out, he didn't really love me. He married me because it helped his business situation."

The horrified expression on Lydia Ann's face said it all.

Before Caroline could explain further, the front door opened.

Michael walked in, grinning broadly. "Special delivery," he said, chuckling. "And I even brought some help."

Simon walked in behind Michael, carrying a basket of baked goods. At the sight of Lydia Ann standing in the center of the room, he stopped short. "Lydia Ann. I didn't expect to see you here."

"Hello, Simon." Lydia Ann nodded. "I'll be working here for a few weeks, helping Caroline get the hang of running a store."

Caroline couldn't help but notice the pleased expression that flashed across Simon's handsome face.

* * * * *

Lydia Ann felt as if she were rooted to the spot. Simon was the last person she'd expected to run into today. And it appeared that he already knew Caroline.

Simon held out a basket. "Mrs. Landis and my mamm sent over a few things for you to munch on while you were getting ready to reopen."

Caroline took the basket from him. "Please tell them thanks." She set the basket on the counter next to the cash register. "I didn't realize the two of you knew each other," she said.

Lydia Ann nodded. "Simon came into Dat's store the other day."

"But I'd heard all about her even before then." Simon grinned. "Her dat talks about her all the time." He chuckled. "I've even heard stories about when you were a little girl."

Lydia Ann felt her face flame, but she didn't say anything.

"Michael, I guess you're the only one who needs to be introduced to Lydia Ann, then," Caroline said. She turned to Lydia Ann with a smile. "Michael's parents run the guesthouse where I stayed. And Simon works there."

Things clicked into place for Lydia Ann. "I've been there." She smiled shyly at Simon. "Emma and I took the girls there to see the farm animals." She turned to Caroline. "Simon showed us around."

"And you didn't see me probably because I'd already left for work," Michael explained. "It's very nice to meet you, though." He grinned and looked from Caroline to Lydia Ann. "Man, the two of you look enough alike to be sisters. Except for your eye color." He paused. "And your clothes."

Lydia Ann burst out laughing and caught Caroline's gaze.

"I consider that a compliment," Caroline said, smiling.

"Did Katie and Mary enjoy their time at the farm?" Simon asked.

Lydia Ann chuckled. "They've barely stopped talking about it. We may have to make a return trip."

"Any time," Simon said, smiling.

"Right now they're in the backyard, playing with the puppy," Caroline said to the men. "I'm not sure who is happier, him or them."

Michael laughed. " 'The puppy'? You mean that poor animal doesn't have a name yet?"

Caroline shook her head. "Not yet. Soon, though."

Lydia Ann stepped behind the counter and ran a dustcloth over the surface.

"Do you want to see the mattress before we bring it in? To make sure we picked up the right one?" Michael asked Caroline.

She nodded. "Lead the way."

The two of them were gone before Lydia Ann could blink, leaving her alone with Simon. She glanced at him then quickly glanced away.

"Are you enjoying your visit?" Simon asked. "I stopped by your dat's store this morning, but he was busy with customers the whole time." He grinned. "Or else he probably would've told me about your new job."

Dat had been pleased when he'd learned she was going to be working. "We'd be happy for you to stay here forever, you know," he'd said. But of course that wasn't going to happen.

"Jah. I think he likes knowing I'm just a few stores down from him." She smiled and tried to shake the feeling of uncertainty in the pit of her stomach. "Thanks again for your tour of the farm the other day," she said.

"Oh, it was my pleasure." He grinned. "So how are you and Leah getting along?"

The personal question threw her off for a moment. "She's very nice." It was true. Even though Leah was very different than Lydia Ann's own mamm, she truly was a kind woman. It seemed she was always doing something for someone else, and Lydia Ann had noticed that she was very well-respected in the community. Even so, seeing Dat with her made Lydia Ann feel strange—like she was an outsider.

"Leah and my mamm have been friends for a very long time," Simon explained. "In fact, I went to school with her sons."

"What happened to her husband?" Lydia Ann had never asked. She only knew that he'd passed on several years earlier.

"He had a heart attack. He worked as a farmer, and one day he just keeled over." Simon shook his head. "He was awfully young. It was so hard on Leah and her boys."

Sadness washed over Lydia Ann. She knew something of being left alone with children. Maybe she and Leah had more in common than she'd realized. "That's awful."

"So, tell me more about you." Simon grinned. "Jeremiah tells me that you're quite a good quilter."

She nodded. "My husband used to say I thought better with a quilting needle in my hand."

He met her gaze. "I'm sorry about his illness."

"Danki. He's been gone five years now."

Simon shrugged. "Doesn't matter how long it's been, does it? The absence is still there."

Lydia Ann looked up in surprise. Most people didn't understand that. "Jah. But we have a happy life in Charm. The girls enjoy school, and our community is so good to us."

"Well, I'm glad you're here." He flushed. "I mean, I know your dad and Leah are glad to have you." He motioned around the store. "And Caroline really needs your help here." He leaned forward conspiratorially. "Michael is afraid she might be in over her head, but, honestly, I think he's happy to have her around a bit longer… even though he'd never say that to her."

Lydia Ann couldn't hide her laugh. "She means well. And I think she's a hard worker." She thought of what Caroline had said earlier, about her husband not ever really loving her. "Besides, she needs to throw herself into a project right now."

Simon nodded. "I think you're right. I don't know much about her, but I do know that when she first arrived at the farm, she looked positively broken."

The door burst open, and a laughing Michael and Caroline walked in. It looked as if perhaps Caroline had found a healing balm in her new friend.

Chapter Eighteen
....

Michael motioned toward the door. "You ready to help me move the mattress?"

Simon nodded. "Sure."

"You ladies just stay out of the way," Michael said. "This is a job for the men."

Lydia Ann and Caroline exchanged amused glances.

"Of course," Caroline said with a grin. "We'll just stay in here and keep cleaning."

Michael chuckled and clasped Simon on the back. "Let's get this done." The two of them walked out to the truck and assessed the situation.

Simon opened the tailgate and glanced at Michael. "I thought that new mattress place offered free delivery," he commented.

Michael smirked. "I know that, and you know that, but Caroline doesn't." He grinned. "I guess it's kind of pathetic for me to go to these lengths to get her to lean on me."

Simon shook his head. "If you really like her, maybe you should just tell her."

Michael drew his brows together. "I think the situation is sort of complicated. I'm not completely sure what she's running from, but I have an idea it isn't pretty." Even though Caroline had explained to him that she was recently widowed, he still thought there might be more to the story. But he knew she needed to share it with him in her own time.

They lifted the plastic-wrapped mattress from the bed of the truck and slowly came through the doorway.

"Just right up the stairs," Caroline directed. "The upstairs is an open floor plan, so you'll see the bed frame."

Once they were up the steps, they set the mattress on its side.

"Whew," said Simon. "Those stairs were steeper than they looked."

Michael nodded. "If you'll hold on to the mattress, I'll take off the plastic."

Simon balanced the mattress and looked around the room. "This is a pretty big space."

Michael ripped the plastic from the mattress. "Yeah. I'm a little jealous that she found this place for rent. I'm still looking."

"Really? Why?"

Michael wadded up the last bit of plastic and tossed it into a nearby trash can. "I miss having my own place. Plus I'm a little tired of my daily dose of Phillip."

Simon shook his head. "Brothers shouldn't fight the way you two do." He furrowed his brow. "I remember when the two of you were friends. Don't you think you can work out your differences?"

Michael shrugged. "He's got such a chip on his shoulder. It was his decision to stay here, and he enjoys it. But he can't seem to get over the fact that I want a different kind of life." Michael motioned toward the bed frame. "Let's get this done."

They picked the mattress up and flopped it onto the bed.

Simon winced and grabbed at his arm.

"I saw that," Michael said. "Are you okay?"

Simon nodded. "It's probably nothing. I've just been having these weird pains lately." He sat down on the mattress. "And I've been so tired too. I'm not sure what's going on."

Michael furrowed his brow. "Have you been to the doctor?"

Simon made a face. "I'd rather not. I might check in with Leah Bellar to see if she can recommend some tea to help raise my energy level." And with that, he turned toward the stairs, stumbling over his feet.

"Steady there," Michael said.

"You know me. Clumsy as always," Simon said before heading downstairs to the women.

But Michael had known Simon for a long time. And he couldn't recall him ever having a reputation for being clumsy.

* * * * *

Caroline sank onto the love seat in the bookstore. It seemed so quiet now that everyone had gone. And the twins had worn the puppy out, so even he was quietly sleeping in his little bed.

She pondered a nap of her own but knew she had plenty to do. Since she hadn't planned to be gone for more than a week, she could really use some clothes. Not to mention bedding. The thought of picking out a cheery new bedding set raised her spirits. Maybe she'd find something brightly colored...or a print. Maybe gerbera daisies. Or even one of those beautiful quilts she'd seen displayed in so many of the little shops in the area.

Lance had insisted that their expensive sheets and duvet back home be white. He preferred neutral colors, a palette that their home reflected. It would be a nice change to finally add some color to her life.

She glanced at her watch. If she hurried, she could make it to a few stores before they closed. And then she planned to come back to her new place and curl up with a good book.

She cradled the phone with her shoulder as she got into the vehicle and pulled out onto the road. She needed to speak to Robyn, and this was as good a time as any. "How are things in Atlanta? Have things calmed down?" she asked when Robyn finally answered.

Robyn sighed. "Not exactly. I have several messages for you. I was just in the middle of writing them into an e-mail. Do you want me to go ahead and send it or read the list to you?"

It had been such a nice day. The last thing Caroline wanted was to hear those messages. "Just e-mail it. That way I can weed through them at my leisure."

"Well..." Robyn hesitated. "There is one thing I thought you should know about right away."

Caroline wrinkled her nose. "What's that?"

"Valerie wants to see you. Her lawyer called to relay the message."

She sighed. "Can you put him off? Just tell him I'm out of town. But *don't* mention where I am, if he asks."

"Sure. No problem." Robyn fell silent. "But, um...do you know when you'll be coming back?"

Caroline hadn't filled Robyn in on her decision to rent a house and open a store. Although Robyn was completely trustworthy, that information was something Caroline preferred to keep to herself. "I'm thinking of staying for a few more weeks. If you don't mind staying on awhile longer, I'd really appreciate it." When Caroline left Atlanta, she'd put Robyn in charge of running things at the house and also logging some hours at the charity she and Lance had started. Robyn planned to eventually transition to full-time work at the charity.

"That's not a problem," Robyn said. "Do you still want me to spend a couple of nights each week at your house?"

"Please. And can you also go to Lance's apartment? Pick up the mail and make sure there are no messages that need to be handled."

Robyn chuckled. "I had that on my list of things to ask you about."

The girl was a lifesaver. "I don't know how I could've gotten through this without you." Caroline thanked her, ended the call, and turned the car into the mall parking lot. Maybe a little retail therapy would help her forget her troubles.

Chapter Nineteen

....

Michael stood on the front porch of the bookstore. He glanced down at his jeans and red polo, wondering if he were overdressed.

Caroline flung the door open with a grin on her face. "I'm almost ready." She waved him inside. As soon as he stepped through the doorway, he could see how much work she and Lydia Ann had done over the past few days. "The wood floors look great," he said, admiring the gleaming finish. "Almost like brand-new."

"Thanks." She stopped on the bottom step that led up to the residential apartment. "I rented a buffer from a place in Lancaster. It was a comedy of errors at first, but between Lydia Ann and me, we finally figured it out."

He chuckled. "I'll bet."

"I'll just be another second." She headed upstairs.

"Take your time," he called. "I'll look around down here." He wandered to the back of the room, where the coffee bar and tables were. This place had some real possibility. He vaguely remembered it from when he was in high school. Mom had mentioned that Lottie hadn't really tried too hard to make the place a success. "I think she was just trying to pass the time until she was ready to move close to her daughter," she said that morning at breakfast. He thumbed the hodgepodge collection of coffee mugs. There were some pretty funny ones there.

"Ready?" Caroline asked, coming up behind him.

He grinned, taking in her denim capris, bright yellow top, and sandals. "You look beautiful." He loved the way she had such a low-key air about her. Most of the women he'd gone out with had been firmly in the high-maintenance category…but not her.

She flushed. "Thanks."

"You hungry? I was thinking we could head to Lititz…or if you don't want to drive all that way, there's a great little place near Strasburg that serves some very tasty Pennsylvania Dutch cuisine. Complete with shoofly pie." He grinned. "My favorite."

Caroline laughed. "I don't know which sounds better."

"I have a fantastic idea." He ushered her out the door and waited for her to lock up. "How about we go to the closer place tonight and plan on heading to Lititz later in the week?" He knew he might be pushing it. Ever since she'd confessed to him that she'd been married and her husband had passed away, he was trying hard to take things slowly.

She narrowed her eyes. "Well, I do want to try both places. And I hate to eat alone." She quirked her mouth into a smile. "So maybe I could go along with that plan."

He chuckled. "I'm not going to argue with that." He pulled onto the highway. "So how were your first few nights in the house?"

"The mattress was very comfy. Thanks." She sighed. "But I do have one complaint."

"What's that?"

"The puppy cries unless I let him sleep with me."

Michael groaned. "Please tell me you didn't give in. You left him in the crate, didn't you?"

"I tried to. I really did." She laughed. "But he is so cute. I finally gave in and got him out of there. He went right to sleep once I put him on a little pillow at the foot of my bed."

Michael shook his head. "He's going to be so spoiled." He glanced over at her while they waited at a stoplight. "And he needs a name."

"I know." She leaned her head against the seat. "I've been trying to find one that suits him."

"Well, you can't just keep calling him Puppy." He grinned. "I know you're more creative than that."

"Maybe. I've actually been thinking of naming him Bandit."

"Bandit?" he asked. "Why?"

She burst out laughing. "You'll make fun of me if I tell you."

"Probably so." He grinned. "But try me anyway."

"Because he stole my heart like a bandit." She joined in with his laughter.

"That might be the cheesiest thing I've ever heard."

She rolled her eyes. "Oh, come on. I'm sure a guy like you has probably heard some pretty cheesy stuff in your day."

"A guy like me?" He pulled into a spot near the front of the restaurant. "What is that supposed to mean?"

Caroline shrugged. "Good-looking. Smart. Funny." She shot him a glance. "You've probably broken a lot of hearts."

He bit his lip. "Not as many as you'd think." He hated to tell her the truth. He'd only been in one relationship. Sure, he'd had his share of dates. But he'd only been serious about one woman. And he happened to be having lunch with her next week.

* * * * *

Caroline couldn't believe how much fun she was having. It had been years since she'd been on a date with a man without worrying about the media or having to feel like she was on display. And she and Michael were so comfortable with each other. It seemed almost like he was an old friend, even though they'd only known one another for a short time.

"Not as many as I'd think, huh?" she asked as he held the restaurant door open for her.

He grinned. "Nope."

By the time they were seated and had ordered, Caroline's stomach was rumbling. "It's a good thing we decided to go ahead and eat here," she said. "Or we might've had to stop at a gas station for me to get a snack."

He chuckled. "Didn't you eat lunch?"

"No. I was so caught up in getting the floors done, I forgot to eat. And then by the time I realized it, it was only a couple of hours before you were supposed to pick me up." She grinned. "By that point, I didn't want to spoil my dinner."

"Well, I think you'll find the food here to be worth the wait," he said as the waitress, a young Amish girl, set their plates on the table.

"Mind if I ask the blessing?" he asked.

She smiled. "Please do." Now that she'd gotten back into the habit of praying, it would seem odd not to give thanks for the food. And now that she saw and felt the difference that praying made in her life, she vowed to never let her prayer life lapse again. "Oh my goodness," she exclaimed as she bit into the meat loaf on her plate after Michael's prayer. "This tastes almost as good as what my grandmother used to make."

He grinned. "Told you."

She took a sip of her Coke. "This settles it. I'm definitely going to have to start running again."

"You're a runner?"

"Used to be." She took another bite.

"Used to be a kindergarten teacher. Used to be a runner." He looked at her curiously. "Why do I feel like you've lived more than one life?"

His words hit so close to the truth, she cringed. "I guess I've just done a lot of different things." But as the words left her mouth, she realized that she wanted to tell him the truth. The whole truth. But this wasn't the spot. She glanced around the crowded restaurant, full of families enjoying their meals. "What do you say about checking out some more of those covered bridges after we eat?" she asked.

He smiled. "Sounds great to me. Maybe we should get our dessert to go and picnic it up."

Caroline laughed. "Yes. Let's picnic it up."

Thirty minutes later, they were back in Michael's SUV. Caroline clutched a doggie bag with two desserts in her lap.

"Which bridge?" Michael asked. "Same one or a different one?"

She thought for a minute. "Same. I liked our little picnic spot."

Once they had everything spread out on Michael's stadium blanket, he reached into the bag and pulled out a Styrofoam container. "Dig in," he said, grinning.

Caroline sighed. "Actually, can we talk first?" Her heart pounded. Suddenly, telling the whole truth about her past didn't seem like such a great idea. But she didn't want to spend more time with Michael until he knew what he was dealing with.

Michael placed the container back on the blanket and regarded her seriously. "Of course."

"Remember how I told you that I was a kindergarten teacher?"

Michael nodded. "Yes. But you're not anymore."

"I worked in a small town in Georgia. Our school won a contest, and some of the Braves baseball players came to school to talk to a few of the classes and hang out with the kids at recess."

"Lucky kids," Michael said.

She shrugged. "I guess." She cleared her throat. "Anyway, Lance DeMarco was one of the players that came to school that day."

"Poor guy. I saw on the news what happened to him."

She froze for a second. "Yeah. Well, anyway, my principal introduced me to Lance. And to make a long story short, we started dating."

"Wow."

"And a few months later, we were married."

Michael let out a whistle. "Okay, I did not see that coming."

Chapter Twenty
....

Michael could barely register his thoughts after the shock. Caroline had been married to Lance DeMarco? He tried hard to process the information.

"Lance was really good at getting his way," Caroline explained. "He was the picture of a smooth talker. The only person he didn't fool was my mama. She saw through him immediately." She shook her head. "Unfortunately, I wouldn't listen. I fell for him hook, line, and sinker."

"What do you mean?" he asked.

"The media was all over our relationship. There I was, this back-woods country girl who taught kindergarten at a poverty-stricken school. And he swooped in like Prince Charming and we fell in love. It seemed like the kind of story movies are made of."

"Wasn't there a TV movie loosely based on it?"

She chuckled. "I think so. Believe me when I tell you that the last thing I wanted was to be in the spotlight. But once we were married, it was like I was on a roller coaster that wouldn't stop. There were always events to go to and appearances to make. Lance became the most recognized athlete in the world. And I was expected to stand next to him and smile, no matter what was going on."

Michael wrinkled his brow. "What *was* going on?"

She leveled her brown-eyed gaze at him. "Can I trust you? I mean really trust you?"

He reached over and grabbed her hand. "You can trust me with your life."

"And you won't tell anyone who I am or what I'm about to say?"

He held his hand up. "Scout's honor."

She nodded. "Well, not too long after we were married, he seemed to change. A lot. He tried to 'fix' me by turning me into some kind of cookie-cutter Atlanta housewife. There were people hired to consult on my wardrobe, my accent...you name it. It seemed like he wasn't in love with me as much as he was in love with the media story of us. After our wedding pictures were in *People*, he got more endorsement deals. His agent said that having such a fairy-tale love story made him even more attractive."

Michael shook his head. This woman had been through a lot.

"When I wanted to start a family and he threw a fit about it, it became apparent to me that we didn't have a real marriage. So for the last two years, we lived apart. He had an apartment downtown near the stadium where he stayed most of the time." She sighed. "I suspected that there were other women but was never certain until..."

"I know. I saw the news stories. Those pictures from the tabloids were pretty incriminating."

"The worst part is that Valerie Stephens was my best friend. But I guess you heard that already."

"Yeah, I saw it. Such an awful story."

She nodded. "I guess she thought she was the only one. Because when the story came out about multiple girlfriends, she kind of lost it."

"So were you there? When she..."

"When she shot him," she finished for him. "Yeah. I was there." She tried to keep the bitterness out of her voice. "Here's the irony.

The reason he was at the house was because he wanted to beg my forgiveness and try to talk me into staying with him. I told him there was no way and followed him outside, arguing. I had no idea she was out there until she'd already pulled the trigger."

"It's a wonder she didn't shoot you too."

Caroline nodded. "That's what everyone says. After the funeral, I couldn't go anywhere. There were paparazzi literally camped outside of my house. That's why I decided to come here." She tugged at a lock of hair. "And color my hair."

"It's a good look for you." He grinned and then grew serious. "I can't imagine what the past few months have been like for you."

"Believe me, that's a good thing. It's like I've been held captive." She squeezed his hand. "But I feel free here. Like I can be myself again."

"I'm glad."

"And now you know why I couldn't let anything happen between us. I needed to make sure you knew what you were dealing with. *Who* you were dealing with. Because I know that is a lot of drama to unload on someone." She gave him a tiny smile.

"Hey," he said softly, "it means a lot that you trust me with it. Your secret is safe with me." He lifted her hand to his lips and kissed it. "And this thing between us can go as slowly as you need it to." He grinned.

"Thanks for being so understanding." She returned his smile.

"You're safe with me," he whispered. "Safe." But he couldn't help but wonder if his heart was safe with her. She seemed far removed from everything that had happened. Did that mean she'd dealt with all those feelings and was ready to move forward? Or would the feelings haunt her later and catch him in the cross fire? One glance at her beautiful face and he knew that, either way, he was already invested. He could still turn back...but he didn't want to.

* * * * *

"You've been awfully quiet the past few days," Leah remarked. "Is everything okay?"

Lydia Ann looked up from the letter from Abby that she was rereading. "I guess I've just been tired."

"Are you sure?" Leah wrinkled her brow. "Because you know you don't have to work at the bookstore if you don't want to. It's probably a lot of work to try and get it ready to reopen." She rocked gently on the porch swing. "We would love to have you at our store."

Lydia Ann smiled. "Danki. But Caroline needs my help." She sighed. "She's truly alone."

Leah nodded. "It's very kind of you to help her out."

"I'm enjoying it," Lydia Ann explained. "It isn't that much different than getting a quilt store ready to open."

Leah fell silent. Finally she turned to Lydia Ann. "It means so much to your father that you're here. I hope you know how much he's missed you."

Lydia Ann chewed on her bottom lip. "I have missed him too."

"There's something else you should know," Leah said. "It means a lot to me that you're here too. But I think I owe you an apology."

Lydia Ann looked at Leah in surprise. "An apology? For what?"

"I should've tried harder to include you in our family, especially after your husband fell sick." She shook her head. "I, of all people, know what it's like to be left behind with two children to raise." She reached over and clasped Lydia Ann's hand. "I should've written you more and offered you more encouragement. But I didn't. Instead, I feared you didn't want anything to do with me."

Lydia Ann didn't want to admit it, but there was a touch of truth in her statement. "It's okay. I had support from Levi's parents and others from the community."

"I wish to extend my apology anyway. I've prayed for you and your daughters for years."

Lydia Ann smiled. "Sometimes that is the best thing anyone can do." Prayer had certainly sustained her over the years.

Dat stepped out onto the porch. "I know two little girls who are going to sleep well tonight," he said, pointing at Mary and Katie, who were chasing each other around the yard. He put his hand on Lydia Ann's shoulder. "They remind me so much of you when you were that age."

Lydia Ann chuckled. "If only I'd have had a twin."

Dat chuckled. "Having Emma and Abby visit during the summer was enough, don't you think?"

She joined in his laughter. "We did have some fun times."

He patted her shoulder. "There are still fun times to be had."

Lydia Ann reached up and covered Dat's hand with her own and looked at her two healthy children playing in the yard. He was right. Sometimes she focused too much on the bad. But there were a lot of good things in her life. And the people who surrounded her right now were a big part of that.

Chapter Twenty-One

Caroline hummed to herself as she brewed a pot of coffee. She felt a million pounds lighter now that Michael knew the truth. The whole truth. She just hoped he didn't wake up and feel weirded out about the whole thing. He'd joked on the way back to her place that he might have to Google her to see how she looked with dark hair. And since he worked in the world of journalism, she suspected that he would probably look at some of the media stories about her. It would be hard not to.

"Good morning," Lydia Ann called from the front.

Mary's and Katie's excited chatter filled the large space.

"I'm at the coffee bar," Caroline said. "Would you like a cup?"

"Jah," Lydia Ann said. "That would be wonderful." She stepped into the coffee bar area. "You look awfully happy this morning."

Caroline smiled broadly. "I am happy."

She couldn't remember when she'd last said that out loud and meant it. It had been ages. Sure, things weren't perfect. She knew there was a long road ahead of her as she dealt with Lance's death and the life she'd left behind. Besides that, she still held on to the fear that someone would learn her true identity and she would lose the peace she needed so much. But having Michael in her life helped a lot. She trusted him to keep her secret and appreciated the way he didn't put any pressure on her. Last night he'd only given her a hug. She appreciated that so much. So many guys would've been pushing her to get physical. But not Michael. He seemed to want to make sure she was comfortable with things between them. Not that she'd mind kissing him…but she knew she wasn't quite ready for that step yet.

"I'm glad to hear it." Lydia Ann smiled. "Do you think we'll be ready for the opening next week?"

Caroline nodded. "I sure do. And guess what? Michael is going to do an article about the store for the magazine he works for. That should really help us out as far as customers go." She'd argued against his idea at first. What if someone figured out who she really was? But he'd promised not to use her name in the article and to only photograph the outside of the store.

Lydia Ann raised her eyebrows. "Michael seems like a good friend to you."

"He is. I think he's one of those elusive 'good guys' who are so hard to find." At least she hoped so. She'd trusted her instincts in the past and had been proven wrong. Michael seemed like the real deal, but after everything she'd gone through, she wasn't quite ready to trust him blindly. But things were off to a good start.

"What's on our list for today?"

"I'd like to brainstorm a little bit," Caroline said. "I wanted to run something by you." She carried two steaming cups of coffee to the table where Lydia Ann was sitting.

"Danki," Lydia Ann said, grasping the ceramic cup in her hands.

Caroline sat down in the chair across from Lydia Ann. "I'm considering having a story hour a couple times a week for kids." She motioned toward the section of the store that housed the children's books. An alphabet rug on the floor and a full toy box beckoned children when they came in the store. "With my background as a kindergarten teacher, I know how much kids enjoy listening to stories. So I thought maybe that might help drum up some business. Perhaps parents would bring their kids for story time and they would purchase coffee and pastries while they waited."

Lydia Ann nodded. "That sounds like a good idea to me."

"I also thought about adding some more merchandise," Caroline explained. "Maybe things that are locally made. Quilts, paintings… things that will catch the eye as people come inside." She pointed at the entrance to the store. "I don't want to have too much, though. Maybe just a few select pieces to display in the front."

"Those all sound like good ideas to me," Lydia Ann said.

Caroline beamed. "Great."

"Miss Caroline," one of the twins called from the other room.

Caroline stepped into the children's area to find Mary and Katie sitting on their knees and hovering over Bandit.

Katie rubbed Bandit's belly, and the puppy squirmed in his bed, clearly enjoying the attention.

"Is Bandit ready to go outside?" Mary asked.

Caroline chuckled. "I think he would love to go outside."

Katie picked up the puppy and cradled him in her arms. "I love you, Bandit," she murmured.

Mary leaned close to the puppy. "Me too."

They headed out the back door with the squirming puppy, chattering back and forth.

"Precious," Caroline observed. "They're so precious."

Lydia Ann smiled. "Gifts from God."

Caroline couldn't help but wonder if she'd ever have children of her own. Despite the way her marriage had worked out, she regretted that she hadn't become a mother yet. She'd been looking forward to being a mom since the day she got her first baby doll as a little girl.

She thought of how Mrs. Landis had told her that her day would come. And she'd like to hold onto that thought, except that so much had gone wrong in her life. She wondered if this dream might be another that went unfulfilled.

* * * * *

"Mr. Landis?" Mr. Sinclair's assistant said over his speakerphone. "Do you have a few minutes? The boss would like to see you."

"Yes. I'll be there in a second." He saved the blog post he was working on about the covered bridges of Lancaster County.

"Hey there," Jenny peeked over the cubicle. "You aren't in trouble, are you?" She grinned.

He shook his head. "I don't think so. And thanks for respecting my privacy."

She laughed. "Michael, everyone hears everything around here. Next time someone buzzes to your speakerphone, pick up the receiver." She winked. "Otherwise, all information is fair game."

"Don't you have some marketing to focus on?" he asked, unable to hide his smile. They might not be romantically compatible, but Jenny was definitely a force to be reckoned with.

She made a face. "Not before I tell you that we have reservations. Monday." She grinned. "So don't make plans."

He raked his fingers through his hair. "Monday isn't good for me. Sorry." Caroline's opening happened to be Monday, and he planned to cover it for the magazine. He hoped to get the owner to sneak away for lunch too.

Jenny's bright smile faded. "You don't have another lunch date, do you?" She furrowed her brow.

He stood. "I'm covering a business opening for the magazine."

Relief washed over her face. "Oh. I'll change the reservation, then. I'll try for Tuesday."

He nodded. "Fine." Something was up with Jenny. He had a sinking feeling that she was intent on trying to rekindle things between them. But he didn't have time to worry about that right now. He had a meeting to get to.

"Michael," Mr. Sinclair said a few moments later, "please have a seat." He pointed a pudgy finger at a worn leather chair across from his massive desk.

"Everything okay?" Michael tried to shake the worry. But if he got let go from another job after such a short time, he wasn't sure his ego would recover. He might have to change career paths.

"Things are more than okay." Mr. Sinclair smiled. "All that Twitting you're doing is working."

Michael bit his lip. *Twitting? Really?* But Mr. Sinclair didn't seem like the kind of man who enjoyed being corrected by someone young enough to be his grandson.

"The businesses that purchase our ads are seeing an upswing in traffic, both to their physical stores as well as their websites. They're crediting you with getting the message out about some of the interesting things to do and see in our area."

"That's great news." Relief washed over him. Maybe he wouldn't be out of a job today after all.

"Even better, ad sales are up. And we're expanding beyond our normal customers."

Michael nodded. "Excellent."

"But that means I'm going to need you to do a little more traveling. So far, your stories and the information you're posting online center around the general area." He pressed his fingers together. "How do you feel about a little road trip?"

"Great."

"Fantastic. I want you to head toward Gettysburg as soon as you get the chance. Tour around, take some pictures. Post them online. Check out some of the restaurants and shops." He peered at Michael. "Does that sound okay?"

Michael nodded. "Sure." He hadn't been to Gettysburg in years. It was an easy day trip from Lancaster. An idea began to form in his mind. He didn't often mix business with pleasure, but this seemed like too good of an opportunity to pass up.

Chapter Twenty-Two
....

Lydia Ann gave one final look around the store. "I think it's perfect," she declared.

Caroline smiled. "I think so too." She gave the glass counter one last swipe with a cloth. "We're ready. Come Monday, we'll be in business."

Lydia Ann looked forward to having customers. It was one of the things she missed about her own shop. She'd been in business for so many years that she'd gotten to know her customers well, especially those from the local area. In many ways, her customers had become her friends. She hoped Caroline would have the same experience. "We sure will."

"I'm more excited than nervous," Caroline said. "Except that I keep worrying we won't have any customers. So I'm going to try to keep busy this weekend to keep my mind off opening day." She grinned.

"Do you at least have big plans for tonight?" Lydia Ann asked.

Caroline smiled. "Michael and I are supposed to go to Lititz. The downtown area looks so neat. We're going to have dinner and just walk around, looking at the shops and sights."

"Sounds like a wonderful time." Caroline had confided in her earlier in the week that she'd gone to dinner with Michael. That dinner must have gone well if they already had another date planned.

The shop door opened and Michael strode inside. "Afternoon, ladies," he said, grinning. "Looks like you're ready for the big day."

Caroline narrowed her eyes at him. "We aren't supposed to leave for a couple of hours. What are you doing here?"

Michael burst out laughing. "I can always count on you to get to the point," he said. "Actually, I came to invite both of you on a little outing."

"An outing to where?" Lydia Ann asked.

"I need to visit Gettysburg for work," he explained. "I need to get some photos of the tour route as well as some of the historic buildings in town. My boss also wants me to visit some of the little shops and eat at a restaurant or two." He grinned. "Tough job, but someone has to do it. And I thought it would be more fun if I had company." He shrugged. "It's only a couple of hours from Lancaster, so we could easily leave tomorrow morning and be back in the late afternoon."

Caroline wrinkled her nose. "I don't know. I'd have to get someone to take care of Bandit. I really can't leave him in his crate for that long."

"I know two little girls who'd love to keep him for the day," Lydia Ann said, imagining the squeals of excitement she would be met with when she told Katie and Mary the news.

Michael grinned. "Okay, that's settled." He turned to Lydia Ann. "And how about you?"

Although she wouldn't mind visiting a new town, she didn't want to be a third wheel. "I'm not sure."

"Simon is going to be awfully disappointed if you say no."

She jerked her head up. "Simon?"

Michael nodded. "I asked him earlier. He didn't want to be a third wheel." He shook his head. "But he mentioned that you might like to go too since you aren't from around here." He grinned. "No pressure, but his happiness depends on whether you say yes or no."

She couldn't stop her smile. "His happiness? Isn't that a little dramatic?"

Michael shook his head. "If he doesn't go, he's going to work an extra shift at the farm. And tomorrow is the day the cow stalls get cleaned out."

She burst out laughing. "Okay, okay, I'll go. I don't want him to have to spend his day cleaning up after the cows. Besides, I know Dat and Leah will be happy to have the girls to themselves for a whole day."

"I'll tell Simon the good news." Michael grinned at her then turned to Caroline. "And I'll see you in"—he glanced at his watch—"an hour and a half." With a final wave, he left the store.

"Gettysburg," Caroline said. "I've always wanted to go there." She grinned at Lydia Ann. "I'm glad you and Simon are going."

Lydia Ann nodded. Her emotions were at war. On the one hand, she was excited about visiting a historic place and even about getting to know Simon a little bit better. But on the other hand, just hearing her name linked with Simon's that way made her feel like a traitor. She remembered Emma's plea that she keep an open mind about things.

Perhaps her cousin was right.

* * * * *

Simon and his mother climbed into their family buggy at the Landis farm on Friday afternoon.

"Did you have a good day?" Mamm asked once they were settled.

Simon nodded. "It was a good day. It wasn't too hot outside, and Phillip and I were able to get a lot of work done out in the back pasture. There's a fence there that needs mending. We made good progress." As much as Phillip and Michael didn't seem to get along, Simon had always had a good working relationship with Phillip. They weren't exactly friends the way he and Michael were, but they worked well together.

"That's nice."

"Michael asked me to go with him to Gettysburg tomorrow," Simon said as he drove the buggy past another dairy farm.

Mamm looked over at him. "Are you going?"

He nodded. "I'd like to go, unless you have something you need me to do." Once he'd learned that Lydia Ann had agreed to go, he'd started really looking forward to the outing.

"I think that sounds nice. I know you and Michael haven't spent much time together since he's been away."

Simon knew that spending time with Michael wasn't exactly the draw to go on the trip. "There are others going too," he explained. "I think you've met Caroline—she was a guest at the farmhouse earlier in the summer."

"Jah, I met Caroline. She seems like such a nice girl," Mamm said. "I understand she and Michael have formed a good friendship."

Simon nodded. "They have grown close. Did Mrs. Landis tell you that Caroline is reopening Lottie Harris's bookstore on Monday? Jeremiah Bellar's daughter, Lydia Ann, is helping her get the shop up and running."

Mamm glanced at him. "Is Jeremiah's daughter going to Gettysburg with you tomorrow?"

The woman never missed anything. He nodded. "She is going.

Since she's not from around here, it seemed like a nice idea to show her around a little."

He caught the tiny smile on Mamm's face. Thankfully she didn't ask him any more questions. But as he put up the horse and buggy for the night, he couldn't help but wonder how tomorrow would go.

A twinge in his hand pulled his thoughts away from Lydia Ann. He didn't want to admit it, but he was starting to get worried. He vowed to push his worries from his mind until next week. The Good Book plainly said that worrying did no good.

And as a man who loved the Lord, he strove to follow those words with all his might.

Chapter Twenty-Three
....

Caroline dabbed on a last touch of lipstick and stepped back to look at herself in the mirror. *Not bad.* She leaned closer. *Except for those dark circles underneath the eyes.* She fished through her makeup bag for some concealer. She knew Michael well enough to know that he would notice them. He probably already had, earlier in the afternoon, but been too polite to point them out in front of Lydia Ann. But once they were alone, he'd want to know why she wasn't getting enough sleep.

Just when things had been going so well, the calls had started. Robyn was frantic. There were loose ends that needed to be tied up back in Atlanta—things Caroline would have to handle in person. Yet she knew that once she went back, her cover would be blown. And she wasn't quite ready for that yet. Especially not now, with the bookstore about to open. To make matters worse, the messages from Valerie's lawyer were becoming more urgent. She said she desperately needed to speak to Caroline…in person.

Caroline finally got the under-eye circles covered, as much as possible without looking like a clown. She knelt down to Bandit, who'd begrudgingly gone into his crate after he'd chewed up a paperback. "I'll be back very soon, sweet boy," she cooed.

The puppy turned his face in the other direction, letting her know in no uncertain terms how he felt about being locked up.

She grabbed her purse and headed downstairs. Tonight she'd decided to dress up a little in a green shirtdress and wedge sandals. She'd decided to wear her hair long and loose, even though she still thought the color was a bit much.

Michael rapped on the door right on time.

"Hey there," she said, smiling.

He let out a low whistle. "I am a lucky man."

She did a little pirouette. "Thank you kindly. You sure know how to boost a girl's ego."

He gave her a quick side hug. "Anytime." He inhaled deeply. "And you smell good too."

She laughed. "You're not so bad yourself." And it was true. She liked that he didn't smell like cologne. Just good old-fashioned soap. Her granddaddy would've said that was the mark of a real man, because real men didn't wear perfume. His feelings about men's cologne had come out one Christmas when Mee-Maw bestowed a bottle of Old Spice upon him.

Michael was definitely a real man. She appreciated that he made no effort to hide it when he thought she looked pretty. He wasn't a game player. And it looked like he'd decided to dress up a bit tonight as well. His khakis were freshly pressed, and his green polo was the same color as his eyes.

"You have a good day?" he asked as he helped her into the car.

She waited until he came around to the driver's side. "Good day." She nodded. "We're ready for Monday. I'm so thankful for Lydia Ann, though. She's been a real lifesaver." The more time she spent with the Amish woman, the more respect Caroline had for her. Despite everything Lydia Ann had endured, she'd continually relied on her faith to see her through.

"I think the opening will be great. I plan to swing by around lunchtime and take some pictures."

Caroline furrowed her brow. "What if no one shows up?"

He reached over and patted her knee. "Don't worry. You've had good advertising. And I think people are going to be excited about an activity for their kids." He grinned. "Do you need me to stay for the reading and do animal voices or anything?" He chuckled. "It's one of my many talents."

She shook her head. "You're a man full of surprises, aren't you? But I don't want to scare the kids."

"Ouch. Don't you know my ego can't take a bruising?"

She laughed. "I'm pretty sure I never have to worry about your ego."

They passed through a residential area before turning onto a main highway. "How long does it take to get to Lititz?"

"Fifteen more minutes, maybe twenty depending on traffic."

She leaned her head against the seat. The warmth of the late afternoon sun coupled with the whirr of the SUV's wheels on the pavement lulled her into silence. Her eyelids were so heavy, she had to fight to keep them awake. Those sleepless nights had caught up with her.

"Take a nap," he said softly. "I'll wake you when we get there."

She couldn't fight it any longer. Sleep washed over her, but not before she recognized the growing feeling inside. She felt safe with him. Completely safe.

* * * * *

Michael glanced over at the sleeping girl in the passenger seat. He'd been reeling ever since her revelation earlier in the week. Lance DeMarco sounded like a real piece of work. Rest his soul, of course.

From what Caroline had told him, she suspected that the marriage had been a sham from the beginning. A PR stunt to give Lance added appeal. The public loved a fairy tale, and what could be better than a dreamy baseball player falling in love with a beautiful girl who came from a poor but proud background? It turned his stomach to think of how she must've felt when she realized the marriage was all a show. He'd watched the TV stories and seen the magazines when the news about Lance's affairs had surfaced. In fact, he'd even seen Caroline. At the time, he'd wondered what kind of man would cheat on a woman like that. She'd kept her head up, no matter whether the cameras caught her putting gas in her vehicle or leaving the supermarket.

And just in the short weeks since she'd first come to Lancaster County, he could see a marked change in her. Her smiles came more easily. She'd started to relax. He hoped he had something to do with that.

Michael parallel parked on the historic main street in Lititz. He glanced over at Caroline. She was still sound asleep. He'd noticed the dark circles underneath her eyes and hated to wake her, but he felt like a weirdo just watching her sleep. He wished he were brave enough to lean over and wake her with a kiss—except that he wanted her to be fully awake for their first kiss. He shook her gently. "Wake up, sleepyhead," he said softly.

She turned her face toward him and smiled through closed eyes. "Five more minutes?" she murmured.

He chuckled. "Am I seeing a glimpse of you as a little girl trying to sleep in for school?"

She sat up and stifled a yawn. "My mama used to say that I was the biggest sleepyhead she knew."

He got out of the car and went around to the passenger side. He opened her door and held out his hand.

Caroline took it and hopped down from the SUV. "Thanks."

"So. The million-dollar question. Do you want to eat first or walk around first?"

"Let's walk around for a bit," Caroline said.

Michael wondered how she'd react if he grabbed her hand. *Only one way to find out.* He reached over and took her hand, hoping she wouldn't recoil.

She didn't. "Nicely done," she said. "Who knew you were such a smooth operator?"

He laughed and gave her hand a squeeze. "Baby steps. I promise."

They walked down the street and stopped to peek into the window of a gourmet food store.

"Look at those adorable aprons!" Caroline exclaimed. "They're so cute."

Michael grinned at her exuberance. "I didn't realize you were such a traditional kind of woman."

She cut her eyes at him. "I'll have you know that I happen to be a great cook. And I *am* a traditional kind of woman." She grinned. "Just with a little bit of an edge."

He laughed. "An edge, huh?" He squeezed her hand as they continued down the street. "Tell me more about your life in Atlanta. There have to be some good parts, right?"

She sighed. "Yeah. There are a few things I miss. I don't think I ever told you that I work with a charity."

"Oh yeah? What do you do?"

"We work to give kids a place to go after school. There are so many kids who don't really have much of a home life. We've opened centers in certain areas of the city, and they're fully staffed. There are tutors to help with homework, coaches who help with organized sports…and each center has cooks on staff so that the kids can take a bag supper with them when they leave."

"Wow. That sounds like an awesome program."

She nodded. "You'd be surprised at the number of children who don't have enough to eat. For some of them, the meals they get at school are their only meals of the day. This is a way to make sure that they have a safe environment as well as some resources to help the ones in need."

Caroline spoke with such passion. Michael knew that if he ever had to look back and pinpoint the moment when he knew his feelings for her were strong, this would be it. "I'll bet you were really involved."

She nodded. "Especially the last couple of years. Once I stopped traveling with Lance, it gave me more time to devote to my work." She shrugged. "After we married, I found that I really missed teaching. So this gave me a way to still work with kids even though I wasn't in the classroom."

Hand in hand, they crossed to the other side of the street.

"Look." Caroline pointed at a historical marker. "It's the oldest pretzel factory in the United States."

Michael dropped her hand and pulled out his camera. "That's awesome. I'm going to have to get a picture for the magazine."

Caroline scooted out of the way. "Just don't get me," she said.

He chuckled. "Don't worry. I'm aiming the lens at that gigantic statue of a pretzel." He snapped a couple of shots of the pretzel with the historical marker in the background. "Perfect."

"Too bad they're already closed for the day. I'll bet they taste yummy."

He nodded. "It's been years since I was here, but they certainly do." He motioned down the street. "You getting hungry?"

"You must be reading my mind."

They stopped in front of a little Italian restaurant.

"This okay?" he asked.

Caroline nodded. "Better than okay."

He hated to drop her hand, but they couldn't fit through the door at the same time. He opened the door. "After you," he gestured.

She walked past him, granting him a still-sleepy smile.

Once they'd ordered, he leaned forward. "So what gives? Are you not sleeping well? Is Bandit keeping you up?"

Caroline laughed. "I can't blame Bandit. He's actually a good sleeper as long as he's not in his crate." She smiled.

"Then what's the problem? If it's the mattress, I think it's under warranty. We can take it back."

She furrowed her brow. "It isn't the mattress." She sighed. "It's just…" She trailed off, an uncertain look on her face.

He reached across the table and took her hand. "You can tell me. Maybe I can help."

She regarded him for a long moment. Finally she nodded. "I've been getting a lot of calls from back home. I guess there are some things I need to deal with there. Things that need to be handled in person."

"I figured you might say something like that."

She gave him a half smile. "Guess you can't really run from your problems. And you can only hide from them for so long before they track you down."

"Look at it this way," he said, "at least no one here knows who you really are." He squeezed her hand. "You can go back and take care of what you need to. Then come back. We'll figure out a way to keep anyone here from ever knowing."

She bit her lip. "There's more to it than just that." She sighed. "Valerie wants to see me. I'm guessing to apologize or to explain? Or something like that."

"How do you feel about seeing her?"

She shrugged. "I can't say that I'm surprised. I mean, clearly she wants to ease her conscience."

"And?"

"A few weeks ago, I would've said no way. That it wasn't my place to see to it that she feels better about things."

"What's changed?"

Caroline gave him a wan smile. "Lydia Ann. I'm just amazed at the way she seems to get through everything with an incredible faith in God. And we were talking the other day about forgiveness. Something she said has stuck with me."

"What's that?"

"That she always tries to live her life knowing that if you're praying for someone, it's hard to be mad at them." She played with the straw wrapper. "So I've been giving that a try. I've been praying that the Lord will help me to forgive Lance. And I've been praying that Valerie will find some kind of peace." She met his gaze. "I guess once I got here, I realized that my faith wasn't as strong as it used to be. And I've been trying to fix it."

"Then I guess you know what you have to do."

She nodded. "I have to go to Atlanta. And meet with the woman who killed Lance."

Chapter Twenty-Four

....

Lydia Ann hadn't felt so light and free since she was a teenager. Leah and Dat had been thrilled to keep the girls and Bandit for the day.

"Anybody want to drive through McDonald's before we hit the road?" Michael asked as they left the Landis Farm.

"Ladies?" Simon turned to them from the front passenger seat. "Do either of you want to stop?"

Caroline and Lydia Ann exchanged glances.

"I had a Pop-Tart before I left," Caroline said.

Lydia Ann smiled. "And we had a big breakfast this morning. Katie and Mary helped with the cooking, which meant pancakes—their favorite."

Simon chuckled. "Mine too."

"Okay, then, I guess the next stop is Gettysburg," Michael said.

Caroline leaned over toward Lydia Ann. "I'm just going to warn you—I might fall asleep."

Lydia Ann laughed. "That's fine."

"I don't want you to think I'm rude." She grinned and slipped some oversized sunglasses out of her bag. "But I'm completely exhausted."

"Don't feel bad," Michael said. "She fell asleep on the way to Lititz last night too." He chuckled. "I'm hoping it wasn't a reflection on how much fun she was having."

Simon laughed. "And all this time I thought you had a way with the ladies."

Lydia Ann turned to Caroline. "A nap sounds wonderful. I might try for one too."

Caroline smiled and leaned against the window. "Wake me before we get there so I can see the sights," she said.

Lydia Ann leaned her head back against the seat and shut her eyes. She was far too keyed up to go to sleep, though. She finally sat up and watched the passing scenery. A sign that advertised Hershey reminded her of the letter from Emma she'd stuffed into her bag. She pulled it out to see what her cousin had to say.

She quickly read the latest family news. Abby felt wonderful, and her belly was just beginning to protrude. Noah had been working on a new set of paintings inspired by some of the covered bridges they'd seen in Lancaster County. And Emma was considering adding a coffee bar to their store. She'd liked the idea a lot when she visited the bookstore.

The last sentence of the letter jumped out at Lydia Ann. *I hope you and Simon Zook have become friends. He's such a nice man....*

Lydia Ann quickly folded the letter up and shoved it back into her bag.

* * * * *

Simon watched Michael and Caroline talking and laughing near the Gettysburg National Military Park entrance sign. Michael was taking pictures for his magazine and trying to convince Caroline to get in one of the shots.

Simon glanced over at Lydia Ann and caught her eye.

She grinned. "They seem to have grown pretty close," she said, stepping closer to Simon.

He nodded. "It looks that way."

"It's nice to see two people so happy," she observed.

"And how about you? Are you happy?" Simon asked, looking into her blue eyes.

A pretty blush covered her face. "Jah. Each day when I wake up I thank the Lord for allowing me another day with my loved ones." She sighed. "I learned a long time ago not to take a single minute for granted."

"I know what you mean. Since my dat passed away last year, I've spent a lot of time thinking about time. I've come to realize that we must make every moment count, whether it be at our work, with our loved ones, or in our worship."

She gave him a surprised look. "I didn't realize you'd lost your dat so recently."

Simon nodded. "He got very sick last winter and never recovered. By the time he went to the doctor, it was too late. Pneumonia." He shook his head. "It's been a difficult time." Simon appreciated the sympathy in Lydia Ann's eyes. She had such a sweet spirit.

"You two ready?" Michael called. "Let's check out the museum before we head out on the tour."

Simon nodded. He and Lydia Ann followed Michael and Caroline into the vast building.

"Wow," Lydia Ann breathed when they stepped inside. "This might be the biggest building I've ever been inside."

Caroline nodded. "It's not quite what I was expecting, either. Back home, our parks usually have smallish rustic buildings where you can get tourist information. But this…" She waved her arms and spun in a circle, looking at the tall ceilings. "This is amazing."

An hour later, after watching a movie about the events that had taken place at Gettysburg and looking at the many artifacts in the museum, they got back into the SUV.

"Let's take the driving tour so I can get some good pictures for the magazine," Michael said, starting the vehicle. "Does someone have a map?"

Lydia Ann handed her map to Simon. "Here you go," she said.

"Anybody want to get out and climb up the hill to that marker?" Michael asked ten minutes later, pulling the car over and putting it in PARK.

Lydia Ann glanced up at the steep hill. A tall monument was barely visible midway up the incline.

"I'll go with you," Simon said.

"Ladies?" Michael asked, glancing into the backseat.

Caroline shook her head. "I think I'll stay here."

Lydia Ann was relieved. She didn't want to seem like a spoil-sport, but the last thing she wanted to do was climb that steep path. "I'll keep her company." She glanced at Caroline.

Michael turned off the engine and tossed the keys to Caroline. "If you get hot and need to run the AC, feel free." He grinned. "Just don't run off and leave us."

She chuckled. "Then don't be gone too long," she warned.

The men headed up the pathway toward the monument.

Caroline sighed. "I'm so glad you didn't want to go up there. That looks too steep for my tastes."

"Mine too." Lydia Ann grinned. "It looks like you and Michael have become pretty good friends."

Caroline nodded. "He's not like anyone I've ever met before. He has such respect for me and is so understanding," she said. "I guess you could say that isn't what I'm used to."

Lydia Ann furrowed her brow. She remembered what Caroline had said about her marriage being troubled. "I'm sorry you've had such a hard time."

Caroline pulled off her sunglasses and met Lydia Ann's gaze. "Can I tell you something?" she asked.

"Of course," Lydia Ann said.

"The only other person around here who knows this is Michael," Caroline explained. "So please don't tell anyone."

Lydia Ann reached over and patted Caroline's hand. "Don't worry. Whatever you say will stay between us."

Caroline sighed. "A few years ago, when I was a kindergarten teacher, my school won a contest," she began.

Lydia Ann listened intently and soon found herself lost in the story of loss, betrayal, and a woman who never thought she'd be happy again.

Chapter Twenty-Five

....

Relief washed over Caroline. She'd been afraid the truth about her past life would be so shocking to Lydia Ann that she'd not want to remain friends. But Lydia Ann seemed genuinely sympathetic.

"That must've been a horrible experience," Lydia Ann said.

Caroline nodded. "I always thought that when I fell in love, it would last forever. I didn't expect to fall in love with a fraud." She shook her head. "He really did a number on me." She shook her head. "But even so, he didn't deserve what happened to him."

"I know what you mean about thinking love would last forever," Lydia Ann remarked. "Levi was the picture of health when we married. I never expected that in such a short amount of time he would be so sick." She smiled. "But he loved me. Of that I'm certain."

"That must give you such comfort," Caroline said. "I know that in his own way, Lance cared about me. He just cared about himself more." She shook her head. "You know the Bible passage about love being patient and kind? That's what I'm looking for now."

"And do you think you'll find it?"

"I hope so. Because I've seen enough happy couples to know that there's nothing like being in love with your best friend." She smiled. "That's what I want. Not some unrealistic fairy tale, but the kind of relationship where the conversation is easy, the affection is natural, and the Lord is in the center." She grinned. "Does that sound crazy?"

Lydia Ann laughed. "No. It sounds pretty perfect to me."

Michael opened the driver's side door. "You two really missed out," he said. "I got some great pictures."

Simon climbed into the vehicle, grinning. "It was a little steep, though."

Caroline caught the look Simon shot at Lydia Ann. She wondered if there might be sparks between the two of them. She'd have to ask Michael later whether he thought so. It would be nice to see Lydia Ann find someone to love after everything she'd gone through. And Simon seemed to have a good head on his shoulders, not to mention a tender heart. He was the kind of man who had a heart big enough to love Lydia Ann's children as his own too.

An hour later, Michael had gotten several pictures for the magazine. "I'm pretty sure I have enough, but let's make one more stop," he said, pulling the vehicle into a parking spot. "This is the location of Pickett's Charge." He pointed at a row of cannons. "Let's get out and walk for a bit and then we'll head into town to look around."

Caroline had vague memories of her fourth-grade teacher, Mr. Watson, telling the class about Pickett's Charge. If she remembered correctly, he'd even shown them slides of his own visit to Gettysburg. Back then, she'd never imagined she'd ever leave Hiram, much less visit a place that seemed as far away as Pennsylvania. "Sounds good to me."

Lydia Ann and Simon headed toward a monument.

Michael grabbed Caroline's hand. "Come on. Let's check out those cannons over there," he said, pointing toward a long row of Civil War artillery pieces. "That would make a great shot for my magazine article."

He pointed his camera and clicked a few times. "These will

be great shots," he said, grinning. "Come here for a second." He motioned her to him.

She stepped closer to him, and he pulled her close.

"Self-portrait," he said, laughing and turning the camera around to take a picture of the two of them.

She put her face next to his and grinned.

He snapped the picture then checked it. "Not too bad. A little off-center, though." He held up the camera and showed her the screen. "But I think we make a great pair."

She had to admit, they looked pretty happy together.

* * * * *

Michael held up the camera again. "Go stand next to the cannons," he directed.

Her face grew cloudy. "I'd rather not."

"Come on. It won't go in the magazine or anything. It'll just be for me—to prove that you were here." He grinned.

"Fine." She stomped over and put one hand on a cannon. She threw the other hand in the air, striking a Vanna White pose. "Cheese," she said.

He snapped several pictures in succession.

The last frame captured a beautiful Caroline, her head thrown back in laughter with the summer sun glinting off her blond hair. "Perfect," he said, holding the camera screen so she could see it.

"Have you two had enough?" he called to Simon.

His friend turned from where he and Lydia Ann stood, reading a plaque on the side of a monument. "We were just deciding that we're a little hungry."

"It's a good thing, because we're going to two different restaurants." Michael chuckled as he caught their surprised expressions. "First we're going to a little hole-in-the-wall place on the main drag that's supposed to have the best french fries in this part of the country," he said. "It's called Hunt's Café, and their specialty is something they call 'battlefield fries.' Does that sound okay with everyone?"

Caroline nodded. "Sounds yummy to me."

The four of them got back in the SUV, and Michael headed toward town. "Once we're through eating, we can stop at the National Cemetery," he said. "And then we're done unless there's something else one of you wants to see."

Twenty minutes later, they'd ordered two large orders of fries covered in cheese.

"These are so good," Caroline said once the waitress brought them their order. "But why are we going to another restaurant?"

"For the article I'm writing. I want to showcase more than one eatery," Michael explained.

"That makes sense," Simon said. He held up a cheese-smothered fry. "Although these are pretty tasty."

"Just don't get too full. I have a feeling the food at the other place is just as good." Michael pulled out his camera and snapped a couple of pictures of the restaurant's interior. "Okay. I know everyone hates to leave good food behind, but we should get going." He pulled out enough cash to cover their bill and ushered his friends out of the restaurant.

"So where are we headed next?" Caroline asked once they were on the way.

"A place called the Dobbin House Tavern. It's supposed to be really neat to see. It was established in 1776 and is the oldest structure in Gettysburg today." He slowed the car to a stop as they came to a red light. "It served as the first stop on the Underground Railroad north of the Mason-Dixon Line and also was a field hospital during the Battle of Gettysburg."

"Someone's been doing his homework," Caroline said teasingly. "But seriously, that's a lot of history."

Michael nodded as he turned into the parking lot. "No kidding. We're going to eat in the tavern, but there is also a fancier dining option upstairs."

"What a beautiful place," Caroline exclaimed once they were out of the car and standing in front of the large stone building.

Once they were inside and seated, a waitress came right over with menus and a basket of warm bread. "Welcome to Gettysburg," she said, smiling. "I always recommend starting with the King's Onion Soup." She gave them a moment to look over their menus then quickly took their orders.

"Thanks for coming today," Michael said after the waitress left. "It wouldn't have been much fun alone."

"It's been a nice day," Lydia Ann said, smiling shyly.

He'd grown to like her over the few times he'd been around her at the bookstore. And from what he could see, Simon had too. He knew the Amish were private about their dating lives, but he was pretty sure Simon wouldn't mind telling him if there was something going on with Lydia Ann.

"Yes, it has," Caroline agreed. "It's taking my mind off Monday. I still can't believe the store is about to open."

"You're ready," Michael said, glancing over at her. "I predict you'll have more shoppers than you know what to do with."

She laughed. "Let's hope so."

The waitress placed heaping platters on their table.

Michael brushed Caroline's hand with his own as they both went for the ketchup bottle. He locked eyes with her for a split second. His pounding heart surprised him. He'd gone so many years without feeling much of a connection with anyone. But that had changed when he met Caroline.

And he couldn't help but worry that her upcoming trip to Atlanta had the power to alter that somehow.

Chapter Twenty-Six

....

Caroline took a sip of coffee, enjoying the quiet of her empty store. "Lord, please let the opening go well," she prayed. That had been her constant prayer over the past few days. She hadn't realized until last night how much she had invested in the store. Not financially, but emotionally. She needed the store to be a success. Even if it didn't make a profit, she wanted it to be full of happy people. Happy, coffee-drinking, pastry-eating people who enjoyed looking at the books and the knickknacks. Who brought their happy children to play in the children's area and enjoyed coming in for story time.

Yes. She needed it to go well—so that she would feel like she could stand on her own two feet. For once.

The front door opened, and Lydia Ann peeked her head inside. "Hello," she called. Her face broke into a wide grin when she saw Caroline. "I had a feeling you'd be ready to go extra early this morning."

Caroline chuckled. "I didn't sleep much last night." She held up her mug of steaming coffee. "So I finally decided to just get up."

Lydia Ann put her bag in a drawer beneath the counter. "Leah is going to bring Mary and Katie over later. I figured we might have our hands full this morning."

"I keep telling myself that we're ready, but I still feel nervous."

Lydia Ann poured herself a cup of coffee and sat down across from Caroline. "Don't be nervous. I think this is going to be a wonderful-gut day."

Caroline couldn't help smiling. "I hope so." She fell silent. "I'm a little worried—worried that someone might recognize me." She was glad she'd been able to share her identity with Lydia Ann while they were at Gettysburg. Now that Michael and Lydia Ann both knew the truth, Caroline no longer felt like she was deceiving them.

"I don't think you should worry about that," Lydia Ann said. She took a sip of her coffee. "You've been here for weeks and no one has figured it out."

Caroline smiled. "Lydia Ann, I can't thank you enough. You've been such a big help to me here." She motioned around the spotless store. "And you're such a good friend to me." She shook her head. "It's been so long since I had a real friend, I'd almost forgotten what it felt like."

Lydia Ann returned her smile. "I'm glad I could help."

Caroline glanced at her watch. "It's about that time," she said, standing. "Let's just hope we actually have some customers."

An hour later, Caroline leaned against the stool behind the counter. The store was full of smiling, laughing people milling around. They'd sold a few books and a lot of coffee.

Lydia Ann grinned at her from across the room, where she was showing Leah around. The Amish woman was definitely in her element today, the way she'd been talking with customers and ringing up sales.

"If you're through daydreaming, maybe I could get a few pictures," Michael said.

Caroline jerked her head up and stared into Michael's green eyes. "I didn't see you come in."

He chuckled. "When I walked in, you looked like you were a million miles away."

"I was just looking around the store and realizing how blessed I am." Caroline grinned at him. "I have good friends, a store that makes people happy, and the world's best puppy. What more could a girl ask for?" And to think that just a few weeks ago, she'd been afraid that she'd never feel happy again.

"You never know what God has in store for you," Michael said. He held up his camera. "Now, how about some pictures?"

"Just don't put me in them."

He narrowed his eyes. "Come on. At least let me get one of you out front with the new sign."

She bit her lip. "Only if you promise it will never get printed."

"Fair enough."

She followed him outside and posed for a couple of pictures. Her smile was a little broader than normal. And she knew it had something to do with the man on the other side of the lens.

* * * * *

Lydia Ann and Leah looked out the back window of the store and watched Mary and Katie chase Bandit around the yard.

"They sure love that puppy, don't they?" remarked Leah.

Lydia Ann chuckled. "Jah. I'm afraid we might have to get one when we get back to Charm."

Leah turned to her, her brow furrowed. "I've been meaning to talk to you about that." She sighed. "Have you given any thought to staying here?"

"The girls return to school in a few weeks. I guess we could stay until closer to their start date," Lydia Ann said.

Leah shook her head. "That's not what I meant. I'd like for you to consider staying in Lancaster County." She fixed her brown eyes on Lydia Ann. "For good."

Lydia Ann stared at her, openmouthed. *Stay here?* "Oh, I couldn't."

Leah patted her on the arm. "Just think about it. There is a lot here for you. Jeremiah would love it. I would love it. The rest of our family would love it. And you seem to be enjoying your job here." She smiled. "Just something for you to consider."

Stunned, Lydia Ann walked Leah to the door. Staying in Lancaster County hadn't crossed her mind. Once Leah was gone, Lydia Ann busied herself with customers. She gave the coffee area a good cleaning as soon as there was a lull.

"Afternoon," a voice said from behind her. She turned to see Simon, a grin on his face.

"I just left Jeremiah's store and thought I'd stop by here on my way back to the farm. I had to pick up a few things for Mamm and Mrs. Landis. I guess they've decided to throw a big celebration dinner tonight."

She smiled. "That's nice. Caroline will like that."

"It's for you too. I've already invited Jeremiah. He said he'd pass the word along to Leah." He grinned. "I'll be there also."

"It sounds like a nice evening." She couldn't help but feel excited about the prospect of spending more time around Simon. He had proven himself to be such a kind man. He was a good friend and a good son, and his faith in the Lord was strong.

Simon chuckled. "And Katie and Mary can help me feed the calves before dinner. I know they'll love that."

She nodded. "Jah, they will." Lydia Ann gestured toward the overflowing trash can. "Things have gone very well today. We've had a lot of customers."

"I know. I spoke to Caroline out front. Michael just left to go back to his office." He smiled. "I'd better go. I'll see you tonight."

Lydia Ann watched him leave and thought of Leah's request that she consider staying in Lancaster County. She couldn't help but wonder what Simon would think about it.

Chapter Twenty-Seven

....

Michael watched as Caroline got out of her vehicle. "One of our guests of honor has arrived," he said, smiling.

She shook her head. "I can't believe your parents did this. They're so sweet."

He walked over to where she stood. "Well, they're proud of you, that's all. And so am I."

Caroline's face lit up with a smile. "Thanks. That means a lot."

"I think Simon is finishing up in the barn. Lydia Ann's daughters are helping him." He chuckled. "My mom took one look at them and declared that she's officially ready to be a grandmother."

Caroline laughed. "And what did you say?"

"I told her that Phillip is the oldest."

She nodded. "Is he dating anyone?"

"There was a girl he used to be crazy about. But she moved to Philly about a year ago for a better job. They dated all through college, though."

"So Phillip went away to school?"

"Not as far away as I did. But yes. He has a business degree." Before Michael could say more, Lydia Ann came out of the barn, followed by Katie and Mary.

"We'd better get inside before anyone gets any dirtier," Lydia Ann said, laughing.

"Miss Caroline," Katie said, tugging on Caroline's sleeve. "We named the baby cows. Mine is called Spot and Mary's is Blackie." She giggled. "Aren't those wonderful-gut names?"

Caroline smiled down at the child. "They sure are." She turned to Michael. "I'm going to go in and see if your mom needs any help." She followed Lydia Ann and the twins into the farmhouse.

Michael stepped into the barn. "Do you need any help?" he asked.

Simon looked up from where he was washing out the large bottles. "No. I'm just finishing up here." He grimaced. "But can I talk to you about somethin'?"

"Of course." Michael sat down on an overturned bucket.

"I'd like to keep this just between us for now."

"You have my word."

Simon sighed. "I've been having some odd pains. First in my leg and now in my arm." He rubbed his jaw. "At first I tried to ignore them, but I wonder if it's time to get things checked out."

Michael regarded his friend seriously. "It's probably nothing. But maybe it would be best to go see a doctor."

Simon nodded. "I figured that's what you'd say." He grinned. "I guess I'll make an appointment for next week."

"If you want to catch a ride with me, just let me know."

"I appreciate it."

"Anytime," Michael said. He motioned toward the house. "Now let's get inside. I think there's quite a meal waiting for us."

Once everyone was gathered around the table, Dad stood from his spot at the head of the table. "We're so glad you could all join us for dinner tonight," he said. "I understand that Caroline and Lydia Ann have done a wonderful job in fixing up the bookstore and getting it ready for today's grand reopening."

Michael glanced at Caroline, who was seated next to him.

She smiled, her pretty face flushed from the attention.

He leaned over. "I told you my parents were proud," he whispered.

"Lydia Ann says you're originally from Georgia," Jeremiah Bellar said to Caroline.

She nodded. "Yes, sir. I grew up in Hiram. It's a very small town northwest of Atlanta."

Michael knew that the last thing Caroline wanted to do was talk about her past. "Mrs. Zook, this chicken pot pie is amazing."

The older Amish woman smiled modestly. "Danki. The recipe has been in my family for years."

Caroline rewarded him with a grateful grin.

* * * * *

The buzz of conversation around the table was a far cry from the lonely meals Caroline had gotten used to over the past couple of years. She'd forgotten how it felt to belong. As she looked around the table, she felt real connections. These people had come together to celebrate her bookstore. Their kindness was like a warm blanket on a cold day.

"I'm planning to come by the store tomorrow," Mrs. Landis said. "Will there be anything special going on?"

Caroline nodded. "Tomorrow afternoon we'll have children's story time. It's the first one, so I'm a little nervous."

"Michael tells me you worked as a kindergarten teacher," Mrs. Landis said. "I'm sure you'll do well."

Caroline grinned. "I'm really looking forward to it."

Mrs. Zook came out of the kitchen with a large platter. She set a beautiful shoofly pie in front of Caroline. "I hear this is one of your favorites," she said, smiling.

Caroline nodded. "I'd never tasted anything like it before visiting here. I'm going to have to add shoofly pie to my recipe book, that's for sure." The closest thing Caroline could compare it to was pecan pie, but the heavy molasses gave shoofly pie a very unique taste.

"I can't thank you enough for this special dinner," Caroline told Mrs. Landis once everyone had finished eating and they were clearing the table.

Mrs. Landis smiled. "We believe in celebrating when those we care about have good things happen." She took a stack of plates from Caroline's hand. "Now you get out of the kitchen. I suspect Michael is looking for you anyway." She flashed a knowing grin.

Caroline walked outside in time to tell the Zooks and Bellars good-bye. "See you tomorrow," she called to Lydia Ann.

Michael turned to her once they were gone. "Are you up for a walk tonight?" he asked.

She smiled. "Maybe a short one." She did need to walk off the heavy meal. Besides, she wanted to tell Michael about her upcoming travel plans.

"How about we drop your car off at your place first?" he asked.

"Sounds good. Let me just run inside and tell your parents good-bye."

Fifteen minutes later, she parked her car at the bookstore and climbed into Michael's waiting SUV. "What do you have in mind?" she asked.

He grinned. "We've visited a covered bridge from the outside, but we've never walked through one. And it's only about ten minutes away." He reached over and patted her on the leg. "If you need to take a quick nap, I'll understand."

She couldn't hide her laughter. "Stop it. I don't always fall asleep in the car. I promise."

"You could've fooled me."

"Besides," she said seriously, "I needed to tell you something anyway."

He reached out and turned down the radio volume. "What's that?"

"I'm leaving on Thursday for Atlanta," she explained. "I made my reservation before I came over to the farm." She sighed. "I talked to Lydia Ann about it today. She's fine with running the store for a couple of days without me. She told me tonight that Leah would be happy to pitch in if she needed extra help."

"Which airport are you flying out of?" he asked.

"Harrisburg. It's a little closer than Philadelphia—plus I was able to get a flight out after work on Thursday."

"I hope you'll let me take you to the airport," he said.

She furrowed her brow. "I don't want you to have to go to any trouble."

"Don't be silly. It's no trouble." He grinned. "Besides, I like to feel useful."

"Well, I'd love for you to take me. I get back on Sunday night."

"I'll clear my schedule." Michael chuckled. A few minutes later, he pulled into a parking space and turned off the engine. He reached over and took her hand. "I hope everything goes well in Atlanta," he said softly.

She hoped so too. Ever since she'd booked her ticket, she'd tried to keep from worrying about what might be waiting for her back home. "Let's not think about it tonight."

Michael squeezed her hand. "Sounds like a plan to me." He jerked his chin toward the covered bridge in the distance. "You ready to go for a walk?"

She nodded. "Sure."

They climbed out of the vehicle.

"Cool park," Caroline commented, pointing at the park adjacent to the parking lot. "That would be a great place to picnic too."

"Maybe we'll have to do that sometime," Michael said with a grin. He grabbed her hand. "Come on before it gets too dark to see anything." Hand in hand, they walked toward the bridge. The setting sun seemed to make the red bridge almost glow.

"This one doesn't allow vehicle traffic," Michael explained, pointing at the pedestrian-only sign.

They walked into the bridge. The sun's fading rays kept them from walking into total darkness.

"You know, legend has it that James Buchanan met his fiancé at this bridge," Michael said. "But she died before they could be married."

"That's so sad."

Michael stopped walking midway through the bridge. "It is. He never married and went on to become our only bachelor president."

She grinned. "Is that a little historical tidbit you're using in one of your articles?"

He chuckled. "You caught me. You want to know another one?"

"Absolutely." She couldn't hide her smile.

"The covered bridges here are also known as 'kissing bridges' because they've provided seclusion for so many sweethearts over the years." He winked.

"Kissing bridges, huh?"

He pulled her to him. "Yes," he whispered. "Kissing bridges." He tipped her chin upward.

A delicious shiver ran up Caroline's spine. She'd wanted this moment to happen for so long.

Michael bent down and covered her lips with his.

Caroline sank into the kiss and let herself get lost in his warmth. As the kiss intensified, she was struck by the feelings behind it.

He pulled away, an almost drunken smile on his face. "Well, that was something."

"Indeed." She grinned. She could count on one hand the number of men she'd kissed. Lance had kissed with a lot of experience but not a lot of passion. Back in college, Jordan Evans had kissed her every chance he'd found during the months they were together. His kisses had neither experience nor passion. And she didn't even want to think about her first kiss on the night of her junior prom. It had been an awkward mashup of braces and nerves that had turned her off kissing for years.

But kissing Michael felt right. Felt real. Made her weak in the knees and caused her heart to race like she'd just run a sprint.

He pulled her to him and held her tightly. "I hope you know how much I care about you," he whispered. "I've been wanting to do that pretty much since we met." He let her go and locked eyes with her. "But I wanted to wait until I was sure you were ready."

She smiled. "I care about you too. And I'm glad that we built a friendship first. It makes this even better."

"I'll say," he said, taking her hand. "And now you're leaving."

"Just for a long weekend," she said as they strolled slowly back toward the entrance of the bridge. "And then I'll be back."

"I'm already counting the minutes." He stopped and pulled her into another kiss.

Chapter Twenty-Eight

....

Simon sat anxiously in the waiting room, flipping through a magazine. Doctors always made him a little nervous. He glanced at the clock on the wall. Hopefully he'd be done and waiting outside by the time Michael came back.

"Mr. Zook?" the nurse said. "The doctor will see you now."

He rose from his seat and tossed the *National Geographic* onto the table. He followed the woman to a little exam room.

She took his blood pressure and temperature and recorded them on a chart. "Dr. Meadows will be right with you," she said, before shutting the door behind her.

Simon sat stiffly on the exam table and thought briefly of Lydia Ann. He enjoyed spending time with her so much. He'd thought about telling her about his appointment, but she'd dealt with enough burdens of her own. No need to heap more upon her.

The door burst open, and Dr. Meadows entered. "Good afternoon, Simon."

"Dr. Meadows." Simon nodded. The last time he'd seen Dr. Meadows, it had been for a sprained ankle. He had a feeling that whatever ailed him this time might be more difficult to treat.

"What brings you here today?" The doctor sat down on his rolling stool and looked expectantly at Simon.

Simon cleared his throat. "It's probably nothing." He sighed. "But I've been having a couple of unusual symptoms. First, I've been having a weird numbness in my leg. But it isn't like the normal kind you get when your foot falls asleep. It's more painful than that. Sometimes it feels like a knife or something."

Dr. Meadows drew his brows together and made some notes on the chart. "Go on," he encouraged.

"And the other thing is, it doesn't matter how many hours I sleep at night, I'm still tired." He shook his head. "I just can't figure it out. I've tried taking extra vitamins. I've even started trying to get some extra sleep. But nothing seems to help."

Dr. Meadows looked seriously at Simon. "I'd like to refer you to another doctor."

"Another doctor? Why?"

"I'd like for you to see a neurologist. Just to check everything out."

"What could it be, Doctor?"

Dr. Meadows folded his arms over his chest and leaned against the counter. "Your symptoms are consistent with something called multiple sclerosis. But you need to have a few tests run to be sure."

Simon's heart pounded. He'd hoped there would be an easy answer. And it didn't sound like he was going to get one. "If it is… multiple sclerosis… Is that—I mean, can it be fatal?"

Dr. Meadows sighed. "MS is one of those things that affects people in different ways. You could have an episode now and never again. Or they could be years apart. Or it could end up becoming debilitating." He patted Simon on the back. "Don't worry, though. I'll set you up to see the neurologist, and after that, you should know more about what to expect."

Once he had his next appointment scheduled, Simon stood in front of the medical clinic. He tried to keep his breathing even. Getting a ride with Michael had seemed like a great idea, especially since they were going in the same direction. But now he wished he'd come alone…because he knew Michael would ask what the doctor had said.

Multiple sclerosis.

Just the words sounded scary. He paced the length of the sidewalk.

Michael pulled his vehicle next to the sidewalk and rolled down the passenger window. "Sorry I'm late. Hope you haven't been waiting long."

Simon climbed into the vehicle and fastened his seat belt. "I just got finished. Thanks for the ride."

Michael weaved through traffic. "Is everything okay?"

Simon looked out the window, watching the familiar sights pass by. But now he looked at them with new eyes—the eyes of someone who might have a serious illness. It was amazing how just that possibility could change the world. "He's sending me to another doctor, to run some tests." He glanced over at Michael. "So no news yet."

Michael seemed to accept that answer. "Well, just let me know when your next appointment is. I'd be glad to drive you."

Simon nodded. "Thanks." Except that he knew he needed to face the next appointment alone.

* * * * *

"It's so nice to see you again," Jenny said to Michael once they were seated at the restaurant.

He smiled stiffly. Ever since they'd left the office, he'd been uncomfortable. And being in a restaurant where they had spent so much time together in the past made him even more uneasy. "I'm glad you're doing well," he said. He picked up a menu, hoping their food would come quickly once the order was placed.

She reached over and tugged the menu from his hand. "Why do I get the feeling you're not too happy to be here?"

He sighed. "It isn't that. It's just that this seems weird." He motioned between them. "It's been years."

"Yes. Years. And yet here we are, back in our old hometown." She grinned. "Both single."

He bit his lip. This would be a good opportunity to tell her that he was dating someone. But he didn't want to hurt her feelings. Besides, a huge part of the reason they'd broken up in the first place was because of her unreasonable jealousy. So finding out that he was happily dating someone now probably wouldn't sit well with her. "Let's just order; then we can talk." He gave her a half smile. "I have a lot of work to do at the office before I leave." And he had to leave a little early today anyway so he could get Caroline to the airport on time. At the thought of her going back to Atlanta, his stomach tightened. What if she never came back?

Once they'd placed their orders, Jenny leaned toward him. "Do you want to know a secret?"

He looked into her familiar eyes. "What's that?"

"I'm the reason you got the job at the magazine. Mr. Sinclair had someone else he wanted to make an offer to. Someone with more social-media experience." She took a dainty sip of water. "But I told him I could vouch for you. That you were a great writer and photographer." She giggled. "You were pretty good at other stuff too, but I kept that to myself."

Michael raked his fingers through his hair. He wished she hadn't told him that. "Thanks for giving me a good reference. I think I've proven to Mr. Sinclair that I'm a good fit for the position." He decided it would be best to leave her reference to their former relationship alone. No need to dredge up the past.

The waitress set down an appetizer of spinach dip and pita chips in the center of the table. "Your food will be out soon," she said with a smile.

"Remember when all we could afford was appetizers?" Jenny asked. "Back in college, we'd get all dressed up and go out for appetizers and water." She laughed. "Those were the days, huh?"

He scooped some dip onto a chip. "They were. I'm glad they're past us."

At her crestfallen face, he wished he'd chosen his words better. "I don't mean anything by that. Just that those were some tough years." And best forgotten.

She met his eyes. "Michael," she began, reaching for his hand, "there's something you should know."

He didn't like the turn this conversation was taking. "What?"

"I'm still in love with you. I guess I never stopped." She gripped his hand tightly. "I know I messed up all those years ago. I was stupid. I should've gone with you to DC. We'd still be together now."

Michael's eyes widened in shock. "I don't know what to say, Jenny. Our splitting up was mutual. We gave it our best shot." He shook his head, thinking of the way she'd make accusations if he so much as mentioned another woman. Once she even went so far as to show up unannounced at his DC office because she was certain he had a secret girlfriend at work. Of course, he didn't. For some reason, trust had never come easily for Jenny, and being in a long-distance relationship had nearly pushed her over the edge. "But you know we weren't compatible enough to make a real go of it." He pulled his hand away from hers. "Don't you remember how much we fought, especially that last year?"

She leaned closer to him. "Surely you aren't going to tell me that you haven't thought about me over the years."

Michael closed his eyes for a moment, hoping God would give him the right words. "We had a special thing once. But I don't see us getting back together." Even if he didn't have an interest in Caroline, he never would've struck things up with Jenny again. He was a firm believer in learning from the past. And while he and Jenny had had a good relationship their senior year of high school, by the time they'd left college and entered the "real world," the relationship had run its course.

His phone buzzed on the table. Before he could grab it, Jenny picked it up.

"Who's Caroline?" she asked.

He pried the phone from her hand. He'd have to call Caroline back. This was certainly not the right time. "She's the woman I'm seeing."

Jenny's gaze turned icy. "Is it serious?"

He sighed. "I knew this wasn't a good idea."

"No, it's fine. I'm happy for you. In fact, you're right, I'm sure." She forced a smile. "We're better off as friends."

Michael looked at her suspiciously. She'd gone from "I still love you" to "Let's be friends" a little too quickly for his liking.

"I'm serious, Michael." She grinned. "Just ignore what I said earlier. I don't know what I was thinking. I guess seeing you again has just been a shock."

He regarded her for a long moment. "No problem."

"So, tell me about this Caroline. When are you going to bring her by the magazine to meet your coworkers?"

"She stays pretty busy. She just opened a bookstore near Bird-in-Hand."

The waitress set their plates on the table.

"This looks delicious." He smiled at Jenny. "Good choice of restaurant."

"I remembered that it used to be your favorite. We had some great times here."

They ate in silence for a moment.

"How are your parents?" Jenny asked. "And Phillip?"

"All doing well."

"I run into Phillip from time to time." She took a sip of water. "I felt bad for him when Amanda decided to move to Philly. I thought for sure he'd put a ring on her finger before she got the chance." She shook her head. "But he didn't." She chuckled. "Maybe you Landis boys are more alike than you think."

"Phillip's fine. He enjoys his work." But something about her comment struck him. Maybe part of his brother's bitterness did have something to do with Amanda. Michael made a mental note to talk to Phillip about it. Of course, there was a good chance Phillip wouldn't take kindly to his interference. But he could at least try.

After they finished lunch, Michael and Jenny walked back to the office in downtown Lancaster. Despite the early morning rain, it had turned out to be a beautiful day.

"This was fun," Jenny said outside the office building. "We'll have to do it again soon." She turned to go inside and then abruptly turned back to face him. "This Caroline person is a lucky girl." Jenny gave him a smile and then was gone.

Michael pulled his phone out of his pocket to check his voice mail. He was the lucky one. Women like Caroline didn't come along every day. And he was going to try his best not to screw it up.

Chapter Twenty-Nine
....

"Are you okay?" Caroline asked.

Michael had been quiet ever since he'd picked her up from the bookstore.

"Just a long day at work, I guess." He grinned. "I finally pulled all the pictures off my camera, though. I got some great ones at Gettysburg and of your store opening."

She nodded. "I'm sure they're all good ones. But feel free to delete the ones of me."

He chuckled. "Don't worry, I'll put them in my own personal folder. They won't go on Facebook or Twitter or anywhere else."

"They'd better not." She could only imagine. She'd seen the pictures from Gettysburg. With her hair pulled back into a ponytail instead of long and blond, she looked like her old self. If those got out to the public, it would be a disaster.

"You worry too much." Michael reached over and patted her denim-clad leg. "You ready for this trip?"

She sighed and leaned her head against the leather seat. "Not really. I just want to get it over with."

"Are you going to visit her?"

No need to clarify who "her" was. "Yes. I think it's the right thing to do. Not the easiest thing, but the right thing." Caroline had spent the better part of the day pondering what she would say to

Valerie when they came face-to-face. But she still hadn't come up with the right words.

Michael pulled into a space at the airport.

"You could've just dropped me off," she said.

He reached over and took her hand. "I could have. But I'm not going to." He leaned over and gently kissed her mouth. "I'm going to miss you so much," he breathed.

"I'll miss you too." She traced the back of her hand over his jaw. "But I have to go, or I'm going to miss my flight."

Michael grabbed her small suitcase from the backseat. "This is all you're taking?" he asked as they headed toward the building.

She shrugged. "I didn't bring much with me." She grinned. "I only planned to be gone for a week, remember? I'll come back with a much bigger suitcase. And then you won't have to see me wearing the same outfits over and over."

He chuckled. "No complaints from me about your outfits. I happen to think that you always look beautiful."

"Then I guess I shouldn't bring that little sundress I had in mind to try and impress you with, right?" she asked, an innocent grin on her face.

"Well, I mean, of course I'd love to see you in a sundress." He laughed. "But you don't have to worry about impressing me."

Once she was checked in for her flight, she met him at the big board that displayed the departing and arriving planes. "Time to go," she said.

He pulled her to him in a hug.

She loved how it felt to have her head against his chest. So warm. So safe. For a minute she wished he were going with her back to Atlanta.

But she knew the demons that waited on her there were hers and hers alone.

* * * * *

Lydia Ann brought two steaming mugs of coffee over to the brightly painted table where Leah sat. "Here you go," Lydia Ann said.

Leah took the mug and set it down in front of her. "Danki." She smiled. "I hope you didn't mind my coming to help today."

Lydia Ann shook her head. "I'm glad for the help. Things have been pretty busy this week, so I'm sure today will be more of the same." Lydia Ann was surprised at just how much she enjoyed Leah's company. When she'd agreed to come to Lancaster County to visit Dat, it hadn't occurred to her that she might actually develop a relationship with Leah. But now that she was here, she was surprised at how close she and Leah had become. They had a lot in common. Not that she would ever replace Lydia Ann's own mamm or anything, but it was nice to have a motherly figure around.

"Katie and Mary sure seem to have made themselves at home here," Leah observed, pointing to the children's area where the little girls were reading to Bandit.

"Jah. They've taken to Caroline. I think her background as a teacher has helped." Lydia Ann pulled out a letter from Abby. She'd hoped to have time to read it this morning before things got busy.

"Is everything okay with your family back home?" Leah asked, motioning at the letter.

Lydia Ann nodded. "This is from my cousin Abby in Shipshewana. Emma's sister."

"I've heard you and Jeremiah speak of Abby."

"She and her husband, Jacob, are expecting their second child. They already have a little girl, Clara." She met Leah's understanding gaze. "She wrote to tell me that she thinks Emma and Noah are going to pursue adoption. Another couple in their district adopted a few months ago."

Leah set her mug on the table. "And Emma and Noah have no children of their own?"

Lydia Ann shook her head. "They're going on three years of marriage. Emma would never say so, but I can tell it saddens her that they don't have children. And they would be wonderful parents."

"You never know what the good Lord has in store," Leah said with a smile.

Lydia Ann nodded. "That's exactly right. Just a few months ago, I wasn't even considering a visit to Lancaster County."

Leah smiled. "But we're so glad you did." She took a sip of coffee. "Have you given any more thought to making a permanent move?"

Lydia Ann bit her lip. "I haven't made any decisions yet." She smiled at Leah. "But I'm thinking about it."

"I know things are different here than what you're used to. Moving to a new place is always an adjustment. But you fit in so well with everyone here." She smiled. "And Katie and Mary have made friends of their own with the Staltz girls next door."

Lydia Ann returned her smile. She'd been nervous when Leah introduced her to her sons and daughters-in-law, but she'd been pleasantly surprised to find that she got along well with them. She'd been around them a few times at the house and at church and could tell it wouldn't take much effort to become real friends. "Everyone has made me feel so welcome."

The bookstore's front door opened, and two women came inside.

"I'll go see if I can help them," Lydia Ann said. "Will you tell Katie and Mary to take Bandit outside to play?"

Lydia Ann walked toward the women with a smile. She knew she could be happy in Lancaster County. There seemed to be a lot for her in Pennsylvania. But she knew that part of her hesitation had to do with Simon.

There was no denying how much she enjoyed his company. And that alone might be enough reason for her to return to Charm at the end of the summer.

Chapter Thirty

....

Caroline had tossed and turned all night. There had been a time when the immaculate Atlanta mansion was her favorite place in the world. But last night she'd missed the sweet sound of Bandit's breathing. She'd missed the clip-clop sound of the horses and buggies that passed outside her window. And she'd missed knowing that Michael was just a few miles away at his parents' farmhouse.

She stumbled into the giant bathroom and flipped on the light. The deep whirlpool tub beckoned her. If she could move this tub into her place in Lancaster County, life might be perfect.

Caroline filled the tub with hot water and added her favorite bubble bath to the mix. She sank into the hot bubbles and tried to relax. Today would be a test. There was no way around it. She was meeting with Robyn first to go over messages. Then the lawyer was supposed to stop by—and a couple of Lance's former teammates.

And then, after lunch, it would be time to face Valerie.

Caroline ducked her head underneath the water and enjoyed the silence. The only sound in her world now was the whirring of the whirlpool.

Her ringing cell phone brought her back to the surface. That would be Robyn, telling her she'd arrived.

Twenty minutes later, dressed and clutching a cup of coffee,

Caroline padded into the office. Memorabilia from Lance's career lined the walls.

Robyn looked up from her perch in one of the oversized recliners. She set her iPhone down and smiled. "Good to see you. You look great."

Caroline gave her a half smile. "Thanks." She sat down at Lance's massive desk. "Give me a rundown of everything."

Robyn began ticking off messages and household items. She'd found a new landscaping company a couple of weeks ago after the company they'd been using had gone out of business. The garage door had been sticking again, and someone was coming out to look at it on Monday.

Once Robyn was through with her list, Caroline smiled. "Thank you for all your help. How are things with the center?"

Robyn nodded. "Going really well. Are you planning to stop by while you're in town?"

"If at all possible. I'd like to talk to them about the possibility of expanding."

Robyn raised her eyes. "Expanding?"

Caroline nodded. "I've become attached to the Lancaster area. I'd love to look into the possibility of opening one there. The part of the county I'm staying in is pretty rural, but the city of Lancaster might be a good fit for a center. I'd like to at least look into it."

"Are you planning on staying there for a while?"

Caroline sighed. "I'm not sure. I like it there. A lot." She waved her hand around the room. "But I'm not quite ready to sell this place yet." She grinned. "I guess my future is kind of up in the air."

"That's kind of nice, though, isn't it? Kind of exciting?"

Caroline nodded. "I'm enjoying myself right now." She smiled.

"I got a dog. His name is Bandit. And I know I've only been gone for a day, but I miss him."

Robyn laughed. "I'm the same way about my cat. Can't imagine going home and her not being there."

After Robyn left, Caroline wandered around the house. She stopped in front of the large picture of herself that hung in the hallway. It was her bridal portrait. She peered closely at it. Were there still traces of that naive small-town girl in her today? Back then she'd thought true love conquered all, just like in the fairy tales. And now...she wasn't sure if she even believed in true love. Could Michael make her believe again? His kisses had certainly felt as if they were true.

Only time would tell.

* * * * *

"Hey there," Jenny said.

Michael turned from his computer and nodded. "Hi." He turned back to his computer. He was trying to select some Gettysburg pictures to go along with his article. He'd use the rest for the blog and the Facebook page.

Jenny grabbed the guest chair from the corner and slid it next to Michael. "Whatcha workin' on?" she asked.

He motioned toward the computer. "Just choosing some shots."

"Let me see them. I can help you choose." She bumped against his arm. "Just like old times, right?"

These kinds of situations never worked out well. His experience with women told him that. There was no way of declining her help without coming across as a jerk. But he really didn't want to spend any more time with her than he had to. "Yeah. Old times." He glanced at her. "But I know you have your own stuff to work on." He grinned. "Deadlines, you know."

She let out a tinkling laugh. "I'm all caught up. Now we just need to get your piece finished, and this one will be a wrap."

He clicked through a few pictures. It would be tough to narrow it down. He'd taken a ton while they were at the battlefield.

"Michael," Mr. Sinclair said over the intercom, "can you come in here for a second? The organizers of a half marathon are on the phone. I'd like you to be in here while I talk with them about ways we can help them promote their event." He cleared his throat. "I know you're on a deadline, but it will only take a second."

Michael glanced at Jenny. "I'll be right there." He expected her to go back to her cubicle, but she stayed put. He hurried toward Mr. Sinclair's office.

Thankfully, the conversation didn't take long. "I'd be happy to post the information about the event on our Facebook page as well as on our Twitter feed," he said. "And if you'll email me a flyer, I'll get it on the event calendar in the magazine."

That seemed to satisfy Mr. Sinclair and the organizers. "Thanks, Michael." Mr. Sinclair waved him out of the room as he lifted the receiver.

When Michael returned to his desk, Jenny was gone. He breathed a sigh of relief. Now he could finish his task in silence and get out of the office at a decent time. Although with Caroline in Atlanta for the weekend, it wasn't like he had big Friday-night plans waiting for him.

Chapter Thirty-One

Caroline took a breath. This was it.

The guard led her through a door. "Right this way," she said. "Just pick up the phone to talk to her." The guard motioned to a spot next to the wall. "I'll be standing there. Just signal me if you're ready to leave before time is up."

Caroline nodded. She tried to ignore the pounding in her head. Then she spotted Valerie, seated behind a Plexiglas wall.

Valerie smiled tentatively when she saw Caroline approaching. She was already holding onto her phone receiver.

Caroline sat down across from Valerie, trying to calm her nerves. The whole experience seemed unreal, like a bad dream. After a long moment, she reached out and picked up the phone receiver. For a split second, she wished she'd thought to bring a Lysol wipe with her but quickly pushed the thought away.

"Thank you for coming," Valerie said quietly. "I wouldn't have blamed you if you'd ignored my request."

Caroline chewed on her bottom lip. "I decided it was in my best interest to hear you out." She met Valerie's gaze. "I'll be honest— I'm searching for closure at this point."

Valerie shifted in her seat. "I would like to apologize. For everything." Her voice broke. "I had no right to have a relationship with

Lance in the first place. And then to snap like that…" She shook her head. "You have to believe me when I tell you I'm sorry."

Caroline had practiced her speech in the car on the way over, but she couldn't remember how it began. She gripped the phone tightly. "You were my friend." She shook her head. "No. I *thought* you were my friend." She swallowed hard. "I guess I don't get why you were so surprised to find out there were other women besides just you."

Valerie bit her lip. Tears threatened to spill from her dim blue eyes. "Because I was your friend, I knew that your marriage was all but over. So when Lance asked me to have dinner with him at his apartment, I said yes."

Caroline didn't want the details. She didn't want to know how her friend and her husband had developed a secret relationship behind her back. But she needed to learn the truth. That way maybe she could finally be free and move on.

"I thought he loved me. He made it sound like the two of you were about to officially split up." Valerie shook her head. "I was so stupid."

"Yes, Valerie, you were." Caroline kept her voice calm. "I've never understood why a woman would choose to get involved with a married man. Because if he'll cheat on his wife, chances are he'll cheat on you someday too."

A mixture of hurt and anger flashed across Valerie's face, but behind the safety of the Plexiglas, Caroline felt brave. "And furthermore, I don't get how you thought this would end well for you. And then to shoot him like that. All you did that day was ruin lives. Yours included."

Valerie's face flamed. "Don't you think I know that? I've been reminded of it every single day since it happened. I didn't even go over there intending to shoot him. But I was just so mad. So tired of the way he could walk through life and see everything he touched turn to gold. He never cared who he hurt along the way."

"I still don't understand. Couldn't you just walk away? Is it really better this way?" Caroline gestured at the Plexiglas.

"I couldn't walk away. He said he loved me. But then when that love was put to the test, he didn't want anything to do with me." Valerie spit the words out bitterly.

"Put to the test?" Caroline asked.

Valerie put the phone down and slowly rose from her seat.

Caroline couldn't hide her gasp.

Valerie's round, pregnant belly looked almost like a basketball hidden underneath the standard-issue prison garb.

* * * * *

"Pregnant?" Michael asked.

"Yes," Caroline whispered, clutching the phone. "Can you believe it?"

"No. How are you holding up?"

"I don't have the feelings you might expect. I mean, I'm not jealous or whatever. I'm mostly just sad." She paused. "Is it okay for me to talk to you about this? Because if it makes you uncomfortable, I understand."

"Of course it's okay. You can say anything to me; you know that. In fact, I think you need to talk about it. Get it off your chest."

"Okay. But if it weirds you out in any way, just let me know and I'll shut up." She'd already unloaded so much on Michael. What if this were too much for him to take?

"You're funny," he said. "I promise it won't weird me out at all. Now, tell me the whole story."

She paced the length of the master bedroom. "I've always wanted children. I love kids. No." She shook her head. "I adore them. That's one of the reasons I went into early childhood education. I liked the idea of helping to shape children during their formative years." She tugged absently on a lock of hair. "And these past years with the media spotlight, I've always tried to be a good example." It was true. She'd visited schools all over Georgia, talking about everything from staying in school to abstinence. Lance used to laugh at her and tell her that she wasn't Miss America with a platform. But she'd always felt it was her duty.

"So why didn't you have kids while you and Lance were married?"

She picked up on the strain in his voice. It was hard for him to talk about this with her. She knew she shouldn't have brought it up. "Lance didn't want to." He'd refused to have a family with his wife but apparently hadn't had any qualms about having one with Valerie.

"Are you mad? Now, I mean?"

She sighed. "I think I might be thankful—now that I know how things turned out. I still want to be a mother. Someday. But I want my children to have a good dad. The kind who will be involved in their lives." She flopped down on the bed. "And in hindsight, I know Lance wouldn't have been that."

"Sometimes God's plans are better than yours."

Michael's words were simple but their meaning profound. "That's something I've really been learning lately."

"So how did you leave things with Valerie?" he asked.

"Oh. I haven't told you the craziest part." This still blew her mind. "She asked me to raise the child."

Michael was silent.

"Did you hear me? Are you there?" Caroline held the cell phone out to check to see if she still had service bars.

"I'm here," he said in a quiet voice. "Just surprised."

"Join the club." Caroline fluffed her pillow and lay back on it. "She told me that she knew what kind of person I was and that since she wouldn't be able to raise the child herself, I was the perfect person." Just saying it out loud seemed unbelievable.

"What did you tell her?"

Caroline sighed. "I didn't know what to say. She really doesn't have any family. Lance's parents live in Florida at a retirement community. He has a brother, but he's a bachelor who can barely keep himself out of trouble, much less provide a stable home for a child." She paused. "And then there's me. The woman who's always wanted to be a mother."

Chapter Thirty-Two
....

"Simon," Dat said, "I'm so glad you could join us for dinner."

Lydia Ann kept her eyes on her plate. She'd been surprised when Dat came home and announced they were having company. And she was even more surprised to find out that company was Simon.

"Did anyone come help you feed the baby calfs today?" Katie inquired.

Simon grinned at Katie's question. "I had a couple of helpers today, but they weren't as good as you and your sister."

Katie beamed. "Maybe we can come back soon to help you."

"That sounds like a wonderful-gut idea, Katie," Lydia Ann said.

Simon nodded. "How about tomorrow?" he asked. "The bookstore is closed tomorrow, isn't it?"

Lydia Ann nodded. "It is."

"Please, Mamm," Mary said. "Can we visit the farm?"

"I don't see why not," she said, smiling at Simon.

"How were things at the bookstore today?" Dat asked.

Leah smiled. "We had a steady stream of people." She glanced at Lydia Ann. "It was fun to help out."

"Caroline will be back on Monday," Lydia Ann explained. "But you're welcome to stop in anytime."

"Miss Caroline reads books to the kids," Mary piped up. "She's really good at it."

Thursday's story hour had been a hit with everyone in town, but especially Mary and Katie. They'd loved the funny voices Caroline had made as she read the stories. Lydia Ann could see how much her friend loved kids.

"This food is delicious," Simon said. "Thank you for having me."

Leah smiled. "You're welcome."

Once they were finished with the meal, Lydia Ann jumped up to clear the table.

"Let me help." Simon turned to Leah. "We'll take care of this."

Leah looked from Simon to Lydia Ann and smiled. "Danki."

"Thanks for helping me," Lydia Ann said once they were in the kitchen.

"I'm not usually fond of doing the dishes." He grinned. "But for you, I'll make an exception."

She chuckled. "I appreciate that." As they stood side-by-side at the sink, she was struck again by how his nearness unnerved her. It was the same feeling she'd had the day they visited Gettysburg. She'd only experienced that tingly feeling in her stomach one other time, and that was when she'd first gotten to know her husband, Levi.

Once all the dishes were clean, she glanced at Simon. "I hear Michael's big Gettysburg article is coming out in a couple of weeks."

He nodded. "I think that's right." He smiled. "That was such a fun day."

"Jah. I had a wonderful time." She smiled.

Simon returned her smile. "I guess I should be going," he said.

She followed him into the living room so he could tell Dat and Leah good-bye.

He turned to Lydia Ann at the door. "I hope you'll bring the girls to the farm tomorrow."

"We'll be there bright and early." She grinned and stepped outside onto the porch.

Simon motioned toward the porch swing. "Do you want to sit down for a moment?"

She nodded. "Just a moment, though. I need to go put the girls to bed." She chuckled. "If I can get them away from Bandit." She sank next to him carefully, so as not to brush against him.

"Lydia Ann, I just wanted to tell you that I'm glad I met you," he began.

She blushed. "I'm glad I met you too." Even though she'd always been certain that she would never be interested in another man, meeting Simon and spending time with him had made her reconsider the wisdom of her certainty.

"I wonder if you think you'll ever be ready for another relationship, though," he said. "Because I understand if that's not something you're interested in."

She sighed. "I used to think the answer to that would always be no." She glanced over at him. "Watching someone you love battle an illness is one of the worst things you can ever imagine. It's something I would never want to go through again. I felt so helpless. I couldn't do anything for him." She wiped away a lone tear. "And getting used to him not being around took so much time. I honestly thought that that was my one-and-only chance at love."

"Even though you were so young? I mean, you were only twenty-one when Levi passed away, right?"

She nodded. "I was. But you have to remember that by the time I was twenty-one, I'd lost my mother to an accident, become the mother of twins, and dealt with the illness of my husband." She waved her hand toward the front door. "And my dat had remarried and moved."

"So what you're saying is that even though you were only twenty-one, you'd done a lot of living...and dealt with a lot of sorrow."

She smiled. "Exactly. I don't want any more sorrow. Just happiness for me and my girls. And recently I've started to wonder if happiness for us might mean sharing our lives with someone." She met his gaze and felt the flutters in her stomach. She wasn't completely sure she was ready to give her heart to another man. But she knew the idea was at least worth considering.

He stood. "I'm glad we had this talk." He gave her a bright smile. "At least I know that you're not closed off to the idea of love."

She returned his smile. And when she went back inside, she was glad Dat and Leah didn't comment on what she knew was a goofy look on her face.

* * * * *

Simon got to the farm extra early on Saturday. He'd not been able to sleep well the previous night because his mind kept drifting to Lydia Ann. After their conversation, he couldn't help but think of a future with her. But he knew she planned to return to Charm at the end of the summer. The thought hovered over him like a dark cloud.

"Good morning, Simon," Phillip said, entering the barn. "I'm surprised to see you here already."

Simon grinned. "Mornin'. I thought I'd get a jump on things, and Mamm didn't mind coming a little early too, since we're only working until noon today."

Phillip nodded. "Is the milking finished?"

"Almost. I'm just sending the last cows into the room now." He set to work, concentrating on the task at hand. Lydia Ann and the girls would be there any minute.

Twenty minutes later, he was just finishing when he heard the sound of a buggy coming up the driveway. He stepped outside.

"We're here to help you," Katie said, scrambling to the ground.

Mary ran over to her sister and grinned. "I'll bet the baby calfs have missed us."

"Do exactly what Mr. Simon tells you, okay?" Lydia Ann said, coming to stand next to her daughters. She smiled at Simon.

He returned her smile. "Let's take care of the kittens first. Does that sound okay?"

The little girls squealed in response.

"Follow me," he said. He'd saved some milk this morning so they could put it in the big bowl for the kittens. "Can one of you pour this milk into that big bowl?" he asked.

"I will," Katie said. She carefully poured the milk.

Tiny kittens seemed to come out of the walls. They scurried over to the milk bowl to drink.

"Look at their little pink tongues, lapping at the milk," Mary said. "Can I drink my milk that way?" She looked up at her mother.

"It would take you a long time to finish your milk if you drank it that way," Lydia Ann said, laughing.

Katie squealed. "Look at that one. He jumped all the way in!"

A tiny calico kitten, overwhelmed by the excitement of fresh milk, had scrambled right into the bowl.

"One of you can take him out of the bowl if you'd like," Simon said. "But don't let him scratch you. He's very excited."

Mary leaned over and carefully plucked him from the bowl. She set him next to the other kittens at the bowl's edge. "He's all covered in milk, from head to toe," she said.

"He had a milk bath," Katie said, giggling.

Simon glanced over at Lydia Ann. "Dinner last night was fun."

Her cheeks turned pink. "Jah. I'm glad you could come."

He motioned toward the calves. "Are you ready to feed the babies?" he asked.

Mary and Katie worked with him to get the bottles prepared.

"You're both doing a great job," Simon said as they each held a bottle for a calf.

"I thought I heard little ones," Mrs. Landis said, coming out to the barn. "Good morning, Lydia Ann. I see you brought Simon some visitors."

Lydia Ann grinned. "They love helping."

Mrs. Landis smiled. "Do they enjoy helping in the kitchen too? Mrs. Zook and I are about to make pretzels. Would you like to help us?" she asked the twins as they finished feeding the calves.

Katie and Mary nodded excitedly.

Mrs. Landis laughed. "I'll take that as a yes. Girls, come with me. We'll get your hands washed and see if we can find aprons for you." She grinned at Simon. "Why don't you take a break? Show Lydia Ann around the farm."

Simon glanced at Lydia Ann and smiled. "Okay."

"And when you're through, come to the kitchen," Mrs. Landis said, "for some fresh pretzels."

Mrs. Landis, Katie, and Mary headed out of the barn, leaving Simon and Lydia Ann alone.

He looked over at her, suddenly nervous. They hadn't had much time alone together.

Simon's heart had been broken once. He wasn't sure if he was ready to risk it again….

But he couldn't help but think that Lydia Ann was worth it.

Chapter Thirty-Three

Caroline pulled her hair into a ponytail and put an Atlanta Braves baseball cap on her head.

Today had "disaster" written all over it.

When she'd met with Greg on Friday, she'd been flooded with memories. Lance and Greg had been best friends for so many years, even serving as best man in each other's weddings.

And when he'd let her know that the team planned to honor Lance during today's game, she'd promised to be there, thinking she could sit in one of the suites and watch the tribute from afar. But then he'd told her they planned for her to throw out the first pitch. And it had already been advertised to the media, so she really didn't have a choice.

So there would be no viewing from afar. Instead, she'd be right in the center of the action. Right where she didn't want to be.

It was almost like old times. The old "DeMarco" jersey that Lance had custom-made for her still fit like a glove. She paired it with khaki shorts and running shoes.

Her running shoes, which hadn't seen much running lately. Running used to be something she did just for her. Lance had always tried to get her to take yoga or Pilates with the other players' wives, but she'd been a runner since high school. Maybe it was time to start again.

She looked once more in the mirror. An extra drop of Visine had cleared her bloodshot eyes. After she'd hung up with Michael last night, the tears had started. The whole experience of meeting with Valerie, learning about the pregnancy, and dealing with Lance's estate had been overwhelming. Even another hot bath hadn't helped.

She'd finally found comfort in her tattered Bible. It was the one she'd gotten at VBS one summer when she'd successfully learned all the required memory verses. She'd used it through high school, and it still contained notes and pictures scribbled on attendance cards. She'd forgotten about it after it had been put on a shelf along with a couple of textbooks from college. But last night she'd pulled it off the shelf and opened it.

Lydia Ann had said there was nothing so big that the Lord couldn't handle it. That was a good thing, because the problems Caroline faced were certainly enormous.

And it had helped. She'd read first one verse, then another. The words calmed her. Gave her hope. Allowed her to finally sleep after praying that the Lord would take away her pain, even if just for a night.

She'd dreamed of Mama. The two of them had been drinking coffee in the bookstore. She couldn't remember what they'd talked about, but she woke up happy. Warm. Content.

And now, with that comforting memory fresh, she would face the baseball team and their wives. She would throw out that pitch for Lance. Lance, who'd been a terrible husband but wasn't a horrible man. He'd cared deeply for his friends. Given back to the community. And made a mistake that had eventually cost him his life.

She would honor him today. She hadn't been able to do so at his funeral. The hurt on that day had been too new, too fresh. But now that she had some distance, she could accept that his legacy was more than just another cheating athlete. She would throw out the pitch, from the same mound he'd thrown from so many times, and she would only remember the good times. The charity they'd established together that would go on helping underprivileged kids for many years to come would be his legacy.

That and an unborn child she hadn't decided whether she could raise.

Thirty minutes later, she arrived at the stadium. Although she hated to have a driver, the organization had sent a car for her.

When she walked out on the field, the crowd cheered. The team stood at attention. The announcer called her name.

Caroline walked slowly to the mound, clutching the ball in her hand. *This is for you, Lance. This is good-bye.* She hurled the ball with all her might and watched it land neatly in the catcher's mitt.

Good-bye.

* * * * *

Lydia Ann couldn't help but wonder if Mrs. Landis had somehow sensed that she and Simon might like to spend some time together. Was it obvious to everyone that they shared a special bond? Had others noticed that she snuck glances at him when he wasn't looking?

If so, what must they all think of her?

"Would you like a tour?" he asked, grinning. His blue eyes seemed even bluer today.

She returned his smile. "Jah. I'd like that." The truth was, she'd like anything that meant she could spend extra time with him. She'd even clean out the cow stalls...or at least stand back and watch while he did it. Somehow, confessing to him last night that she would be open to the possibility of finding love again made her more aware of his presence.

He motioned toward the barn door. "If you don't mind walking a bit, I'll take you out and show you where the puppies are."

Lydia Ann nodded. "I enjoy walking." She chuckled. "Mary and Katie will be upset if they find out I saw the puppies without them."

He laughed. "Maybe they can come out later."

They walked along in silence for a moment.

"I can't believe how the summer is speeding past," Simon said finally.

She looked over at him. "I know. Do you think time seems to go by faster as you get older?"

He chuckled. "I do. When I was a boy and looked forward to my birthday, it seemed to take forever to come. But now, I blink and a whole month has passed."

"I think I see it even more because of Katie and Mary. They are truly growing up before my eyes."

"You're a wonderful mother."

She blushed. "Motherhood has been a blessing from God. I love them so."

"Things are sure going to be quiet after you've gone back to Ohio," he said, stopping at an old rickety building and turning toward her.

She looked into his eyes. "There's something I've been meaning to tell you."

"What's that?" He leaned against the building.

"Leah and I have been talking…about me staying in Lancaster County with the girls." She smiled. "For good."

His blue eyes widened in surprise. "Really? You are considering that?"

"Jah. I've missed Dat a lot more than I realized. And we feel at home here." She shrugged her shoulders. "I would miss Charm, of course."

Simon kicked at a loose stone on the ground. "Well, you know I would like it very much if you lived here." He gave her a shy grin. "I like the thought of spending more time with you."

She gave him a wide smile. "I like that thought too."

Lydia Ann hadn't expected this. Even in her wildest dreams, she'd never thought she'd meet another man who made her so happy.

Life was full of surprises.

Chapter Thirty-Four

. . . .

"It's kind of nice, isn't it?" Mom asked. "Our whole family together for church and lunch."

"Just like when you were boys," Dad said, looking over his shoulder at Michael.

Michael and Phillip sat in the backseat of the old family sedan. Mom had driven the same car for years. Back when Michael was in the seventh grade, he used to get her to drop him off around the corner from the movie theater so his friends wouldn't see.

"Michael, I hear you work with Jenny," Mom said. "How is she doing?"

He felt Phillip's eyes on him. "She's doing well. Looks the same as she did when we were in college." She acted the same too, but he didn't want to get into that with his family.

"Please give her my regards," Mom said. She turned toward the backseat. "Maybe you should set her up with Phillip." She grinned.

Phillip grunted. "That won't be necessary, but thanks."

After Mom turned back around, Michael glanced at his brother. There was no way he'd ever set Jenny up with Phillip. And Phillip knew it. They might not be as close as some brothers, but some things would just be too weird. There was definitely a man code. Most guys would never set up a serious ex-girlfriend with a brother or good friend.

Phillip leaned over. "Mom doesn't know it, but I'm actually seeing someone."

Michael eyed his brother. "Is Amanda back?"

"No. This is someone you don't know," he said in a low voice. "I haven't brought her around to meet Mom and Dad. Yet."

"Yet. So does that mean this one warrants a family meeting?" Even though they'd had their differences, Michael wanted to see his brother happy.

Phillip shrugged. "More than anyone in a while. Since Amanda."

"Do I get to know her name?" Michael grinned.

"Hannah. She's a nurse." Phillip's normally solemn face twisted into a smile.

Michael knew it was huge for Phillip to open up to him about something personal. There had been a time, back in their younger years, when the two of them had shared everything. But once they went to different colleges and he moved away, their relationship was never the same.

"I'm happy for you, man. I'd love to meet her sometime."

Phillip eyed him warily then nodded. "I'd like that. Maybe we can all hang out sometime. You and Caroline are seeing each other, right?"

"Yeah. She's out of town right now, but I'd love for the four of us to do something sometime."

Phillip nodded in agreement.

Dad pulled into the driveway.

"Can you let me off?" Phillip asked. "I'd like to take a nap this afternoon."

"Sure," Dad said, slowing to a stop.

Mom turned around. "Will you join us for supper tonight, dear?" she asked.

"No thanks," Phillip said. "I'll see you at breakfast, though." He climbed out of the car and headed into his house.

Michael leaned his head against the seat. He'd kind of hoped Phillip would invite him over to watch baseball or just hang out. But at least they'd finally had some sort of conversation that hadn't ended with anyone storming off in anger. That felt like progress. And the fact that Phillip was willing to go on a double date spoke volumes.

Maybe there was hope for them yet.

* * * * *

Lydia Ann sat on the porch, gazing out into the yard. Her time in Lancaster County was coming to a close. It wasn't that long ago that she'd been grumbling to Emma about how miserable the summer was going to be. And now she was actually considering turning her short visit into a permanent stay.

As much as she tried to tell herself that her growing friendship with Simon shouldn't have any bearing on her decision, she knew better. Yesterday had been so much fun. Simon always made her feel so happy inside. And they had a lot to say to one another.

Just like with Levi.

She and Levi had known each other since they were just a little older than Mary and Katie. But it wasn't until they were teens that they'd begun courting. She still remembered the night he had asked her to go for a buggy ride with him after a singing.

From that day on, she'd known she would end up married to him. They could talk and laugh about everything. It seemed like they never ran out of things to say.

And Levi had been more than just her husband. He'd been her best friend. They'd shared the good and the bad.

After getting to know Simon, she got the same feeling. He was the kind of person she would choose to be friends with. His character was strong. And when he spoke of his faith in the Lord, it was obvious that it was a true faith.

Katie and Mary liked him too. They'd even made him a special pretzel yesterday. He might not have realized it, but she knew what high praise that was.

"You enjoying some quiet time?" Leah asked, stepping out of the house.

Lydia Ann smiled. "Jah. Just thinking."

"Mind if I sit with you?" Leah motioned toward the empty spot on the porch swing.

"Go ahead."

Leah perched on the swing. "Katie tells me the three of you had a lot of fun yesterday at the farm."

Lydia Ann nodded. "They love the animals. And Mrs. Zook and Mrs. Landis let them come inside and learn to twist pretzels."

"Did you enjoy your visit with Simon?"

Lydia Ann felt her face grow hot. "Jah. He's great with the girls. He's very patient with them as they learn to care for the animals."

Leah smiled. "I've known Simon since he was just a little boy. He went to school with my children."

"That's what he told me."

Leah sighed. "Did he tell you about Sarah?" she asked.

Lydia Ann shook her head. "No. I don't guess I've heard about her." Her stomach tightened.

"As far as I know, she's the only girl Simon ever courted. But she left town." She glanced at Lydia Ann. "I think it broke his heart to let her go."

Lydia Ann mulled over this news. She hated to hear that Simon had ever gone through heartbreak. But it did explain a little bit more about him. She'd noticed that he always seemed a little hesitant with her. He must be worried that she might leave, just like Sarah had. "Thank you for telling me about his past," Lydia Ann said. "Knowing about the things someone has dealt with can help you understand them better."

Leah smiled. "You're right. Sometimes you have to deal with the past in order to enjoy the present."

Lydia Ann couldn't help but think of Caroline. She was in Atlanta, dealing with her past right now. *Lord, please watch over Caroline. Give her the strength to deal with whatever she is facing.*

Chapter Thirty-Five
....

Michael looked at his watch. *She should be here by now.* He rose from his spot on the airport bench to look at the arrival board. He found her flight. Delayed. *Figures.*

Every time he'd ever flown through Atlanta, he'd managed to be delayed. Why should it be any different for Caroline?

His phone buzzed. He glanced down, and though he didn't recognize the number that flashed on the screen, he answered it.

"Hey there," Jenny said. "Thought I'd check to see if you might want to grab a bite to eat tonight."

"Thanks, but I can't. I'm actually in Harrisburg. I had to pick up someone from the airport." No need to tell her who. Friday at work, Jenny had managed to bring up Caroline twice. He got the distinct feeling she wasn't going to let it go until she actually met her. And he would rather that meeting *not* take place.

"Oh." The disappointment came through the phone. "That's fine. I was just thinking of getting some of our old classmates together."

"Maybe some other time."

His platitude seemed to satisfy her. He clicked the phone off and paced, lost in thought.

After their last conversation, he'd gotten the impression that Caroline was seriously considering raising Lance and Valerie's child. He couldn't quite wrap his head around that concept. On the one hand, he could see how unselfish it would be, providing a loving, stable home for the other innocent victim in the whole mess. But at the same time, how would that impact her life—and his? He raked his fingers through his hair. It was too much for him.

"Michael," a voice called.

He looked up and grinned. "You are a sight for sore eyes." He lifted her into an embrace and twirled her around.

She giggled. "A girl needs to twirl every now and then," she said when he put her back on her feet. "I've missed you."

He pulled her to him. "And I've missed you." He grabbed her hand. "Now let's get out of here."

Caroline hung back. "I have a couple of checked bags." She winked. "My sundress. Remember?" She clung tightly to his hand as they walked to baggage claim.

He laughed. "Of course. Now we'll just have to plan a night out for you to wear it."

Her face lit up. "Sounds perfect." She grinned. "But you know what I want to do tonight?"

"What's that?"

She grinned. "When we get to Lancaster, let's drive through Five Guys and get burgers…then swing by and pick up Bandit…then go to my place and eat and catch up."

"That sounds like a good plan to me, but I have a little surprise for you."

She furrowed her brow. "What?" she asked as they stood side by side at baggage claim.

He shook his head. "Uh-uh. Patience, please."

She made a face but didn't press. "There they are," she said, pointing to two pale-blue, paisley-printed suitcases.

"You must have brought a whole closet full of sundresses," he grumbled, lifting one suitcase and then the other to the ground.

She wrinkled her nose. "I'd just as soon not have to go back to Atlanta for a while." She shrugged. "So I brought a few things I might need." She took the handle of one of the suitcases. "Now let's go. I can't wait to see my surprise."

He loved the way her brown eyes lit up when she was excited about something. "Lead the way," he said.

* * * * *

Caroline was happy to be back. Being with Michael almost made her forget about Valerie's gigantic, pregnant belly.

Almost.

She still couldn't believe it. She'd wanted to ask Valerie more questions, but her time had been up. Caroline couldn't help but wonder if Lance had planned to tell her about the baby. And she also wanted to know what his reaction had been to learning that Valerie was pregnant. He'd been so adamant that he wasn't ready to be a father. Had that changed when he learned he was actually going to be one? So many questions and no real answers.

Caroline had no idea how to make a decision about whether to raise the child. On the one hand, it seemed crazy to consider it. But on the other hand, it seemed wrong not to.

Michael pointed at a row of vehicles. "I'm over there," he said.

She followed him to his SUV. "Is the car running?" she asked.

"I wanted it to be cool." He grinned.

Caroline laughed. "Silly, I'm not going to melt."

He lifted the back end of the SUV and there sat Bandit.

"Oh my goodness," Caroline exclaimed, scooping the puppy into her arms. "He's grown so much."

Michael laughed. "You've only been gone for three days."

She pulled the wriggling dog to her and nuzzled his soft fur.

Bandit rewarded her by licking her on the nose.

She looked at Michael. "Thank you so much. This makes me so happy." She laughed. "I've missed him so much."

"The million-dollar question is, did you miss me or Bandit more?" he said as they started toward the airport exit.

Caroline giggled. "That isn't fair. I missed you in different ways. I missed your conversations and his puppy breath." She glanced over at him. "How's that for an answer?"

"Sounds like a cop-out to me." He reached over and patted her leg. "But I'll take it."

"Anything exciting happen at work on Friday?"

Michael shook his head. "Not really. I'm helping to promote a half marathon that's coming up in the fall." He shrugged. "That's about the only new thing going on."

Caroline sat up a little straighter. "You know, I might need to get some information about that. I'm thinking of taking up running again."

"Have you done a half marathon before?"

She shook her head. "The longest race I've ever done was a 10K." She grinned. "But the upside is that if I start training for a half marathon, I can eat all the shoofly pie I want to."

He laughed. "I guess that's one way of looking at it." He glanced in his rearview mirror and switched lanes. "I'm not much of a runner, but I'll cheer for you at the end."

Caroline grinned. "That sounds perfect. You and Bandit can be at the finish line." She scratched the puppy behind the ears. After the excitement of their reunion, he'd fallen asleep in her lap.

"Great," Michael grumbled. "You'll probably kiss him first."

She laughed. "Please tell me you aren't jealous of this tiny little puppy."

He glanced over at her. "I can think of ways for you to make it up to me once we get back to your house."

At the thought of kissing him, she blushed. "You can? Well, I'll do my best." She grinned.

Michael flipped on his blinker. "Five Guys still sound good to you?"

"Yum," she said. "I'm totally starved. By the time I got to my gate, it was too late to grab anything to eat. And then, of course, we were delayed. We sat on the plane forever before we took off."

"Flying is a pain," he said, pulling into the drive-thru line.

She nodded. "Especially flying alone." She grinned. "Maybe next time I have to fly somewhere, I can take someone with me."

"Like me?" he asked.

She shrugged. "Or Bandit. You know, most flights let one dog fly in the cabin as long as they're crated."

He groaned. "You're impossible."

She leaned over and kissed him on the cheek. "I'm kidding. Of course I'm talking about you." She grinned. "I'd never subject Bandit to the stress of flying."

Michael burst out laughing. "I've missed you. A lot." His face grew serious.

She watched the emotions play across his face. "I missed you too. It was a hard trip."

He reached over and took her hand. "I'm sure facing the team and the fans was difficult. I'm proud of you for keeping your head high."

She sighed. "The easy thing to do would've been to say no. I could've said I wasn't ready." She shook her head. "But, honestly, I think the whole scene helped me to get some closure."

"You think so?"

"I think I've finally accepted everything. Lance was a big part of my life. Things didn't turn out the way I expected them to, but he and I still did a lot of good together. The foundation that we established has helped a lot of kids. So I'm trying to just focus on the good things." She glanced over at him. "When I threw that ball out today, I sort of felt like it was my way of really letting go of the past. I'm done."

"Except for the trial. And the baby."

She nodded. "Yes. And those will be tough to deal with. But I feel a peace now that I didn't feel before."

"I'm glad."

Caroline grinned. "Now let's order burgers and not talk about anything serious for the rest of the night."

He laughed. "You've got a deal."

Chapter Thirty-Six

....

Lydia Ann stuck her head through the doorway of the bookstore. "Caroline?" she called.

"I'm in here," Caroline said from the coffeepot.

Lydia Ann grinned. "I want to hear about your trip." She walked over and poured herself a cup of coffee.

"It went okay." Caroline motioned to a chair. "Sit down and I'll tell you."

Lydia Ann sat across from her. "Was it strange to be back?"

"Kind of. I mean, there are things I miss. Mostly material things, though." Caroline shook her head. "I guess that sounds stupid. But some of the stuff in my house, like old family pictures and books that I love and certain things that I've had forever…I miss that. It was nice to be around it again."

"That doesn't seem strange. There is a reason the saying says 'comforts of home.' I think that the things we surround ourselves with—the familiar things—have a way of bringing us comfort." Lydia Ann thought of her own kitchen in Charm. Her mamm's mixing bowl sat in the cabinet. Every time Lydia Ann used it, she thought back to when she was a girl and helping Mamm cook. So she could understand where Caroline was coming from.

"But I missed you and the girls. And Bandit." Caroline smiled. "And Michael." She shrugged. "Overall, I'm glad I went back. I had

LOVE FINDS YOU IN LANCASTER COUNTY, PENNSYLVANIA

to get some things settled with Lance's estate. And the baseball team honored Lance at Saturday's game, so I had to be there for that." She met Lydia Ann's gaze. "And I went to see Valerie."

When Caroline had first mentioned going to see the woman who'd shot Lance, Lydia Ann had been surprised. "How did that go?"

A shadow crossed Caroline's face. "I was angrier than I thought I'd be. I mean, for all his faults, Lance certainly didn't deserve what he got." She managed a smile. "But I thought about what you said—about it being difficult to be angry at the people you pray for. I think that helped me." She bit her lip. "But there was something I didn't expect."

Lydia Ann was glad to hear that she'd helped in some way. "What's that?"

"Valerie is pregnant."

A gasp escaped Lydia Ann's throat.

"My thoughts exactly."

Caroline had shared how much she'd always hoped to be a mother. Learning of the pregnancy must have been very difficult. "How are you holding up?"

"It was a huge shock. Made even bigger when she asked me to raise the child as my own." Caroline's brown eyes filled with tears. "And now I'm left with an impossible decision."

Lydia Ann didn't even try to hide her surprise. She couldn't imagine how Caroline must feel. "So you're considering it?"

Caroline nodded. "There's no one else. If we go too far down the family trees, I'm afraid we'll find people who say yes just because the child will be entitled to part of Lance's money." She sighed. "That was one thing Valerie and I agreed on. The baby deserves to be raised in a home where it's loved. Not in a home where it's seen as an easy meal ticket."

"You're in a difficult position."

"On the one hand, I've wanted to be a mother for so long. I keep wondering if this is my chance. But on the other, I don't know if raising Valerie and Lance's child is something I can handle."

Lydia Ann shook her head. "I will be praying that the outcome is the best for everyone involved."

"Thank you."

No matter the situation, prayer was always the answer.

* * * * *

Caroline took another sip of her coffee. "Enough about that. How was everything here while I was gone?"

Lydia Ann smiled. "Fine. Leah came and helped me on Friday. There wasn't any trouble."

"Thank you so much for handling things for me. And I can't thank you enough for letting Katie and Mary keep Bandit."

Lydia Ann laughed. "They had so much fun. When I went to their room to wake them on Friday morning, he was right in the middle of them. All three, sound asleep." She shook her head. "Katie told me they'd planned on letting him sleep in his little crate. But he cried, so they let him out."

Caroline grinned. "He's a little stinker. I'm glad they had fun, though." She glanced around. "Where are they, anyway?"

"Leah is going to bring them by a little later." She smiled. "They've really taken to her."

"And how is Simon?"

Lydia Ann's face grew pink with happiness. "He's fine. Dat invited him to dinner on Friday, and Saturday I took the girls to the farm to help him."

Caroline raised an eyebrow. "How was that?"

"It was a nice day. The girls enjoyed themselves." She grinned. "And so did I." She cleared her throat. "I told Simon that I'm considering staying in Lancaster County for good."

"You are?" Caroline asked. "That's wonderful." She smiled. "And I expect he was pleased to hear that news."

Lydia Ann nodded. "I think he was." She turned questioning eyes toward Caroline. "How about you? Are you moving back to Atlanta once the trial is over?"

Caroline had tossed and turned all last night thinking about it. "I don't know. I guess it makes sense for me to move back there. I have a house, and I've been really active in the foundation that Lance and I started." She sighed. "But at the same time, I really like it here." Even when she took Michael out of the equation, she was happy in Lancaster County. The peace she'd found here might be worth the trouble of relocating for good.

"The good thing is that neither of us have to decide today." Lydia Ann smiled.

Caroline rose from the table. "Right." She glanced at the wall clock. "Especially now, when we're just opening for business."

As if on cue, the bookstore door opened and a couple walked in.

Caroline pasted on a smile and went to greet them. It was good to be back.

Chapter Thirty-Seven

....

"You given any thought to that reunion I mentioned last week?" Jenny asked from the cubicle entrance.

Michael looked up from the blog post he was working on. "Huh?" It took him a minute to register what she meant. "Oh. Right." He leaned back in his chair. "Just let me know if you guys are going to get together. And where." He grinned at her. "I'll try to make it if I can."

She narrowed her eyes. "I kind of need more input from you than that. I mean, I was doing it for you."

His eyes widened. "Don't go to any trouble or anything. I thought maybe it was something you'd been planning for awhile." The last thing he wanted was to be indebted to Jenny for anything.

Jenny sank into the guest chair. "I don't mind. I think it would be fun for you to see the old gang." She smiled. "You could bring your new girlfriend."

She'd been so persistent about wanting to meet Caroline. It seemed like the more he declined, the more she pushed for an introduction.

He shook his head. "I don't think so. She's pretty busy these days."

"Come on. I'm sure she'd love to hear stories about you from back then." Jenny smiled broadly. "And I have a ton of stories to tell."

Michael grimaced at the thought of Jenny telling Caroline about him. He didn't care to reminisce about high school. He remembered it as a terribly awkward time when he didn't really know who he was. His late twenties might not be perfection, but he knew he wouldn't want to be seventeen again. "We'll see." He turned back to his computer, hoping his answer had placated her enough to get her to leave.

"Are you ashamed of the fact that you dated me or something?" Jenny asked.

He looked up at her in surprise. "Of course not. But that was a long time ago. Years ago, in fact." Michael shrugged. "We've both moved on. Caroline knows that you and I work together, though."

"I hope it doesn't bother her that you work with an old girlfriend." Jenny let out a tinkling laugh. "So many affairs start in the workplace these days. I know I wouldn't want the guy I was dating working with an ex."

Michael sighed. "Caroline trusts me. So it's fine."

Jenny stood. "That's good." She paused before she left the cubicle. "I still might try and get everyone together. I'll let you know."

Michael watched her walk off and tried to shake the uneasy feeling he was getting. Jenny wouldn't give up. He was certain he wasn't sending mixed signals to her. But she didn't seem to be getting the hint.

He sighed and turned his attention back to his work.

* * * * *

Caroline locked the front door after the last customer left the bookstore. "Man. It's been some kind of week." She sank onto the love seat.

"Sales were up this week," Lydia Ann said as she removed the money from the cash register. "The grand-opening publicity that Michael did must have worked."

Caroline nodded. "It sure did." She'd been pleased with the work he'd done. "And I think the children's story time is really catching on."

Lydia Ann counted the cash into stacks. "It seems that way. Even though children don't actually spend money, their parents do." She placed the stacks carefully in the bank deposit bag. "How would you feel about offering hot tea as well as coffee? I had a couple of customers ask about that today."

"I think it sounds like a great idea. In fact, let's see if we can purchase it from your dad's store. I know he and Leah carry a big selection." Caroline emptied the last bit of coffee from the still-warm pot.

"I'll talk to him about it tonight." Lydia Ann picked up some stray books and placed them back where they belonged. "Do you have big weekend plans?"

Caroline couldn't hide her excitement. "Actually, yes. Michael and I are getting dressed up and going out tonight." She'd been looking forward to this night all week. It had been a long time since she'd gotten all fixed up for a fun night out.

"Where are you going?" Lydia Ann glanced over her shoulder as she put a book on the top shelf.

"The Revere Tavern. Michael says it's a historic place and very romantic." It had been his idea, which made it even better. The fact that he cared enough about her to plan a special night out meant a lot.

Lydia Ann grinned. "That sounds like a wonderful night."

Caroline nodded. "I think so. I'm usually pretty low-key, but every now and then it's nice to do something special." She straightened the row of coffee mugs. "After dinner, we're going to downtown Lancaster to an art gallery. It should be fun."

"When you're with the right person, anything can be fun." Lydia Ann laughed.

Caroline nodded. "I guess you're right about that."

Lydia Ann dusted off her hands. "I'd better go see if the girls are ready. We're going to walk over to Dat's store and ride home with him." She pushed open the back door.

"Wait a minute," Caroline called. "How about you? Are you doing anything special this weekend?"

Lydia Ann turned back and smiled. "Tomorrow I'm supposed to take Mary and Katie back to the farm. After they've fed the calves and played with the puppies, Simon and I are going to take them to see the train."

Caroline grinned. The steam engine that ran through Strasburg was very popular, especially with children. "Are you going to the train museum?"

Lydia Ann nodded. "Jah. I think we're going to ride the train too." She grinned. "It won't be as fancy as your night, but it will be fun."

"What was it you said? Anything is fun with the right person?" Caroline chuckled.

Lydia Ann blushed. "That's right. I hope you have a wonderful evening." She stuck her head out the back door and called to Mary and Katie. "Girls, it's time to go. Come on inside."

Caroline collected Bandit from the twins and carried him upstairs with her. She loved it when she had plenty of time to get ready for a night out. Especially on a Friday. There was something special about a Friday afternoon when the workweek was over and fun Friday night plans loomed. And tomorrow, she could sleep in.

Life was good.

Chapter Thirty-Eight

....

Michael walked into the kitchen at the farmhouse.

Phillip let out a wolf whistle. "Somebody has a hot date tonight."

Michael scowled at his brother. "I'm probably not the only one," he said, adjusting his tie.

"I think he looks nice," Mom said, grinning. "I should take a picture."

Phillip snickered.

"It's not prom or anything," Michael said, laughing. "I think we can do without turning this into a Kodak moment."

"Where are you headed?" Mom asked.

Michael explained that Caroline wanted to get dressed up for a night out, so he was taking her to a nice dinner and an art gallery.

"Bring her by here before you go," Mom pleaded. "Then I can get a nice picture."

Phillip jerked his head toward Mom. "Don't argue with her, Michael. Or she might decide to just show up at the restaurant and take the pictures there."

The brothers laughed together.

"I don't see why that incident was so funny to you two," Mom said huffily. "Just because I was out of film on your prom night didn't mean I wasn't going to get pictures."

Michael and Phillip exchanged glances. The night Mom had

tracked them and their dates down at Red Lobster and had them pose for pictures was legendary in the family.

"The best part is that all our pictures have those poor lobsters in the background. Swimming around the tank with their little claws tied together." Phillip started laughing again.

Mom couldn't hide her smile. "Okay. Maybe it was a little over the top to come to the restaurant." She shook her head. "Someday you will both understand. I just hated for that moment to go undocumented." She scowled. "And I told your dad to buy film that week, but he forgot."

"Don't tell me you're rehashing the great prom-picture debacle," Dad said, coming into the kitchen. "I never thought I was going to hear the end of it." He winked. "But I never forgot film again."

"That's because now that we have a digital camera, we don't need film anymore." Mom chuckled. She turned to Michael. "But will you bring Caroline by before dinner?" she pleaded. "Please?"

Michael rolled his eyes. "Of course." He kissed Mom on the cheek.

He really had to get his own place soon.

* * * * *

Caroline brushed on an extra coat of mascara. It had been so long since she'd worn full makeup, she almost didn't recognize herself.

She grabbed a mirror so she could check out the back of her hair. It hung in loose curls down her back.

She bent down to kiss Bandit. "It's crate time for you, buddy." She scooped him up and put him inside the crate.

He looked at her with sad eyes.

"Extra treats and kisses when I get home, I promise." She reached her hand through the door and gave him one last pat.

She looked in the full-length mirror hanging on the back of her closet door. The turquoise sundress fit tightly at the waist, then flared. The hem landed just below her knees. A little higher than she'd worn in awhile, but surely it was like riding a bike. She paired it with strappy silver sandals and grabbed her silver clutch, the one she'd bought two years ago for the ESPY Awards and hadn't carried since. Perfect.

The doorbell rang, and she headed downstairs. She flung the door open to see Michael clutching a bouquet of gerbera daisies in a variety of colors.

His smiled grew broader as he checked her out from head to toe. "Wow. You are absolutely beautiful."

She beamed. "Thanks." She took the flowers from him and motioned him inside. "These are so pretty. My favorite, you know."

He grinned. "I know."

She set the bouquet on the counter and turned to face him. "You look pretty hot yourself," she said laughing. "Or is it unladylike for me to describe you as 'hot'?"

Michael chuckled. "It works for me." He pulled her to him and planted a kiss on her waiting lips. "But if I'm hot, you're scorching." He raised an eyebrow. "I'm just sayin'."

She looped her arm through his. "Let's go."

"We have to make a stop before we go to the restaurant, though. Mom wants to take a picture," he said sheepishly.

She grinned. "Awesome. That's so sweet."

He furrowed his brow. "I was afraid you'd be annoyed."

She shook her head. "Nope. Not at all." She followed him to the

SUV and waited while he opened her door. "It's nice that you have a family who cares about you so much that they want do document the special moments in your life."

He climbed into the car and started the engine. "I guess you're right." He leaned over and kissed her on the cheek. "Does that mean that tonight is a special moment?"

She smiled at him. "Every moment with you is special."

* * * * *

Simon watched as Lydia Ann, Katie, and Mary walked around the train display on Saturday morning.

Katie said something and Lydia Ann threw back her head and laughed with her daughters.

This was more dangerous than he'd expected. Not only had he fallen for Lydia Ann, but Katie and Mary had him wrapped around their little fingers.

Every moment he spent with the three of them was special. And scary.

Lydia Ann hadn't decided yet if she was going to stay in Lancaster County. Which meant that in just a few weeks, the three of them could be hundreds of miles away.

And he'd be here. Alone.

He'd gone down this road before, just a few years ago. He'd put his heart on the line only to have it broken. When Sarah had chosen the English lifestyle over a life with him in Lancaster County, it had been so hard on him. On the day she made the choice, he'd told himself he would never be in that situation again—even if it meant a lifetime alone.

Yet here he was, spending more time with Lydia Ann and her

daughters. And it was too late now. He'd already become attached to them.

"Let's ride the train," Katie exclaimed, tugging on his sleeve. "It's getting ready to leave."

He grinned down at her. "Okay."

Lydia Ann came over to where he stood. "How long does the train ride last?" she asked, fiddling with the tie on her kapp.

"I don't think the ride takes too long. It pretty much just goes down the track and then comes right back." He motioned at Katie and Mary. "But they are so excited, I don't think the destination matters much."

Lydia Ann laughed. "It sounds like fun."

"Can I sit by the window?" Mary asked as they were boarding.

Katie jumped up and down. "And me too?"

Lydia Ann raised her eyebrows and looked at Simon. "Jah. One of you can sit next to Simon, and one can sit next to me," Lydia Ann said.

Mary slipped her hand into Simon's. "I'll sit with you," she said.

He felt his heart melt. "Let's go."

* * * * *

Lydia Ann watched Simon and Mary laughing as they looked out the window.

He pointed out various landmarks to her, and she nodded.

This man had truly won her over. As much as she'd always said there would never be another man in her life after Levi, she could see now how narrow-minded she'd been. Simon was wonderful with the girls. It made her heart sing to see them laughing and talking with him.

For so long, she'd felt robbed. Levi had died when Mary and Katie were so small. He'd barely gotten to know them at all. And much of the time, he'd been too weak to spend much time with them. So Lydia Ann had always wondered how it would feel to truly be a family.

And now, thanks to Simon, she was getting a little taste of it.

"Mamm," Katie whispered in Lydia Ann's ear.

Lydia Ann looked down at her daughter and smiled. "Jah?"

"It's nice to have Mr. Simon with us, isn't it?"

"Very nice."

Katie snuggled against Lydia Ann. "I am going to miss him very much when we go back home. Aren't you?" She looked up at Lydia Ann.

Lydia Ann nodded. "What would you think about staying here?" She'd been wondering how to broach the subject with her girls. Maybe one at a time was best.

Katie looked at her with wide eyes. "You mean like *live* here?"

"Jah. I've been away from Dat for a long time. And you like spending time with him and Leah, right?"

Katie nodded. "But I will miss my friends at school."

"I know. I'll miss my friends too. But we'll make new friends here."

The child smiled. "We already have Mr. Simon. And Miss Caroline. And Bandit."

"So if I decide for us to stay here, you will be happy?"

"Jah. And so will Mary." She leaned against her mother. "She likes it here too."

Lydia Ann cast another glance at Mary and Simon, who appeared to be discussing a herd of cattle they'd just spotted out the train window.

Today had been a tiny glimpse of the happiness that a life in Lancaster County could hold. And it was enough to convince Lydia Ann that even though they'd miss their friends from Charm, it would be worth it.

Chapter Thirty-Nine

....

Caroline poured some extra creamer in her coffee and sat down at her favorite table. The round table had a striped motif, alternating red, blue, green, and yellow. The pair of mismatched chairs was painted a glossy red. Something about the colors automatically cheered her up.

She expected Lydia Ann any minute. One of her favorite morning rituals had become sitting with Lydia Ann and enjoying a cup of coffee before the store opened for the day.

Lydia Ann's friendship surprised her. She'd had friends before. Sally from junior high had shared the same taste in boy bands. That had been enough to sustain a friendship that lasted until they were juniors, when Sally had become joined at the hip with the star football player. And in college, she and her roommate had bonded over the experience of knowing no one else and sharing a bathroom.

But for the most part, close friendship had been elusive for Caroline.

Especially once she'd married Lance.

At that point, she'd never been certain if women wanted to be her friend because they genuinely liked her or because they sought access to the mythical world of professional sports, where the men were handsome and rich.

Valerie was the perfect example. She'd worked in PR at one of the companies Lance did endorsements for and had almost imme-diately struck up a friendship with Caroline. After everything that had happened, Caroline couldn't help but wonder if their whole friendship had been a ruse on Valerie's part. Caroline would prob-ably never know for sure.

"Somebody is lost in thought today," Lydia Ann said.

Caroline jumped at the sound of her voice. "I didn't even hear you come in."

Lydia Ann smiled and poured herself a cup of coffee. "The girls are with Dat and Leah again today. They'll be in soon." She grinned. "Otherwise I might not have been able to sneak up on you."

Caroline laughed. "True. They don't tread lightly." She took a sip of coffee. "But they sure are cute."

Lydia Ann sat down. "They are. We've been talking about when we're leaving, though." She sighed. "I've talked to them about stay-ing here, but I'm not sure what we're going to do."

"Still haven't figured it out?"

Lydia Ann shook her head. "I want to make sure I'm staying for the right reason. I don't want to uproot our lives unless I honestly believe it is the best thing for my family."

"That makes sense." Caroline pushed a stray hair from her face. "I guess we both have big decisions to make." She put her coffee mug down on the table. "Can I ask you something? And you'll give me a straight answer? Not sugarcoated?"

Lydia Ann stirred her coffee. "Sometimes we need that sugar-coating to help an answer go down better." She smiled.

"I'm really struggling with the idea of Valerie and Lance's child." She shook her head. "Deciding whether or not to raise the baby seems like an impossible decision."

Lydia Ann nodded. "It is not going to be easy for you, either way you go."

"Your husband died when the girls were young. How hard has it been to raise them alone?"

Lydia Ann sat quietly for a moment. "I had a lot of help. Levi's parents were around. And you met Noah, my cousin Emma's husband. He was Levi's cousin. Noah and his parents helped out a lot too."

"So they had plenty of father figures around?"

"Jah. Noah stepped in as much as he could. He played with them, especially when they were toddlers. Katie used to be terrified of horses. Noah helped her learn to love them. He'd lift her up to pat the horse on the head." Lydia Ann smiled at the memory. "But even though I had help, there were hard times."

"So it wouldn't be something you would do by choice?"

Lydia Ann furrowed her brow. "There have been many times… are still many times…when I have to make decisions alone. It would be better if I were making those decisions with their father."

Caroline nodded. "I can see that." She sighed.

"Your situation is different, of course." Lydia Ann took another sip of coffee. "I get the sense that you see this as your duty. And maybe it is." She met Caroline's eyes. "But I hope you realize that if you choose this, your life will change forever."

"In some ways, my life has already changed forever. I wanted to be a mom for so long. And now I have the chance."

Lydia Ann shook her head. "I think the thing to take into consideration isn't what's best for you. Because the thing that's best for you may very well be to raise this baby as your own so you'll have something to focus on. Something to cling to. But I think the thing you have to consider is what is best for the child."

Caroline fell silent and considered Lydia Ann's words. Parenthood was about putting the child's needs above your own. At least that was how it seemed to her. "I think that's the trouble."

Lydia Ann furrowed her brow. "What do you mean?"

"The ideal situation would be to find a couple to adopt this baby. A couple who have no interest in the fact that the father was a superstar. A couple who will love the child and raise it to lead a good life." She shrugged. "The problem is, I don't know that such a couple exists."

Lydia Ann bit her lip. "I may know the answer."

* * * * *

Lydia Ann felt sorry for Caroline. The decision would not be an easy one. Especially considering that Caroline had wanted a child of her own for such a long time.

And from what Lydia Ann knew of Caroline, she would love the baby with all her might, despite the situation. Not everyone would be able to do that.

But even so, she could see that if there were a better alternative, Caroline would seriously consider it. "My cousin Emma is considering adoption. She and Noah don't have any children of their own."

Caroline widened her eyes. "That might be a good solution." She shook her head. "But do you think they would want to take a child under these circumstances?"

"Emma wouldn't care about the circumstances involved. She would just see a baby who needs a mother." Lydia Ann took her cup to the sink and rinsed it out.

"A baby who needs a mother," Caroline repeated. "And I'll bet

Emma and Noah wouldn't have feelings one way or the other about the fact that Lance was a celebrity."

Lydia Ann shrugged. "I can't imagine that they would."

"I have another trip to Atlanta scheduled in a couple of weeks," Caroline said. "I have to tie up some loose ends. While I'm there, I'm supposed to meet with Valerie again and tell her my decision." She rose from the table. "She begged me to help her with the situation. Otherwise, the baby goes into state foster care."

"Do you want to discuss it with her?" Lydia Ann asked.

Caroline nodded. "I do. I think she would be thrilled at the thought of Emma and Noah adopting the baby."

Lydia Ann smiled. "I won't mention it to Emma until you've spoken to Valerie. I don't want to get her hopes up."

"And there are probably a thousand layers of red tape to make something like that happen," Caroline said. "But I have a great lawyer. He's made a lot of money from us over the years. I have no doubt he can take charge of the situation if needed." She smiled. "Thanks for talking this out with me. I feel like a load has been lifted."

Lydia Ann walked to the counter and wiped a smudge from the glass. "I'm glad to help."

Chapter Forty

....

Michael stopped at the crosswalk and waited for the light to change. He'd had a tough time waking up today. Thankfully, there was a Starbucks near his office to provide him with a much-needed mid-morning coffee break.

His cell phone buzzed on his hip. He pulled the phone from its holster and glanced at the number. He recognized the area code as a DC number, so he picked up.

"Could I speak to Michael Landis?" a deep voice said.

"Speaking."

"This is Harold Blaze with the *Washington Daily Journal*."

Michael's heart quickened. "Hello, Mr. Blaze." Michael had interviewed with the *Daily Journal* before he ever left DC.

"I'm sorry to just now be getting back with you. But we've had an opening here that I thought you might be interested in."

They almost never had openings. In fact, the only way Michael had scored an interview in the first place was because his boss had an "in" with the editor there. "I'm honored."

"Is the e-mail address I have for you still current? I can send you a job description and you can see if it might be something you'd be interested in. But with your background and experience, I think it would be a good fit."

"Yes, sir. Please send it over."

"I'll include an official offer letter, which will explain the salary and benefits. I think it's a package you'll be pleased with."

"Thank you. I'll be looking for it." Michael clicked off his phone and leaned against the brick building. His emotions were mixed. So mixed.

If this had been two months ago, it would've been a no-brainer. This was easily a dream job for him. But now…so much had changed. And he couldn't help but think maybe it was all God's way of teaching him about what was really important. He was glad that he'd come back home. Spending time with his family had made him realize how much he'd neglected them. He never wanted that to happen again. And meeting Caroline had given him a new perspective on things. He'd never had much of a desire for a home and family of his own. But since he'd met her, he'd come to realize that his idea of what it meant to be successful had shifted.

He walked into his office building and sat down at his cubicle. His eyes went to the picture of himself and Caroline, hugged up together on his parents' front porch. As much as he'd complained about his mom's incessant need to document things by taking pictures, he was glad to have the moment captured.

She was laughing, and he was glancing over at her with adoration written all over his face. It was a perfect moment.

He sighed. And now, to be faced with a decision like this one. It just seemed unfair. But he opened the e-mail from Mr. Blaze anyway and printed the offer letter.

The very generous offer.

He'd have to talk to Caroline about it later.

Normally, he loved to share things with her. But this time, dread washed over him.

He'd tried hard to avoid having to define their relationship before it was time. But it appeared that this job offer might make it a necessity.

And even though he was pretty sure where he stood with her, he wasn't sure enough to know what the outcome of the conversation would be.

* * * * *

Caroline finished reading a Dr. Seuss book to the children and put it back on the shelf. "Thanks for being such good listeners today," she said.

"Miss Caroline," a little blond-haired girl tugged on her sleeve. "Can you read another story?"

Caroline smiled down at the girl. She couldn't be more than four. "Sure. Do you want to hear another Dr. Seuss?"

The little girl shook her head. "*Fancy Nancy*, please."

Caroline reached for the popular book and grinned. "Okay. One more story." As she read, she kept an eye on the little girl. She sat at rapt attention, laughing at her favorite parts.

For a long moment, Caroline honestly felt as if she could feel the emptiness inside her from having never carried a child. A little blond girl—that had always been her dream. She'd have Caroline's crooked smile and Lance's athletic ability. But that dream had been replaced with other dreams.

And although now Caroline knew she was in a happy place, she couldn't help but feel like a child would complete her life. To love and be loved unconditionally. Was she making the right decision about Valerie and Lance's child? Or was her own fear holding her back from raising a baby who needed her?

She quickly finished the story and smiled at the kids. "That's all for today. But if you come back next Tuesday, we'll pick a new story."

The kids cheered.

"Are you okay?" Lydia Ann asked as Caroline made her way to the cash register.

She nodded. "I'm fine. Just second-guessing myself. That's always been one of my special talents."

Lydia Ann smiled. "Pray about it. Eventually you will reach a decision that gives you peace."

"I know you're right. But these days when I pray, I feel like I must sound very whiny." She twisted her mouth into a smile. "I need to work on that. Praying not just when I need or want something, but when I'm thankful and feeling blessed."

Lydia Ann fingered the tie on her kapp. "Without ceasing."

Caroline nodded. She'd asked one time about the kapp Amish women wore. She'd learned that they were prayer kapps to help remind them to be in constant prayer. And although Caroline might not take up the practice of wearing one, it shouldn't mean that she couldn't have a more active prayer life. "I know it's short notice, but what are you doing tonight? Do you have plans?"

Lydia Ann shook her head. "Nothing special that I know about. Leah mentioned going to Target to get a few things, and I thought I might go with her." She glanced at Caroline. "Why?"

"I thought it might be fun to have you over for dinner." She grinned. "I've been bragging to Michael that I'm a good cook, but he doesn't seem to believe me. I thought you and Simon might want to come over too. And Katie and Mary are welcome to stay as well. Bandit would love the attention."

"That does sound fun." Lydia Ann grinned. "Katie and Mary will probably want to go with Leah, though. They love Target."

Caroline laughed. "Girls after my own heart."

Chapter Forty-One
....

Simon pulled up to the bookstore in his buggy just minutes before Michael got there. "Hello," he called.

Michael waved. "How's it goin'?" he asked, walking over as Simon climbed out of the buggy.

"Pretty well."

"When's your next doctor's appointment?"

Simon grimaced. "Next week." He'd already decided not to tell anyone what was happening until he had a certain diagnosis. And he definitely planned to go alone.

"If you need me to drive you, just holler."

The two of them walked up the steps to the store.

Simon's symptoms had lessened over the past week, except for the fatigue. It didn't seem to matter how many hours of sleep he got each night, he still felt run-down. "Thanks. I think I'll just drive myself. You know how those appointments can take awhile." He grinned. "And I don't like for anyone to have to wait on me."

Michael nodded. "Okay. But if you change your mind, the offer stands." He rapped on the door of the store. "I have no idea what she's cooking tonight, but I hope it's edible."

Simon chuckled. "You don't have much faith in her, do you?"

"I have tons of faith in her. But she's already told me that her cooking skills are rusty. And I looked at the oven in this place. It's older than we are." He grinned. "So I have Domino's on speed dial just in case."

"I heard that," Caroline said, swinging open the door. "And you can just turn your phone off, mister." She swatted at Michael.

Simon hung back, watching the two of them interact. He didn't remember ever seeing Michael so happy.

"Simon," Lydia Ann said, walking into the room, "I'm glad you could come."

He grinned. "Did you have a busy day?"

She nodded. "Jah. We had a lot of children today for the story time."

Simon glanced around. "Speaking of children, where are Katie and Mary?"

"They're with Leah. But they'll be sad they missed you."

He grinned. "You'll have to bring them to the farm soon. We just had a new calf born."

"Maybe Saturday," she said, smiling. She motioned toward the closed kitchen door, where Caroline had gone. "I'm going to go see if she needs some help. I'll be back in a minute."

He watched her leave.

"Everything okay?" Michael asked.

Simon glanced at his friend and nodded. "Fine."

"You and Lydia Ann seem to get along well," Michael observed. "Is there more to the story than just friendship?"

Simon rubbed his jaw. "I think so. I care a lot about her. And her daughters." He shook his head. "But at the same time, spending time with her and getting closer to her is tough."

Michael furrowed his brow. "Why? It sounds pretty great to me."

"Because I'm afraid she's going to leave soon. She's considering staying here, but when it comes down to it, I'm not sure that's going to happen."

"That's tough." Michael shook his head. "But I know what you mean. It's hard to let yourself get close to someone while knowing it's likely you'll be ripped apart."

Simon shrugged. "I guess at some point you have to take a leap of faith, just like with anything that's important. There's always an element of uncertainty."

"No guarantees," Michael mused.

Simon pondered his friend's words. There were no guarantees in this life. The Lord didn't even promise them tomorrow. So maybe it was time he stopped fretting about the future and focused more on the present.

* * * * *

Michael ate the last bite of poppy-seed chicken on his plate and wiped his mouth with a paper towel. "Okay. I take it all back. You're totally a good cook." He grinned at the pleased expression on Caroline's face. "This was delicious."

Simon nodded, still chewing. "It is very good. And I'm not just saying that because Lydia Ann told me to."

Lydia Ann burst out laughing. "Don't listen to him. It's so good I might need to borrow the recipe."

"Mama used to make it on my birthday," Caroline said. "And it became my go-to meal when I had company."

Michael grinned. "Well, I can see why."

Caroline stood and began to clear the table. "I didn't have time to make dessert, though. Sorry."

Lydia Ann stood to help but Michael shook his head at her.

"I'll help her." He stood. "You stay here and keep Simon company." He grinned and grabbed a couple of dirty plates. He followed Caroline into the kitchen. "Thanks for dinner," he said, putting the plates down on the counter.

"No problem." She smiled. "I told you I enjoy cooking. Just wait until you taste my apple pie."

He grabbed her around the waist and pulled her to him. "I'll bet it could give Betty Crocker a run for her money." He nuzzled her neck. "I missed you today."

She giggled. "Stop it. Lydia Ann and Simon are just on the other side of the door."

He kissed her cheek. "They're busy making googly eyes at each other," he whispered. "They've probably forgotten we're here."

Laughing, she indulged him in a quick kiss. "I highly doubt it." She grabbed his hand. "Now come on and act right."

He followed her into the other room, where Simon and Lydia Ann sat talking quietly.

"Does anyone want some coffee?" Caroline asked.

Lydia Ann shook her head. "Actually, Simon and I were just talking. He offered to drop me off on his way home." She smiled. "I need to get back to Dat and Leah's before Mary and Katie's bedtime."

"Oh, of course," Caroline said. She turned to Michael. "How about you? Do you need to leave now, or do you want me to put on a pot of coffee?"

He grinned. "I guess I can stay a little while." He winked. "If you insist."

Caroline playfully shoved him. "You're impossible."

Simon and Lydia Ann stood.

"Dinner was very gut. Thank you for inviting me," Simon said.

Lydia Ann motioned toward the remaining dishes. "I'd be happy to help with those before we go, though."

Caroline shook her head. "You helped so much with dinner." She smiled. "You haven't even been home today, and I know you must be tired after the long day we had."

"It was a full day," Lydia Ann agreed.

Michael and Caroline walked to the door and watched Lydia Ann and Simon climb into the waiting buggy.

"See you tomorrow," Caroline called. She closed the door and turned to face Michael.

Even though he wanted nothing more than to take her in his arms and kiss her, he knew that he needed to talk to her about the job he'd been offered today. He'd tried to put it out of his mind during dinner, but it had been hanging over him all day.

He knew he'd feel much better when it was out in the open....

Especially if he and Caroline were on the same page about things.

Chapter Forty-Two

....

Lydia Ann glanced over at Simon's handsome profile. "I appreciate your taking me home tonight."

Simon grinned. "It isn't a problem. I'm happy to do it." He looked over at her. "Would you want to go get an ice-cream cone or something? Or do you need to get straight home?"

The chance to spend a few minutes alone with Simon was too good to pass up. "Ice cream sounds great." She chuckled. "As long as you don't tell Katie and Mary. They would eat ice cream for every meal if they could."

"Smart girls."

They rode in companionable silence.

The sun hadn't quite gone down yet, and Lydia Ann enjoyed the last gleaming rays of light. "It sure is a beautiful night," she remarked.

"Made better by good company," Simon said with a smile, guiding the buggy into a parking lot.

Once they had their ice-cream cones, they sat down at a picnic table outside the dairy bar.

"This is one of my favorite things about summer." Simon waved his strawberry cone in the air. "Cool ice cream after a hot day."

Lydia Ann nodded. "Back home, we have a little general store that sells scoops of ice cream. It's right down the street from where my quilt shop is…" She trailed off momentarily. "Or at least, where it used to be. Before the tornado."

"Do you miss Charm?"

She shrugged. "I miss the people. There is something comforting about a place you've known since childhood, isn't there?"

Simon nodded in agreement. "Sure. Many of the people around here have known me since I was born. Leah, for example." He grinned. "If you asked her to, she could tell you about the time I got my head caught in the Landises' fence." He shook his head. "I was seven and I'm still not sure how it happened. It went through the space just fine. But it wouldn't come out."

Lydia Ann laughed.

"Michael and Phillip tried pulling me out, but I yelled so much, Mr. Landis came out to see. He really had to work to get me free. And, boy, was Mamm upset with me. She sat me down and gave me a lecture about the dangers of goofing off." He grinned. "But I heard her laughing about it later when she told Dat. So I knew she wasn't really that mad."

Lydia Ann's mouth twisted into a smile. She could imagine how cute Simon must've been as a little boy. "I guess people and places that are familiar just can't be replaced."

He caught her eye. "But there's also something exciting about new people and places, don't you think?"

She felt her face grow hot. "I suppose so."

His blue eyes bored into hers. "I know so." He stood. "I guess we'd better get going. Mary and Katie are probably waiting up for you."

Lydia Ann followed him to the waiting buggy.

He held his hand out and helped her climb inside.

The feel of her hand in his took her breath away. She glanced over at him as they headed toward home.

Home.

Lancaster County felt like home to her now. And the man sitting next to her had a lot to do with that. She'd told Levi once that she would follow him to the ends of the earth. And now, she felt that way again.

Lydia Ann knew that the friendship between her and Simon had grown into something more.

Something real.

Something that felt a whole lot like love.

* * * * *

Caroline sank onto the cushy love seat and watched Michael play with Bandit on the rug.

"I can't believe how he's grown," Michael said. "And he's so spoiled." He chuckled as the dog turned over on his back and put his feet up in the air. "He knows just how to ask for a belly rub, doesn't he?" He rubbed the puppy's belly and grinned.

Caroline knew she could get used to this, and the thought scared her a little bit. She could see a future with Michael—but she knew how many obstacles stood in their way.

Eventually her true identity would come out, and she didn't want Michael to have to deal with that. Then there was the little matter of Valerie and the upcoming murder trial. Not to mention the baby that Caroline had to come to a decision about.

No, a future for her and Michael wouldn't be easy.

But her mawmaw used to tell her that anything worth having was worth working for. And maybe she'd been right.

Michael rose from his spot on the floor and sat next to her. He turned toward her and gave a little grin. "I hate it when people say 'We need to talk,' but…" He trailed off. "We need to talk."

She furrowed her brow. "What's up? Did you secretly hate my cooking?"

He shook his head. "Nope." He laughed.

She detected an undercurrent of seriousness in his tone. "Then what?"

Michael cleared his throat. "A few months ago, I interviewed with a big news outlet in DC. My old boss got me the interview just before I came to Lancaster County." He chewed on the inside of his lip. "I didn't expect to hear anything. They didn't even have an open position, so I figured the guy was just doing it out of professional courtesy."

Caroline didn't respond. She had the familiar feeling that the rug was about to be swept from beneath her.

"He called me today and offered me a job. A really great job." Michael raked his fingers through his hair. "It has an incredibly generous benefit and salary package. They'd even pay to relocate me and give me a housing allowance until I found an apartment."

She nodded, trying to ignore the sudden tightness in her chest. "That's great," she said, forcing a smile. "Sounds like a really good opportunity." She'd started to lean on him. Depend on him. And now he was going to leave. She tried to keep her face neutral. "It would be tough to turn that down."

He drew his brows together. "That's what I wanted to talk to you about." He reached for her hand. "Caroline, I know we haven't exactly defined things between us."

Caroline gave him a smile. "I appreciate the fact that we haven't rushed into anything." They'd spent the months getting to know one another slowly. She'd always thought the best relationships were built on the foundation of friendship. And it had been just that way with the two of them.

"I know. I think it's important for us to take things slowly, especially given what you've gone through." He squeezed her hand. "But just because we're taking it slowly doesn't mean that I'm not crazy about you."

She felt a sense of relief at his words. Even though his actions told her that he cared a lot for her, hearing him verbalize it made her feel better. "I'm glad to hear it. Because I'm pretty crazy about you too."

He leaned over and kissed her lightly on the lips. "That's why I'm going to turn the job down."

Caroline smiled broadly. "Are you sure that's what you want? I mean, aren't you even a little tempted?"

Michael shrugged his shoulders. "I realize what a good opportunity this is. They have a great reputation for doing the kinds of stories I've always dreamed of covering." He shook his head. "But now that I've met you and been able to spend time with my family, I just don't think that accepting the position would be the right decision for me."

Caroline was touched that he was willing to sacrifice a career move for her. When she'd been married to Lance, she had gotten so used to being at the bottom of his priority pile. This was a wholly new experience.

Michael took her hand again. "I'm glad we talked about things, though. I wanted to make sure you and I were on the same page about our relationship and where it might be going."

She nodded. "I'd very much like to see where this goes. I feel like

I get to know you better with each passing day." Her mouth turned up in a smile. "And I hope you feel that way as well."

He nodded. "Sure do. I feel closer to you with each passing moment."

Michael pulled her against him, and she leaned her head against his chest.

It might not have been a declaration of love, but it was a start. She hadn't felt so safe, so secure, in a very long time.

And that feeling was one that she planned to hang on to for as long as possible.

Like forever.

Chapter Forty-Three

Simon walked numbly out of the doctor's office. He'd spent a good part of the past few weeks trying to forget about today's appointment. And for the most part, it had worked.

But today, he'd had to face up to the fact that everything wasn't okay. He'd seen it on the neurologist's face after the examination.

He wished he could be relieved about finally having a diagnosis. But he wasn't.

Instead, all he could think of was Lydia Ann.

Lydia Ann, who'd seen her husband battle cancer and lose.

Lydia Ann, who'd sat on the porch swing with him a few weeks ago and said that she would never want to watch someone she loved suffer again. Because she couldn't handle the pain.

Lydia Ann, who'd gone with him for ice cream the other night and made him feel like the most special man in the world.

He climbed into the buggy, halfway wishing he'd let Michael drive him. His hands shook today, but it had nothing to do with the multiple sclerosis he'd just officially been diagnosed with.

It had to do with fear. Fear of the unknown. Fear of a disease he didn't know much about.

And fear of telling Lydia Ann that she was involved with yet another sick man.

He wondered how to tell her.

And then a different kind of sick feeling came over him. Lydia Ann would never walk away from him once she found out about his illness. She would stay with him, a silent prisoner of the situation, because she was a good, kind woman. Not the kind who would leave a man because of an illness…even if she wanted to.

While that knowledge might make most men happy, it did the opposite for Simon. He couldn't do that to her.

Lydia Ann could never know about his illness.

And that meant there was only one thing he could do.

* * * * *

Lydia Ann hummed to herself as she cleaned the display of knick-knacks at the front of the bookstore. The past few weeks had been some of the happiest she'd had in a long while. She'd developed close friendships with Leah and Caroline. Her relationship with Dat was as strong as it had been when she was younger. And Simon…Simon had become someone she couldn't imagine her life without. She had so many blessings to count these days.

Yesterday's church meeting had been a good one. She felt as if she fit into the community well. And last night she and Leah had made homemade ice cream as Dat helped Mary and Katie catch fireflies.

Things seemed to finally be coming together for her.

It helped that she'd finally made a decision about Lancaster County. She'd chosen to stay. No one knew yet, though. She wanted Simon to be the first to hear. She had a feeling he would be the happiest of anyone. And she knew that her decision to move to Lancaster County likely had an important impact on a future for her and Simon. At least, she was pretty sure it would.

"I think there's someone here to see you." Caroline came in from sweeping the front porch. "Simon just pulled up in his buggy." She grinned. "And I'm pretty sure he isn't here for me."

Lydia Ann tossed her dustcloth into the trash and smoothed her skirt. "I'll go see what he wants." She stepped onto the porch and shielded her eyes from the bright July sunlight. "Good afternoon, Simon," she called.

He waved at her but didn't say anything.

She walked over to the buggy. "Are you going to come inside?"

Simon shook his head. "I don't think so." He climbed down from his seat. "Can we sit and talk on the porch?"

Lydia Ann nodded. "Jah. Do you want me to go inside and get you some water?"

"No."

She glanced at his expressionless face. It seemed almost as if the life had gone out of him. "Are you okay?"

He nodded. "I'm just tired."

They sat down in the wicker chairs on the store's front porch.

"I have some news that might make you happy," Lydia Ann said. She couldn't keep the excitement from her voice. "You're the first to hear."

He looked at her with interest. "What's that?"

"I've decided to stay. Mary, Katie, and I are moving to Lancaster County," she said, grinning broadly. "What do you think about that?"

Simon furrowed his brow. "Are you sure that's a good idea?" he asked.

"What do you mean? When I mentioned it before, you thought it was the best thing to do."

He shook his head. "I've been giving it more thought." He met her gaze. "And I don't think it's a good plan. You already have a life in Charm. Why would you want to move here?"

Lydia Ann tried to hide her confusion. She'd been sure that Simon would be thrilled at the news. "But I thought you and I were on the path to getting to know one another better. If I lived here, it would give us more time together."

He drew his brows together. "Once fall gets here, I'll be so busy at the farm—I would barely have time to see you. Maybe not at all." His face was grim. "I just don't want you to make that decision on account of me." He met her gaze. "Because I don't see a future for us."

Lydia Ann drew back as if she'd been slapped. Over the past two months, she and Simon had grown close. He'd never given her any indication that he might not be interested in her until now.

She stood. "I see." She bit her lip, hoping to keep her tears in check until she'd gone back inside. "Thank you for your honesty." She motioned at the store, unable to meet his gaze. "I'd better go check on the girls."

"Lydia Ann…," he started.

She shook her head. "You don't owe me anything." She closed the door tightly behind her as the first hot tear began to fall.

Chapter Forty-Four
....

"Here." Caroline handed a tissue to Lydia Ann. "Do you want me to take the girls over to your dad's store so they won't know you're upset?"

Lydia Ann nodded, dabbing at her wet eyes with the tissue. "Danki. That would be nice."

"You can stay here as long as you like. I can drive you home later."

Caroline had been caught completely off guard by the Amish woman's sobs. They'd been quiet at first but had gotten louder. Caroline had flipped the sign to CLOSED and locked the door. They could close a little early today. She was a lot more worried about her friend than she was her business.

"I don't know what came over him. It was almost like he was someone else," Lydia Ann said.

Caroline sat down next to her friend on the love seat. "There must be some explanation. People don't just turn feelings on and off like a faucet." She pulled out another tissue and handed it to Lydia Ann. "Right?"

Lydia Ann shrugged. "Maybe he's had time to consider the situation more. I bring a lot of memories with me. Mamm's accident. Levi's death. Raising the girls alone." She sighed. "Maybe it was all too much for him."

"I've seen the way he looks at you, though—with the eyes of a man who would fight the fiercest battle to keep you by his side." Caroline shook her head. "It doesn't make sense at all."

"Unless…" Lydia Ann trailed off with a sniff. "Maybe he just decided it wasn't worth the trouble."

Caroline reached over and patted Lydia Ann's hand. "That's silly. I might not be an expert in men.…" *What an understatement.* "But it sounds to me like maybe he's just scared. Didn't you say that the last girl he dated ended up leaving and marrying someone in the city?"

Lydia Ann nodded.

"Then maybe he's just having a bout of cold feet." She smiled. "Give him a few days. He'll probably be miserable and come knocking, begging your forgiveness."

Lydia Ann's sad face brightened. "You think so?"

Caroline tried to sound confident. "Of course." She smiled. "Why don't you go upstairs and lie down? I'll take the girls to your dad's." She paused at the back door. "And maybe I'll stop and get you some ice cream. That always makes me feel better."

"Chocolate," Lydia Ann said softly.

Caroline chuckled. "Of course."

* * * * *

Michael took one look at Simon's glum face and knew that something was wrong. And it was bigger than a busted fence post or broken buggy wheel. "What happened?" he asked.

Simon flipped over a bucket and sat down. "Can I tell you something in confidence?"

"Of course."

Simon met his eyes. "I'm not ready for anyone to know this. Not my family or your family. Not Lydia Ann." He leveled his gaze on Michael. "And not Caroline."

"Just between you and me. I get it." Michael had always been good at keeping secrets. Maybe that was part of what made him a good journalist—he knew not to reveal sources.

Simon stretched his legs out in front of him. "I went back to the doctor this morning."

Fear swept over Michael. He'd been waiting for Simon to tell him what was going on with his health, but his friend had been silent about the situation. Michael had hoped that meant everything was okay, but he could see now that it wasn't. "What did you find out?"

"I have multiple sclerosis."

The words hung in the air for a long moment.

"I'm sorry." Michael didn't know a lot about the disease, but he knew it could cause a lot of problems.

"I'm still trying to digest the news." Simon took off his hat and turned it over in his hands. "The doctor has some options for me. Says it impacts everyone differently." He cleared his throat. "But I asked him about the worst-case scenario." He shrugged. "Because I wanted to know the worst thing I could expect."

Michael met Simon's gaze. "And?"

"Pretty bad. I could end up permanently disabled." Simon shook his head. "And I'm just going to go ahead and tell you that I broke things off with Lydia Ann." The pain in his eyes spoke volumes. "I'm sure Caroline knows, so you'll probably hear about it sooner or later, but I at least wanted you to know my reason behind it."

Michael furrowed his brow. "But, Simon, I know she'll want to help you through this."

"That's just the problem. I don't want her to feel obligated. And I don't want her to have to deal with yet another illness. Not after everything she'd already been through."

"But there's a chance that, with medication, you'll live a long and healthy life. Right?"

Simon nodded. "But there's a chance I won't. I can't put her through that. I won't put her through that."

"She deserves to know."

Simon put his hat back on and stood. "Why? I don't want her to feel like she has to stay with me just because I'm sick. And I know her well enough to know that she'd never leave once she found out." He shook his head. "It's better this way. It's the only honorable thing for me to do."

Michael narrowed his eyes. He felt like his friend was making a terrible mistake. "I still think you owe it to her to tell her what you found out. Is it better that she thinks you don't care about her?"

"It hurts me that she thinks that. But it's better in the long run," Simon explained.

"Won't you miss her?"

Simon stopped in his tracks. "I missed her the minute I left the bookstore. But she deserves more than to be tied down to another sick man. I want her to be happy."

Michael watched as Simon headed toward the pasture.

"*The course of true love never did run smooth.*" The words from a long-ago class on Shakespeare came to him.

Only time would tell if Simon and Lydia Ann could get back on a smooth course.

Michael couldn't help but be thankful that things between him and Caroline were on the right track.

But just to be safe, he knocked on the wooden fence post he passed on the way to the house.

Chapter Forty-Five
....

Michael sat at his cubicle and glanced over the paperwork that Mr. Blaze had sent last week. The man still hadn't called to discuss the position. But Michael was glad he had his answer waiting.

"Hey there," Jenny said, plopping down in the guest chair. "How's it going?"

Michael glanced at her and nodded. "Pretty well. No complaints, I guess." He smiled. "How about you?"

She sighed and pulled the chair next to his. "Not good."

He put the paperwork down and glanced at her. "Anything I can do?"

"Can I trust you to keep a secret?" she whispered.

Michael nodded. "Of course. You know that."

"I think I've outgrown my position here." She shook her head. "I've done everything with this magazine that I possibly can do." She leaned closer. "You know what a micromanager Mr. Sinclair is. He seriously tries to control my every move."

"Have you tried talking to him?" Michael knew that Jenny was good at her job. He'd been working alongside her all summer, and her work ethic was impressive. She might be a little nuts sometimes, but she was at the top of her game work-wise.

She nodded. "I've tried. He always says that things will change, but then when it comes down to it, he still calls all the shots." She rubbed her temples. "I've been here for years. You'd think that with seniority would come more responsibility. The kind of responsibility that means I don't have to run every little thing past my boss." She shook her head. "But not here."

"So what are you going to do?"

She bit her lip. "My resume is out right now."

"Anything local?"

"I'm branching out, actually." She grinned. "DC and Philly, mainly."

He widened his eyes. She'd always said that she'd never move to a big city. "What brought that on?"

She shrugged. "I feel stifled here. It used to be nice and safe, you know? To be back in a place where people had known me my whole life. But lately I've been thinking about expanding my horizons." She smiled. "I guess I'm ready to spread my wings, so to speak."

"That's awesome." And he meant it. He'd always thought Jenny could go far. Maybe someday she'd be doing the marketing for a huge company. Or even a political figure, depending on where she ended up. "I think you can do whatever you put your mind to." He grinned. "You know I've always been a big proponent of following your dreams."

She chuckled. "I remember." Her eyes went to the paperwork on his desk. "Wow. Speaking of following your dreams. Is that an offer letter from the *Washington Daily Journal*?" she hissed.

"Shh." He put his finger to his lips. "It isn't a big deal. At all."

She raised her brows. "Not a big deal? Isn't that where you always said you wanted to end up?"

He shrugged. "Yeah. But that was a long time ago. A lot has changed since then."

"Like her?" She fingered the picture of Michael and Caroline taped to his computer screen.

"Caroline isn't the only reason I'm turning it down. I mean, I just got back here. It's been nice to be reunited with my family." He waved an arm around. "And I like it here."

She stood, still shaking her head. "I can't believe you're actually going to turn down this opportunity." She paused at the entrance of the cubicle. "Because I guarantee that someday you're going to wake up and regret it."

Jenny walked off without another word.

Michael's gaze landed on the *Daily Journal* paperwork, Jenny's words ringing in his ears.

* * * * *

A petite woman burst into the bookstore just before closing, a determined look on her face.

Caroline looked up from where she was sweeping behind the counter. "Can I help you with something?" she asked, leaning the broom against the wall.

"You sure can." The woman glared at Caroline. "I came to see you."

"I'm sorry. Do I know you?" Caroline asked.

The woman stuck out her hand. "I'm Jenny. Michael's ex."

Caroline shook Jenny's icy hand. "Nice to meet you."

"Let's cut to the chase, shall we?" Jenny jerked her head toward the tables in the coffee bar. "Mind if we have a chat?"

Caroline followed Jenny to one of the tables. Michael had mentioned Jenny a few times in passing but had given no indication that she might ever want to visit the bookstore. "What can I do for you?"

Jenny primly crossed her legs and regarded Caroline coolly. "It's what you can do for Michael that I'm here to talk about." She leaned forward and rested her elbows on the table. "I know who you are."

Caroline wrinkled her forehead. "I've never seen you before in my life."

Jenny gave her a sinister grin. "Look. Most of the people you've been in contact with are either dairy farmers or Amish. They aren't exactly up on their pop culture. But I have been a *People* subscriber since I was in high school. As soon as I saw pictures of you with Michael, I put two and two together." She chuckled. "I mean, *Caroline* from *Georgia* who happens to arrive in town soon after Lance DeMarco's death? It didn't take a rocket scientist." She smirked. "A couple of phone calls to a friend of mine at the DMV, and my suspicions were confirmed."

Caroline swallowed. "What do you want?" She tried to keep her face a mask of calm but knew her trembling voice gave her away.

"I get that your privacy is important to you. Sorry about your husband, by the way. Truly tragic." Jenny shook her head. "I'm sure you'd have a lot of chaos on your hands if the media found out where you are. They'd make your life miserable."

Caroline locked eyes with Jenny. "Okay. So I get that you want something in exchange for keeping quiet. What is it?" She had a sinking suspicion that she knew what the answer would be.

"I'm not trying to be mean or unreasonable." Jenny twirled a lock of hair. "But I've known Michael a lot longer than you have. Since we were kids, in fact." She smiled. "I've loved him since fourth-grade science class when he kicked Billy Parker for chasing me with a big toad." She leveled her gaze at Caroline. "And Michael's biggest dream has always been to work for a big publication like the

Daily Journal. When we were in college, he tried to get an internship there and didn't get it. Ever since then, that's been like the brass ring for him."

Caroline crossed her arms. "I didn't ask him to turn the job down." It was true. If he'd told her he was going to accept the position, she would've dealt with it. Maybe not very well, but she would have.

"No, I'm sure you didn't. But I'll bet you didn't encourage him to take it, either."

Jenny might have a point there. "He's happy here."

"Do you want him to wake up one day with regret? And resent that *you* were the reason he didn't follow his dream?" Jenny widened her eyes in question. "If you really care about him, don't you think the thing to do is to encourage him to go after it?"

Caroline chewed on her lip. She wanted to hate this woman… but it almost seemed as if her concern for Michael was coming from an honest place. "I really care about him. And he cares about me."

Jenny's eyes flashed. "If that's the truth, your relationship should be able to withstand him taking his dream job. You've followed your dreams. Why shouldn't he get that same chance?"

Caroline swallowed hard. Had she been selfish by allowing Michael to wave away the job offer like it was nothing? She'd been on the opposite end of that kind of behavior before and had always vowed that she would never act that way. She couldn't help but remember all the times Lance had expected her to sacrifice her own happiness for him. Was that what she was doing to Michael? "What do you want from me?" she asked.

"It's simple, really. I'll keep your secret. No one else needs to know who you really are." Jenny's lips formed a thin line. "But in exchange, you need to convince Michael to take the job." She shrugged. "If your relationship is strong, it shouldn't matter if it has to be long-distance for a while." Jenny rose. "It was nice to meet you, Mrs. DeMarco. I trust that you'll do the right thing here."

Caroline sat in shock.

Even though Jenny had basically blackmailed her, Caroline couldn't help but wonder if she was right. If the *Daily Journal* had always been Michael's brass ring, should he let a new relationship keep him from reaching for it? She'd have a hard time living with herself, knowing that she'd kept him from true happiness.

Caroline knew something about dashed dreams. They always came back to haunt a person. And she didn't want that for Michael.

Chapter Forty-Six

....

Caroline pulled into the long driveway that led to the Landis farm-house. She'd spent the afternoon thinking about her visit with Jenny and fighting the urge to call Michael straightaway and tell him what happened.

Except that the more she thought about it, the more she realized Jenny had a point. It wasn't just that Caroline wanted to retain her privacy. That was important, yes.

But it wasn't as important as Michael taking the opportunity he'd been given. She knew how hard it had been for Michael to come back to Lancaster County in the first place. When he'd accepted the job at the magazine, he'd told her it was temporary, until something came open more along the lines of what he was really looking for.

Like a position at the *Washington Daily Journal*.

She sat in her SUV and prayed that the Lord would give her the right words.

A tap on her window startled her.

Phillip peered into the vehicle, a grin on his face.

"Hey there," she said, opening the door. "I'm looking for Michael. He isn't expecting me."

He motioned toward the barn. "He's out there talking to Simon."

She hoped he was talking some sense into his friend. When she'd asked Michael earlier in the week what Simon was thinking, he'd been evasive. "Maybe there are things going on that we don't know about," he'd said. Except she got the distinct impression that he knew exactly what the deal was and just didn't want to tell her.

And watching Lydia Ann's pain made it difficult to give Simon the benefit of the doubt. She didn't get it. She knew he cared for Lydia Ann. It was plain to see whenever they were together. Something must've made him afraid.

Caroline hurried into the barn.

Michael and Simon were locked in a conversation. It looked so serious, she hated to interrupt. But she was there on a serious mission too.

Simon looked up. "Caroline," he said. "How is Lydia Ann doing?"

She glowered. "She's been better. But she'll be fine."

The pain on his face was so obvious, she almost felt bad. Almost.

"Please give her my regards," he said. He nodded at Michael. "I'll just leave the two of you alone." Simon cast a pleading glance at Caroline as he left.

Once she and Michael were alone, she shook her head. "I still don't get it. He's crazy about her."

"Sometimes things are more complicated than they seem."

Wasn't that the truth? She'd been trying to figure out what to say to Michael all afternoon, ever since Jenny had effectively made her case.

"What's up?" Michael asked. "I didn't expect to see you until later tonight."

They were supposed to catch a movie together, but Caroline didn't feel much like it. "I thought you might like to go out to one of the bridges. Maybe the one with the little park next to it."

He grinned. "Sure." He jerked his head toward the farmhouse. "Let me just change out of my work clothes, though."

She nodded. "I should've called."

Michael pulled her to him and kissed her on the forehead. "Nope. I like the spontaneity." He grabbed her hand. "You can wait downstairs while I change."

They walked into the sunny kitchen.

"Caroline," Mrs. Landis exclaimed. "Are you planning on staying for dinner?" She grinned.

"I'll be right back," Michael whispered, racing toward the stairs.

"No. We're going for a drive. I think we'll probably just grab some dinner while we're out."

"Some other time, then." Mrs. Landis patted her on the back. "We've missed you around here. I keep meaning to get over to the bookstore to visit, but things have been so busy."

"That's fine." Caroline smiled.

"We've been booked solid for the past couple of weeks. And it isn't slowing down anytime soon. People are trying to cram in last-minute vacations before school starts."

Caroline nodded. "I can't believe it's almost August." Time had flown so quickly since she first arrived in Lancaster County.

"I know, dear. But I think you'll enjoy fall here. The leaves are beautiful, and the weather is perfect." Mrs. Landis peered at her. "You are planning to stay, aren't you?"

Caroline bit her lip. If only she knew for sure what her plans were. "Probably."

"You ready?" Michael asked, coming into the room. He'd changed into khaki shorts and a faded green T-shirt that advertised a long-ago 5K.

"Let's go." Caroline smiled at Mrs. Landis. "See you later."

Michael pressed a quick kiss to Mrs. Landis's cheek on the way out the door.

"You want me to drive?" he asked.

She nodded. "Sounds good."

Twenty minutes later, Michael pulled into a parking space. He glanced over at her. "I don't think you've heard a word I said since we left. Is everything okay?"

She opened the car door. "Let's go for a walk."

He furrowed his brow but didn't respond.

They walked hand in hand toward the bridge.

"Have you talked to the man at the DC news outlet?" Caroline finally asked.

Michael stopped walking. "No. He said he'd give me a few days and then call to discuss it." He glanced down at her. "Why?"

She sighed. "I've been thinking." Her heart pounded. What if this was a huge mistake? "I think you should accept the offer."

He drew back as if he'd been slapped. "What?"

"I think you should accept it." She shook her head. "Michael, I know that you want more than to work for a tourist magazine. You've always wanted to cover stories that matter. And this is an amazing opportunity to do that."

"I'm not sure where this is coming from," he said. "Are you having second thoughts about us?"

She bit her lip. "No. I'm not. But I am having second thoughts about your staying in Lancaster County and ending up bitter and resentful that you let your dream pass you by."

He reached out and stroked her cheek. "What if you're my dream?"

She grabbed his hand. "It doesn't work like that. We both know that my future here is uncertain. I'm just renting the store. I have a house back in Atlanta. And a foundation to manage." She shrugged.

"I guess I just realized that if you stay here, I'm going to feel obligated to stay here too." She hated herself for saying it. But she knew that he wouldn't choose the job unless she gave him a reason to. So she'd have to convince him that her feelings weren't as strong as they really were. Sometimes love meant making sacrifices. And in this case, she was willing to sacrifice her happiness if it meant Michael reached his dreams.

"But what about us?"

"We can have a long-distance relationship. I'll come visit you in DC. You can come visit me—either here or in Atlanta." She shrugged. "There is no reason for you to give up your dream on the off chance that I decide to stay here."

His jaw hardened. "So what you're saying is that you don't know if there really is a future for us. Is that what I'm understanding?"

She knew it was for his own good. He deserved a shot at his dreams. A shot at the career he'd wanted for so long. And he couldn't have it as long as he hung around Lancaster County with her. "Yes," she whispered. "I'm sorry."

His long silence killed her. "Let's go." He motioned at the bridge where they'd shared their first kiss. "I don't want to be here any longer."

She walked next to him back to the car. For the first time in weeks, they didn't hold hands. Just walked side by side like two strangers hurrying down a sidewalk.

Unconnected.

Jenny would help keep her identity a secret. And Michael would have his chance at a dream career.

She hoped she'd made the right decision.

* * * * *

Michael hadn't been able to sleep all night. Caroline's revelation had taken him by surprise. In fact, this morning he'd almost convinced himself it had been a bad dream.

Almost.

When he got to the office, he numbly poured himself a cup of coffee and sat down at his desk. He opened the top drawer, and Mr. Blaze's offer letter stared back at him.

Michael put his head in his hands and said a silent prayer that God would show him the way.

"You busy?" Jenny asked behind him.

He turned to face her.

"It looks like somebody didn't get much sleep last night." She smiled and sat down in the guest chair. "Want to talk about it?"

Michael shook his head. "No," he grunted.

"Come on. What are friends for?"

He motioned at the offer letter in front of him. "I guess I'm rethinking this job offer."

Jenny's face brightened. "No kidding? Do you want to hear an amazing coincidence?"

He narrowed his eyes. "What's that?"

"I'm on the verge of accepting a job in DC too." She pulled her chair next to his. "Wouldn't it be great if we were both in DC?"

Michael rubbed his temples. "Congratulations on your job offer. But I'm not at all sure I want to go back to DC."

Jenny drew back in surprise. "Don't be stupid, Michael. This is your dream. It's always been your dream."

He shook his head. "It *was* my dream. But things have changed."

She narrowed her eyes. "You're just confused right now. I'm sure it has to do with Caroline." She gazed at him. "Doesn't it?"

Michael raked his fingers through his hair. "I don't want to talk about it."

Jenny put her hand on his arm. "Michael, she isn't worth it. You deserve to follow your dream and take this job." She smiled. "And this time, I'll be there. You and I can have another chance."

He pulled his arm away. "Jenny, I'm happy to be your friend, but you and I aren't going to get back together. Even if we both end up in DC at the same time."

She wrinkled her forehead. "But, Michael, don't you see? This time it will be different. All the things that didn't work out between us before will work out now."

He shook his head. "We're still the same people. The same incompatible people. That hasn't changed." He leveled his gaze on her. "But I have. Maybe my dream was that I wanted to be a hot-shot journalist who was in the know on the political scene. But not anymore."

She shook her head. "You don't mean that. You can't possibly think that you'll be happy here." She motioned around the cubicle.

"I do. Now what I want more than anything is to be close to my family. To spend my life with the woman I love. And to serve the God who blesses me every day." He shrugged. "When I first came back, I thought it meant I was a failure. But now I realize what a blessing it was that I had a place to come back to. I've finally learned that life is more than a job title." He picked up Mr. Blaze's offer letter and ripped it in two. "And that is why I'm turning down the offer."

Jenny's eyes flashed. She stood and put her hands on her hips. "You're going to regret this decision. And so is your precious Caroline." She stormed off.

Michael tossed the ripped pages into the trash without giving Jenny another thought. The only thing he cared about now was Caroline. He had to make her see that what he wanted, what he needed, what he dreamed about—was right here in Lancaster County.

Chapter Forty-Seven

....

Caroline sat on the plush footstool in the children's section of the bookstore. About ten kids ranging in age from four to ten sat around her, enthralled by the story. She held up the book so they could see the pictures.

"I see a bunny," one little girl called out.

Caroline smiled. "That's right." She pointed to the bunny so everyone would see it. She finished the final page. "The end," she said. She stood and placed the book back on the shelf. "Feel free to play in the toy box," she said, grinning.

Lydia Ann motioned for her to come over to the register.

Caroline hurried over. "What's wrong?" she asked. "Is everything okay?" Caroline peered at her friend.

Lydia Ann's odd expression answered the question. Silently she handed a magazine to Caroline.

Caroline glanced down. "This is Michael's publication, isn't it? Is his article about Gettysburg in here?" She'd been avoiding his calls for days—ever since their conversation on the bridge. By now he'd probably accepted the job offer and was making plans to move back to DC.

"Jah," Lydia Ann said quietly. "But I don't think you're going to like it very much."

Caroline quickly flipped to the center spread that depicted their Gettysburg trip. "These pictures are beautiful." She flipped the page and her eyes widened. The largest picture on the page showed Caroline, her head thrown back in laughter, standing in front of a historical marker. She quickly scanned the print underneath the picture. *Caroline DeMarco, widow of Atlanta Braves pitcher Lance DeMarco, paid a visit to Gettysburg recently. Since her husband's death, Ms. DeMarco has relocated to Lancaster County, Pennsylvania, where she's opened a bookstore.* Caroline dropped the magazine onto the desk. "How could he?" She gripped the counter tightly. "I don't understand."

Lydia Ann pulled a chair over and gently led Caroline to it. "Sit here."

Caroline sank onto the seat and pressed her temples with her fingers. "My head feels like it's about to explode."

"Let me get you some aspirin." Lydia Ann hurried off.

Caroline sat numbly. She'd put her trust in the wrong man. Again.

"Here." Lydia Ann handed Caroline a small white pill.

Caroline popped it into her mouth.

"Drink this." Lydia Ann held a bottle of water to Caroline's mouth.

Caroline obliged.

"Do you want to go upstairs and lay down?" Lydia Ann motioned around the busy shop. "I can close up when the last customer leaves." She jerked her chin toward the wall clock. "It's almost five."

Caroline fought to retain control. She wanted to scream, to throw things. Her life here was so quiet. She'd actually thought she was going to successfully begin again without Lance's life hanging over her. Especially since she'd done what Jenny wanted. She'd told Michael to accept the job in DC. Was putting the photo in his article his way of retaliating?

She shook her head. "No. If I go upstairs, I'll only worry. At least the shop will keep me busy." The shock of betrayal left Caroline with an all-too-familiar numbness. After everything she'd gone through with Lance, she'd wound up devoid of feeling. There were days she wished she could actually feel pain just so she'd know she was still alive. And over the past weeks in Lancaster County, she'd known she was healing because her feelings came back. She'd come through the fog of grief over her mama's death and the sadness over the revelations of her marriage and had actually started to feel like a whole person again. But now, with this unexpected disloyalty, her body had gone back into its protective shell. Caroline felt nothing but numbness.

The minutes seemed to tick past. Caroline fingered her cell phone. Maybe she should call Michael and see what he had to say for himself.

Before she could place the call, an unfamiliar woman with glossy dark hair strode into the shop. "I'd like to have a few words with Mrs. DeMarco, please," she said.

Caroline stood rooted to the spot next to the coffee bar. She peered out from behind a column and watched the determined woman plop her notebook and purse on the counter.

"Is there something I can help you with instead?" Lydia Ann asked sweetly.

The woman sighed loudly. "No. I need Mrs. DeMarco. I have a video crew outside. I'd like to get a statement from her in time for tonight's news."

Before Lydia Ann could respond, the front door burst open.

Michael.

"Where is she?" he asked, scooting the reporter out of the way. "I need to talk to Caroline right now."

The reporter looked him over with a gleam in her eye. "Do you know Mrs. DeMarco? Would you mind answering a few questions about her stay in Lancaster County?"

He glowered at her. "I'm sorry. You won't be getting a statement from me or from Caroline. And there certainly won't be a story about her on tonight's news. Please leave."

The woman narrowed her eyes. "Sir, I hate to tell you this, but there are already several reporters in the area. This will be on the news tonight all over the country." She tossed her glossy hair. "We'll just wait outside for Mrs. DeMarco to emerge." Her high heels clicked against the hardwood floor as she left the store.

"Please, Lydia Ann. I need to talk to her." Michael's voice was heavy with emotion. "I need to explain. It wasn't me. I guess Jenny somehow found out the truth. She was the last one to proof the article before it went to print."

Lydia Ann shook her head. "I think it would be best if you leave too. Give her some time."

A dejected expression crossed Michael's face. "I messed up, big-time. I never should have left those pictures on my computer where Jenny could get to them. Please tell Caroline I'm sorry. And that..." He paused. "And that I'll do anything I can to make it up to her."

Caroline listened from behind the column. She wanted to go after him but stayed where she was. This wasn't the time or place to speak to him. They needed to talk in private. She'd been stupid not to tell him about Jenny and her threats in the first place, but she'd wanted to handle it on her own.

Lydia Ann ushered Michael to the door. She peered outside. "There are a lot of people out there. I think you've done enough." She practically pushed Michael out the door and locked the dead bolt behind her.

"I can't thank you enough," said Caroline, stepping out from where she'd been hiding. "Are there really a lot of people outside?"

"Looks like vans from all the local news stations. Plus an assortment of gawkers." She shook her head. "I'm sorry. I know how much you'd hoped to keep your privacy." She met Caroline's gaze. "When will you speak to Michael? He looks pretty upset."

Caroline nodded. "As soon as I can. Not now, though." She sighed. "And I don't think I'll be able to leave here for a few days. Which is a problem." She glanced at Lydia Ann. "You know I'm supposed to fly back to Atlanta tonight. I guess that's not going to happen." The trip to Atlanta had been planned for a few weeks. She'd arranged to visit Valerie and intended to tell her that although she didn't think adopting the baby herself was the best idea, she knew of a couple who would make wonderful parents. But now it looked like that visit would have to wait.

"Unless…," Lydia Ann trailed off. "Unless we do something a bit crazy."

Caroline's life already seemed to be steeped in crazy. So maybe a little more wouldn't hurt.

* * * * *

Lydia Ann put her hands on her hips and faced Caroline. "I'll be fine. I've actually driven a car before." She grinned. "The wildest thing Levi and I did during our *rumspringa* was learn to drive. He had an English friend who let us borrow his car." She chuckled at the memory. "We drove all the way to Canton and back." It had been a wonderful day. They'd laughed so much.

Caroline sank onto her bed and put her head in her hands. "I can't believe this is happening." She looked up at Lydia Ann with a tearstained face. "I mean, I knew I was probably treading on thin ice when Jenny came to see me. But I honestly believed that she would keep it to herself if I did what she asked." She shook her head. "I guess it goes to show that I'm a real dummy, trusting a person who would try to blackmail me in the first place."

Lydia Ann sat down next to her. "Don't blame yourself. Encouraging Michael to take that job had nothing to do with Jenny's learning your identity and everything to do with you believing he was better off in doing so."

"I was just trying to do the right thing. He shouldn't give up his dreams for me." She sighed. "And now everything is all messed up. My cover is blown. Michael is upset. I'm like a walking disaster."

"Let's think about this. I have no doubt that you and Michael can work this out. But it will be easier to do that if there aren't reporters lurking around." She met Caroline's gaze. "You've heard people around here. They say we look enough alike to be sisters." She smiled. "Except for our eye color."

"And our clothes," Caroline finished, repeating what Michael had said weeks ago when he'd first seen them together.

"So...if I put on your clothes and sunglasses and go get in your car"—Lydia Ann shrugged—"they'll assume I'm you." She grinned. "And you will have time to find Michael, talk to him, and still make your flight."

"No. I can't let you do that."

Lydia Ann wrinkled her brow. "I'll drive your car to a crowded parking lot. Target will work." Target was located in a busy shopping center with a huge parking lot and a special area for buggy parking. Lydia Ann had gone there with Leah a couple of times to pick up prescriptions and household items.

"Once I'm gone, you can take the girls, go over to Dat's store, and call a cab from there. Then tell Dat to pick me up in the buggy parking area at Target." She held up a hand and waved away Caroline's protests. "I'll take my regular clothes in my bag and then run in and change in the bathroom." She pointed at the front of the bookstore. "They'll be waiting for you to come out of the store. Not an Amish woman."

Caroline shook her head. "No. I won't let you put yourself out that way." Her face was grim. "Maybe it doesn't even matter. I can just let them follow me to the airport. My cover is blown now anyway."

"My way would give you a little more time before you have to face the cameras, though," Lydia Ann pointed out. The truth of the matter was, she had a feeling that Michael was waiting nearby. Maybe even at Dat's store. She felt strongly that Michael and Caroline needed to clear the air immediately. She knew that if they were just open with each other, they could work things out. And if she were being honest with herself, she knew part of the reason she wanted Michael and Caroline to work out so badly was because she and Simon hadn't. At least one of them deserved to be happy.

She'd tried to put Simon out of her mind since their talk the other day. But at a time like this, it was hard. Lydia Ann would've liked nothing more than to know that at the end of this stressful day, Simon would be waiting to cheer her up. But he'd made his feelings clear. Or his non-feelings, as the case may be.

"You know, I think I might have a way to handle this situation and keep us both happy," Lydia Ann said with a smile.

Chapter Forty-Eight

....

Michael sat on a bale of hay. "She won't even speak to me," he said. "I've called her cell. I've gone to the store." He shook his head. "She doesn't want to see me at all."

Simon looked at his friend. "Give her some time. You know how badly she wanted to keep her identity a secret." He drew his brows together. "How did it get into the magazine, anyway?"

Michael rolled his eyes. "Jenny. That's the only logical explanation. I've tried to get in touch with her, but she's also avoiding me." He shook his head. "She was so angry at me when she found out I wasn't going to take the job in DC. I'm afraid this is her way of getting back at me."

Simon shook his head. Relationships sure were a lot of trouble. He'd been trying to convince himself that he was better off alone... except that he missed Lydia Ann. So much that he'd considered telling her about his diagnosis. But that wouldn't be fair to her. She deserved a healthy man. She'd been through enough sickness to last a lifetime. His thoughts chased each other like a dog chasing its tail. He knew his decision was the right one, but the doubts were creeping in. "How did Jenny figure out who Caroline really is?"

Michael shrugged. "Jenny always has her nose in a magazine. And I can't tell you how many times she's called everyone in the office over to her computer to look at the latest celebrity scoop online." He rubbed his jaw. "I guess she saw one of the pictures on my computer and put two and two together."

A vehicle outside came to a screeching halt.

Simon exchanged a glance with Michael, and they both ran outside.

Phillip jumped out of his old pickup truck. "It's Caroline," he said, out of breath. "She's been in an accident. I saw her car." He shook his head. "The ambulance was just getting there."

Michael took off toward his SUV, a panicked expression on his face.

"No," Phillip called. "Get in my truck. You're not in any shape to drive."

For a moment, Michael wavered. He took a step toward his own vehicle and then turned around. "Thanks," he murmured to Phillip. He glanced at Simon. "Simon, please go tell Mom and Dad. And I know Lydia Ann will want to know." He met Simon's eyes. "Will you find her and share the news?"

Simon nodded. "I'll say a prayer." He watched as Michael climbed into Phillip's truck and the two of them drove away.

* * * * *

Michael wondered for a minute if he were going to be sick to his stomach. He closed his eyes and willed himself to stay calm.

"Try not to worry," Phillip said. "It will only make things worse."

Michael rubbed his temples. "It's my fault. She trusted me with her life. And I was careless." He quickly brought Phillip up to speed about Caroline's past. "She didn't want me to take pictures of her in the first place. And then the other day, I left them up on my computer while I talked to my boss. Jenny was in my cubicle. I guess she went through them." He shook his head. "I just never dreamed Jenny would recognize Caroline."

"Lance DeMarco? Wow." Phillip stopped at a red light. "He was a great baseball player."

"Whatever. That's not important anymore," Michael snapped.

Phillip was silent for a moment. "Look, I don't blame you for being upset. But this isn't your fault."

"Easy for you to say," Michael mumbled.

Phillip cast a sideways glance at Michael. "I know how much you care about her. It's been obvious from the beginning. And one lesson I've learned over the years is that you should fight for what you love." He sighed. "I haven't always done that. Most of my biggest regrets...no, *all* of my biggest regrets are because I didn't fight for what was most important to me."

Michael looked over at his brother. He actually sounded like a real person, not the grouchy, irritable bear he'd been all summer. "It isn't too late for you, you know."

Phillip grimaced. "I wish that were true."

"What is so bad that it can't be fixed? I mean, the woman who is probably the love of your life wasn't just in a car accident. Seems to me like that would put everything in perspective."

"Always gotta be about you somehow, doesn't it?" Phillip flipped on his blinker to switch lanes. "Maybe the things that have passed me by can't be fixed. Maybe it's been too long." He sighed. "Do you think I wanted to stay here forever and work on the farm? Do you think I wanted Amanda to leave for Philly without me?" He shook his head. "Dad isn't in the best health. But that's something you wouldn't know about. Mom and Dad haven't told you that, ever since his back surgery, he can barely get around. Just like they didn't tell you that we almost lost the farm a few years ago."

Michael sat, stunned. "I don't understand."

"Why do you think they started operating the house as a B&B? Times were tough. We had a couple of really bad years. But they didn't want you to worry. So I did the worrying for the both of us. And when the opportunity came for Amanda to move to the city, there was no way I could go. No way I could leave Dad in the lurch like that. Once Simon started full-time, I took over a lot of the day-to-day operations. And the business side. I've made my peace with it now, but if you'd have shown your face around here a couple of years ago, I probably would've punched it."

Things fell into place for Michael. The bitterness Phillip held toward him. The forced cheerfulness he'd sometimes detected from his mother. Everyone had tried to protect him so he could go off and live his dream. "I'm sorry. I didn't know. If I had, I would've come home straightaway and pitched in."

"What good would it have done? I'm glad you didn't know." Phillip stopped the car at another red light. "I'm proud of you, little brother. Even if I don't show it," he said, his voice softer.

Michael stared. "Thanks. That means a lot."

"I guess it's just been hard for me. I'm the one who stayed here and worked hard to make sure we kept the farm. And you come back for a few measly months and everyone acts like you're a prince or something."

"It isn't like that, and you know it."

"It sure seemed that way to me." Phillip glanced at his brother. "At least at first."

"And now?"

Phillip shrugged. "I had a long talk with Dad last week. He actually thanked me for everything I've done. Said that he didn't know what they would've done without me these past years. And as we talked, I realized that my life isn't so bad after all. I'm proud of our farm. And I've visited the city enough to know that even if I had followed Amanda there, I would've been miserable." He sighed. "Now I've met someone I think I can actually have a life with. Someone who doesn't mind living on a dairy farm." He grinned. "I'm sorry if I've been difficult to deal with."

Michael knew that talking about his feelings wasn't easy for Phillip, but he was glad his brother had shared them.

Phillip pulled underneath the hospital awning. "Now go find her. I'll park the truck and meet you inside."

Michael jumped out of the truck and said a prayer as he ran inside. *Please let her be okay.*

Chapter Forty-Nine

....

Simon climbed down from the buggy and hurried inside Jeremiah's store.

"Good afternoon, Simon," Jeremiah said from behind the counter. "We're about to close for the day, but you can go ahead and make your purchases."

Simon looked down the aisle. Katie and Mary were taking turns walking a leashed Bandit. He breathed a sigh of relief. Lydia Ann must be in the back.

"Can I see Lydia Ann?" he asked.

Jeremiah drew his brows together. "That's not possible," he began.

Simon saw movement from the corner of his eyes. He glanced up in shock. "Caroline? I'm so glad to see you."

She gave him a tense smile. "Why?"

"Philip came to the barn a few minutes ago and told us you'd been in a car accident. But it must've just been a car that looked like yours."

All the color drained from Caroline's face. "An accident?" she whispered. "Oh no." She turned to Jeremiah. "Did you hear what he said?"

Jeremiah grasped the counter, terror showing on his face.

Simon looked from one to the other. "What am I missing?"

"Lydia Ann. She was in my car."

The words took time to register. "You're saying Lydia Ann was the one in the car accident?"

"If Phillip saw my car in a wreck, then yes, it was Lydia Ann," Caroline said.

"Simon, can you take us to the hospital?" Jeremiah asked. "Leah can take Mary and Katie home in our buggy."

Simon nodded. "Let's go." His hands shook, but this time it had nothing to do with his health. His heart ached at the thought of Lydia Ann believing that he didn't care for her. That he didn't see a future with her. What if she were seriously injured—or worse?

He prayed it wasn't too late to tell her the truth.

* * * * *

Michael stopped at the hospital desk. "I need to check on a young woman who was brought in here earlier. She was involved in a car accident. Goes by the name of Caroline Jennings." He paused. "Or Caroline DeMarco."

The receptionist looked at him suspiciously. "Are you family?"

"I'm the closest thing to family that she has."

She narrowed her eyes. "Well, sir, you seem to be misinformed. No one by that name has been brought in here today."

He raked his fingers through his hair. Maybe she'd given a fake name. Or maybe she'd been unconscious and hadn't been able to give a name at all. At this thought, his body went icy cold.

Phillip walked over to stand next to him. "Well? Any news?"

"She says Caroline didn't come in here." He looked at Phillip. "Do you think they would've taken her somewhere else?"

"Ma'am," Phillip said, leaning over the counter, "can you check again? A young blond-haired woman was in a car accident about thirty minutes ago near the intersection of Hartman Bridge Road and Lincoln Highway. They loaded her into an ambulance, and I think they brought her here."

The woman stared at Phillip. "I can check. Just a minute." She hurried down the hallway.

Michael managed a grin. "You always did have a way with the ladies. Especially the *old* ladies."

Phillip clapped him on the back. "Careful, little brother." He patted him on the back a couple of times. "Why don't you go sit down? I'll find out what's going on. And try not to worry."

Michael nodded and walked over to a row of uncomfortable-looking chairs. He sank into a seat and buried his head in his hands. Prayer was the only thing that could help him now.

"Michael?" Phillip said. "You're not going to believe this."

He gritted his teeth, preparing for the worst.

"Michael!" a voice yelled from the hospital entrance. He looked up and saw Caroline running toward him. Simon and Jeremiah followed behind her.

He jumped up. "Caroline." He pulled her to him in a tight embrace, not caring about their audience. "I'm so glad you're okay."

She pulled back. "I am. But Lydia Ann...how is she?"

Michael drew his brows together. "Lydia Ann? I don't understand."

"She's in with the doctor now," Phillip said quietly. "They're running some tests. They'll come out as soon as there is news."

"But she's..." Simon trailed off.

Phillip nodded. "She's alive. And the man who was driving Caroline's car is fine. He needed a few stitches, but that's it."

"The driver was Tom Smucker," Jeremiah said. "He's usually who we hire when we need to go out of town." He nodded in Phillip's direction. "Can you make sure his wife knows about the accident? And that he's okay?"

Phillip nodded and hurried off to the desk.

Michael shot Caroline a questioning look. He didn't quite understand exactly what had happened.

"We called Mr. Smucker to drive her," Caroline explained. "She wanted to drive herself, but I didn't think it was a good idea. She was wearing my clothes, though, so all the reporters would believe it was me." She shook her head. "Lydia Ann wanted to do something to help me have a moment's peace." She looked into Michael's eyes. "And so I could talk to you before I left for Atlanta tonight."

He'd totally forgotten about her trip. "You're not still going, are you?"

She shook her head. "I canceled my flight. I just feel awful that everything happened like this."

"Lydia Ann was doing what she does best," Jeremiah said. "Trying to be of help."

Michael's eyes went to Simon. He'd been silent during the entire exchange. The panicked expression on Simon's face worried him. "Sit down." He led Simon to the waiting area. "Let me get you some water."

Simon shook his head. "I need to speak to Lydia Ann."

"Let the doctors do their job," Jeremiah said. "All we can do is ask the good Lord to watch over her." He began to pace the corridor next to the waiting area.

Michael glanced at Caroline. "Can I talk to you? Privately?"

She shook her head. "Not now. Not until we're sure she's okay." She sank into the seat next to Simon. "Are you okay?" she asked Simon. "You look really pale."

Simon shook his head. "How could I have been so stupid? I never should have told her there wasn't a future for us."

Michael sat down on the other side of Simon. "You were only doing what you thought was best for her."

Caroline wrinkled her forehead. "How could telling her you didn't see a future together be best for her? She's been so upset."

Simon sank into the depths of the chair. He glanced at Michael with haunted eyes. "I guess you didn't tell her."

"I did just as you asked."

Michael listened as Simon explained the situation to Caroline.

"But Lydia Ann would want to know what's going on. Don't you think it's a little unfair for you to make a decision that impacts both of you without even consulting her?" Caroline asked.

Simon nodded. "I've wanted to tell her so many times." He shook his head. "But I didn't want to put a hardship on her."

Michael patted his friend on the back. "It seems like this situation is going to give you another chance to decide whether to share your illness with her. I know what I would do if I were you."

Chapter Fifty

....

Lydia Ann leaned her head against the cool pillow, fighting against a wave of nausea. It could've been worse. So much worse. When that car had come careening through the intersection and plowed into them, she'd been afraid for her life.

The sickening crunch of metal on metal had been followed by darkness. The next thing she'd known, she was being lifted onto a stretcher. And now she was lying in a hospital bed, a little groggy, but thankful to be alive.

"Ms. Raber?" the nurse said. "Do you feel like having some company? There are an awful lot of people waiting to see you."

She tried to sit up, but her pounding head wouldn't allow it. "Jah. Please let them in."

"One at a time," the nurse said.

Dat walked inside slowly. "Lydia Ann," he said, tears streaming down his face. "I was so worried when I heard the news." He came to her bedside and took her hand. "I'm thankful you're okay."

At the sight of his tears, her own eyes grew wet. The only other time she'd seen Dat cry was when Mamm died. "The doctor says I'll be fine. He wants to keep me overnight, though. I have a concussion and some broken ribs." She managed a weak smile. "But I'm okay."

He sat down in the chair next to her bed, still holding her hand.

"Lydia Ann, I can't tell you how much it means that you've spent time here this summer. I've missed you so."

She looked at his weathered face. "I've missed you too." She bit her lip. "I think I owe you an apology."

He drew his brows together. "An apology? For what?"

She sighed. "I should've come to visit you sooner. It was hard for me to accept when you decided to marry Leah. I didn't understand how you could love someone else after Mamm died."

He rose from the chair and kissed her on the forehead. "You don't need to apologize. I should've handled things differently, I guess. Given you more time to get to know her."

Lydia Ann smiled. "She's a wonderful person. And I can see how happy she makes you." She grew quiet. "I guess it took me awhile to learn that just because you moved on with your life, that doesn't mean you've forgotten Mamm."

He shook his head. "I loved Clara so much. Still do. But I know she wouldn't want me to spend the rest of my life alone. She would want me to find happiness." He patted her hand. "And your Levi would want the same for you."

She gave him a weak smile. "It's been a hard lesson. I've wrestled with it and fought against it. But I know you're right. I've been happier this summer than I have in a long time."

"It's a blessing for a father to see his child happy."

"Leah and I have talked about the possibility of the girls and me staying here." She eyed him. "For good."

Tears filled his eyes again. "I will support whatever decision you make. But the thought of my daughter and my granddaughters around my table brings me a lot of joy." He leaned down and kissed her on the cheek. "Now, I think there's someone else wantin' to talk to you. That young man has been falling apart in the waiting room."

* * * * *

Simon stood gingerly in the doorway and looked at Lydia Ann's still figure in the hospital bed. He gently tapped against the door.

She turned her head toward him, and her face broke into a smile.

In that moment, he couldn't help but consider what he almost lost. Not only in the accident, but to his own stupidity. He walked over to her side. "I'm so thankful you're okay."

She blinked. "The Lord was watching over me."

"That He was." He sat down in the chair next to her bed. "Lydia Ann, I need to tell you something."

She held a hand up. "Please let me go first." She gave him a tiny grin. "Since I'm the one all banged up and all."

He returned her smile. "Go ahead."

She cleared her throat. "I've decided to move to Lancaster County anyway. As much as I will miss my old life, I have missed Dat more. I truly believe I belong here now." She smiled. "I hope you and I can remain friends."

He stood. "I hope we can remain more than that." He gathered his courage. "Before, when I told you I didn't have feelings for you…that wasn't the truth." He swallowed. "I was only trying to protect you."

She drew her brows together. "Protect me? From what?"

He sank into the chair. "I'm not well." He met her worried gaze. "I've been diagnosed with multiple sclerosis. The doctor thinks it will be manageable, but there is a chance it will become debilitating."

Lydia Ann gasped. "Oh, Simon, I wish you would've told me as soon as you learned the news." Tears filled her eyes. "You didn't need to try and deal with that alone."

He shook his head. "I didn't want you to have to bear my burden when you've already dealt with so much."

She reached out and took his hand. "I won't *bear* your burden. I will *share* your burden." She smiled. "That is what people do who care about each other. They share one another's burdens."

"But there are no guarantees with this disease. I have no way of knowing how it will impact my life." Simon couldn't help but fear the worst. And he hated the thought of Lydia Ann being stuck in a situation that would only bring her more pain.

She motioned at the hospital bed. "There are no guarantees about anything. But I can promise you that I'll help you deal with your diagnosis however I can."

"Do you think you could help me deal with it…as my wife?" He smiled.

Her eyes lit up. "I can think of nothing I'd like more."

Simon leaned down and kissed her on the cheek. "I believe I can face anything with you by my side. The good and the bad. We'll handle it together." Suddenly the prospect of his illness didn't seem so scary. He knew that with Lydia Ann in his life, he could find the good even in the worst situation. The Lord had truly blessed him.

* * * * *

"I'm so thankful she's going to be okay," Caroline said.

"Me too. I can't tell you how scared I was when I thought you'd been in the accident." Michael raked his hands through his hair. "Knowing it was all my fault."

She shook her head. "You know that isn't true. I should've told you that Jenny had figured things out. That way you could've been on guard. And once I thought about it, I knew there was no way you'd have put my picture in the magazine on purpose." She sighed. "It was just that split second when I saw your name on the photo credit. I was afraid I'd put my trust in the wrong man again."

He grabbed her hand. "But because I was careless, your life has been made more difficult. She never should've had access to those pictures."

"We both know that eventually the truth would've come out. It just happened sooner rather than later."

Michael rubbed his jaw. "Maybe. But I'm still sorry it happened this way."

Caroline took a breath. "I'm the one who should apologize. I chided Simon for trying to make a decision without letting Lydia Ann know all the information. And I'm guilty of the same thing." She met his gaze. "As soon as Jenny came by, I should've called you and told you everything. But a tiny part of me couldn't help but worry that she was right—that if you turned that job down, you would end up resenting me for it."

"I know you only had my happiness in mind," Michael said. "And that means a lot."

She smiled. "I do want you to be happy. And if taking a job in DC makes you happy, then I will support that decision one hundred percent."

He shook his head. "I turned down the job offer." He grinned. "And I have no regrets about it."

"The good news is that once Valerie's trial is over, I won't be news any longer." She grinned. "I'm not saying that I'll ever have a completely normal life, but I should at least be able to move without someone taking a picture."

"I know that is a good thing. But I can't say the idea makes me super happy."

She wrinkled her brow. "What? Why?"

"Because then you won't need to hide under the cover of Lancaster County any longer. You can go back to Atlanta and it will be like none of this ever happened."

"Are you serious?" She pulled her hand away from his. "So you're saying that if you had accepted the *Daily Journal* job, it would've been like none of this ever happened?" She motioned between them. If that was really how he felt, it was better she find out now. She needed to know that she mattered to him.

Michael regarded her seriously. "Actually, I don't know that I'll ever recover from you. I have spent my life searching for a partner. For someone who understands me. Someone who challenges me. Someone who makes me laugh." He pulled her into a hug. "And that person is you." He grinned. "I turned down the DC job because that isn't the life I want. I want a quieter life. The kind where work isn't my focal point. Where I can do something I enjoy but still have a life outside of work."

She nodded. "I just didn't want you to give up your dream for me."

"Don't you get it? You are my dream." He traced her jaw with his finger.

His touch made a shiver run up her spine. "I know what you mean about searching for a partner. I've been searching too. These past few years, I haven't felt like I belonged anywhere. But I feel like I belong with you—and your family." She smiled. "They've taken me in like

I'm one of them...celebrated my success...prayed for my safety." She shook her head. "You have no idea what that means to me."

He leaned down and kissed her gently. "I have some idea." He pulled back, grinning. "Does this mean you might consider making Lancaster County your home?"

She quirked her mouth into a smile. "Maybe."

"Maybe?" He pulled her into an embrace. "Would it help if I told you that I love you? Is that incentive enough to change those Georgia tags for some Pennsylvania ones?"

She grinned. "It might help."

He pulled her in for another kiss, this one more intense.

"Caroline," he whispered, "I love you."

She smiled. "Say it again."

"I love you. More than my camera. More than my SUV. More than my vintage collection of comic books."

She grinned mischievously. "More than shoofly pie?"

"Even more than shoofly pie." He returned her smile.

Caroline enjoyed the delicious warmth that spread over her. Hearing him say those words was like basking in warm sunshine. "I love you too. And I'm not just saying it because you said it." She grabbed his hand. "It's been a lot of years since I've had a home. But you...you're like home to me."

He kissed her again.

Epilogue

....

Caroline sat stiffly in the armchair. She and Michael had debated whether doing a live interview was a good idea. She'd finally decided to answer a few questions. Hopefully it would help to put the past behind her once and for all.

A production assistant hovered over her. "Here's a lapel mic," the woman said. "Just clip that on and you'll be ready to go."

Caroline ran her hand over her smooth new pageboy haircut. She'd gone back to her normal honey-brown color and felt so much more like herself. But these things had always made her nervous. Especially now that it had been so long since she'd been in the spotlight.

"We'll be live in three," the assistant said.

Caroline listened to the countdown, willing herself to stay calm.

"We're here today with Caroline DeMarco," the host said.

The camera panned to Caroline. She managed a smile. "Good morning."

"Caroline, the world still mourns the death of Lance. It doesn't seem possible that it's been more than a year since his death."

Caroline nodded.

"We know that you relocated to Lancaster County, Pennsylvania, soon after his funeral. Would you share the reason behind that move?"

"I guess I was just looking for a change of pace. My mama and I had always planned to visit Lancaster County, so I sought refuge there."

The talk show host nodded. "I remember seeing the media camped outside your Atlanta home. It's no wonder you needed to get away." She smiled. "I understand that you've now permanently relocated. What are you doing there?"

Caroline smiled. "I run a bookstore." Once Lottie had seen how well the place was doing under Caroline's care, she'd sold her the property outright. She said it did her heart good to know that the place she and her husband had loved so much was being so well taken care of.

"That's nice," the host said. "And now that the trial is over, is there anything you'd like to say about the verdict?"

Caroline shook her head. "I've spoken with Valerie multiple times. It was a crime of passion. She is very sorry for what she did, and she will spend the rest of her life in prison, paying her debt to society." There were no words for the sadness of the situation. Lance's life had been cut short. Valerie would spend the rest of her years in jail. The one ray of hope was that the child they'd conceived would only know love.

"Does that mean you've forgiven her?"

Caroline looked into the camera. "Forgiveness isn't easy, especially when someone has done something so awful. But it's necessary. We're commanded to forgive one another as God has forgiven us. So yes, I've forgiven." Forgiveness had been a fight. But with the help of Lydia Ann and Michael, Caroline had come to realize that holding a grudge only hurt herself.

"There were rumors that Valerie was with child and gave birth before the trial. What do you have to say to that?"

Caroline had figured this question was coming. She thought of Emma and Noah and how happy they'd been to finally have a child to love. They'd welcomed the baby boy with open arms. Emma's letters to Lydia Ann were full of happiness. She said that Samuel completed their family and they thanked God for him every day. "There are always rumors in situations like this." She shrugged. There was no reason anyone ever needed to know the truth.

"Is that your way of saying 'no comment'?" The host gave a broad smile.

Caroline didn't respond.

"And how about you? Are you happy?"

Caroline took a breath. There was no way she could convey her happiness in a few short sentences. She'd found a good friend in Lydia Ann, the kind of friend who would help her out in a crisis and laugh with her over a cup of coffee. Even though they came from different backgrounds, they had so many things in common. Watching as Lydia Ann, Simon, Katie, and Mary became a family had been an amazing blessing. And the Landises had become a family of her own. Church with them on Sundays, dinner a couple of nights a week—it was more than she'd ever expected. "I'm very happy," she said. "It took a long while to get to this point, but as a wise friend of mine says, you never know what the good Lord has waiting for you around the corner."

The host smiled. "And one final question for you. Have you found love again?"

Caroline couldn't hide her smile. She'd found the sticking kind of love. The kind that would last through thick and thin. A part of her wanted to reach into her pocket and pull out the ring Michael had given her last week. The antique setting had the diamond from her mama's ring. But there were some things she planned to keep private. "I have found love again." She smiled. "I'm a firm believer in second chances. And I'm thankful I was blessed with a second chance at love."

About the Author

....

 Annalisa Daughety, an Arkansas native, is the award-winning author of five novels. She writes inspirational, contemporary fiction set in historic locations. Her previous works include *Love Finds You in Charm, Ohio,* as well as the Walk in the Park series, set in popular national parks around the country. A graduate of Freed-Hardeman University, Annalisa has spent the past ten years working in the nonprofit sector in marketing and event planning. She is an active member of American Christian Fiction Writers and loves to connect with her readers through social media sites like Facebook and Twitter. She currently lives in Memphis with two spoiled dogs and is hard at work on her sixth novel. More information about Annalisa can be found on her website, www.annalisadaughety.com.

Love Finds You in Groom, Texas
by Janice Hanna
ISBN: 978-1-60936-006-1

Love Finds You in Amana, Iowa
by Melanie Dobson
ISBN: 978-1-60936-135-8

COMING SOON

Love Finds You in Branson, Missouri
by Gwen Ford Faulkenberry
ISBN: 978-1-60936-191-4

Love Finds You in
Sundance, Wyoming
by Miralee Ferrell
ISBN: 978-1-60936-277-5

Love Finds You on
Christmas Morning
by Debby Mayne and Trish Perry
ISBN: 978-1-60936-193-8

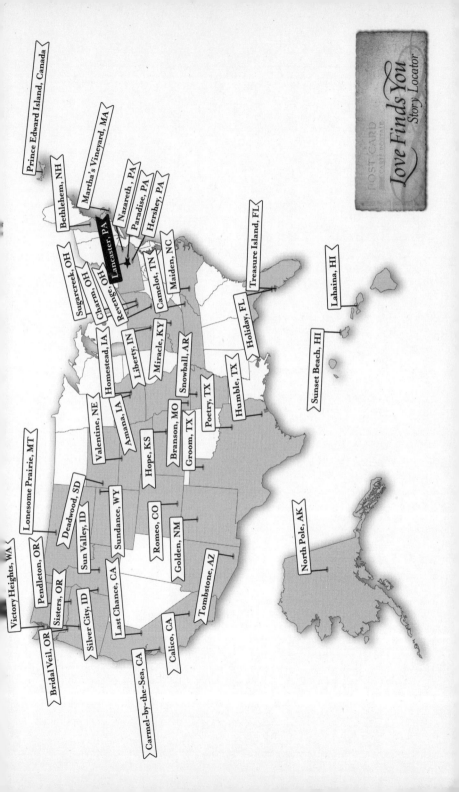